MW00779163

BLACKSNOW ZERO

A Novel
By

Lee Gimenez

RRP

River Ridge Press

BLACKSNOW ZERO
by
Lee Gimenez

This is a work of fiction. The names, characters, places, incidents, and dialogues are products of the author's imagination and are not to be construed as real. Any resemblance to actual persons, living or dead, is entirely coincidental.

BLACKSNOW ZERO
Copyright © 2020 by Lee Gimenez. (www.LeeGimenez.com)

All rights reserved. In accordance with the U.S. Copyright Act of 1976, the scanning, uploading, or reproducing of any part of this book without written permission of the publisher is unlawful piracy and theft of the author's intellectual property. The exception of this is in the case of brief quotations embodied in articles and reviews about the book. Thank you for your support of the author's rights.

Printed in the United States of America.

Published by
River Ridge Press
P.O. Box 501173
Atlanta, Georgia 31150

Cover photos: Copyright by Gary718
used under license from Shutterstock, Inc.

Cover design: Judith Gimenez

ISBN-13: 978-0-578-69159-6

Novels by Lee Gimenez

Blacksnow Zero

The Sigma Conspiracy

Crossfire

Fireball

FBI Code Red

The Media Murders

Skyflash

Killing West

The Washington Ultimatum

The Nanotech Murders

Death on Zanath

Virtual Thoughtstream

Azul 7

Terralus 4

The Tomorrow Solution

Lee Gimenez

BLACKSNOW ZERO

Lee Gimenez

BLACKSNOW
ZERO

30 Days to Zero Hour

Fairfax, Virginia

Bobbie Garcia had killed twenty-four people in his years as a black-ops operative. Tonight would make twenty-five.

He peered through his night-vision goggles and adjusted the focus. The senator's home came into clear view, the shadowy green image of the walled estate visible beyond the imposing gate. Garcia lay prone on a wooded hill, across the desolate road in front of the house. The place was situated on six acres, in a secluded area, and he knew its electronic surveillance was first-rate. But he'd been in black-ops a long time and this job wasn't much different from other wet work he'd done. The target was just higher profile. He'd considered bringing his team on the mission, but decided the less people involved the better.

Taking off his backpack, he pulled out the portable EMP device and adjusted the settings. Clamping his eyes shut, he activated it. Through his closed eyelids he saw the bright flash and felt a tingle of electrical shock.

Quickly stuffing the device back in the pack, he glanced at the house. The flood lights that had lit up the grounds were dark now and the hum of the air conditioning units was silent. The electromagnetic pulse had worked.

Garcia pulled out his Glock, took off the safety and sprinted down the hill. A minute later he was facing the tall, wrought iron gate. He was ruggedly built so the gate presented little challenge. Grabbing the metal bars, he climbed up, vaulted over the top and dropped to the other side with a thud. Scanning the grounds through the goggles, he saw nothing moving.

Avoiding the long driveway that curved up to the front of the estate, he instead zigzagged around the lush landscaping, reaching the back entrance moments later. Hugging the ornate brick wall of the home, he caught his breath and wiped perspiration from his forehead. It was mid-summer and it was hot outside, even at this time of night.

Garcia checked his watch – it read 3:12 a.m. Everyone should be asleep.

He approached a side window by the tall French doors and peered inside the darkened house. The shadowy green image showed a large sitting room, the walls lined with filled bookcases.

Knowing the alarm system was dead, he pulled a glass cutting tool from his all-black uniform and proceeded to cut part of the window pane. That done, he shoved his hand through the hole and unlocked the window. Sliding it open, Garcia crawled in and crouched by a wingback chair. He listened closely, but only heard the faint ticking of a clock somewhere nearby.

Making his way out of the room, he found the wide staircase that led to the second story. According to mission specs, the senator's bedroom was on that floor, off to the right. The man's children were away traveling, leaving only the senator and his wife at home. All Garcia had to do was gas the couple to make them unconscious. Then kill him and take jewelry and cash on the way out. A robbery gone bad. Simple and straightforward, his handler had said.

He crept up the staircase, his heart thudding in his chest. He knew kills were never simple.

Reaching the landing, he turned right, training his weapon in front of him.

A creaking noise behind him broke the silence and he whirled around to find a large man wearing plaid pajamas pointing a gun at him.

Dropping to the floor, Garcia fired two quick shots, the muted sounds of the suppressed gun filling the corridor. The man buckled, his gun clattering on the marble floor. Losing no time, Garcia ran to the prone gunman, whose bleeding body was still. Checking for a pulse, he confirmed the man was dead. But clearly he wasn't the senator. The dead man was much bigger and bulkier. *A bodyguard? The specs hadn't mentioned that. Had the senator been warned?*

His heart racing, Garcia sprinted down the corridor, knowing he had only seconds before the family woke up.

A door opened to his left and a middle-aged, balding man wearing a robe came out, yawning and rubbing his eyes. Senator Carpenter.

Damn it all to hell, Garcia thought. *It was too late, it was all turning to shit.*

Garcia fired, putting three rounds in the man's torso. The senator's eyes went wide, he grunted and clutched his chest. Then he collapsed, his body convulsing.

Garcia heard a woman's scream as he entered the darkened bedroom. A naked, obese woman sat on the edge of the king-size bed staring at him. She yelled again and Garcia put a round in her forehead. A hole appeared there and she slumped to the floor.

Glancing around, he saw no one else. Taking no chances, he sprinted out of the room, checking each of the other bedrooms. They were empty and his mind raced, trying to figure a way out of the mess. He'd killed three people, one of them an armed bodyguard – the 'robbery gone bad' cover was now a stretch.

Finally deciding, he took off his backpack and rummaged through it. Finding the incendiary grenade, he pulled the pin and rolled it down the corridor. In minutes the estate would be in flames.

He ran down the staircase, his weapon trained in front of him. Moments later, he was on the grounds, racing away from the house.

Operation BlackSnow had begun.

***

Garcia was in his cramped Washington D.C. apartment the next morning, working on his computer, when his wife Maria came into his small office.

"What time you get in last night?" she asked, her tired eyes looking sad. Maria was a good-looking woman, with olive skin and shapely figure, but the last couple of years had been difficult for her. Although she was in her mid-thirties, she looked much older.

Saving the file he was working on, he quickly closed the laptop. "After five," he replied, giving her a bright smile.

Maria's expression went from sad to cold. "I want you around more often."

She slouched on the chair across from him, crossed her arms in front of her. "When we moved to D.C.," she hissed, "you told me things would be different. It's been two years and nothing's changed."

He raised his hands in front of him. "You know the military...it's a grind...."

"The hell with the military! We've talked about this before, Bobbie. Put in your papers. You've got your twenty in. You're only forty, still young. With your background in Special Forces, you could get a good job in private security – they pay top dollar."

"I know. Soon, I promise. I just have to finish this one project."

Her dark eyes glared. "Okay. Tell me about it. Tell me what's so damn important that you're gone all the time?"

"I can't talk about it, you know that."

"Just as I thought." Her voice dropped to a whisper. "I want to start a family. I'm not getting any younger. But I want my kids to have a father."

Trying to placate her, he said, "I promise, as soon this project is done, I'll put in for retirement from the Marines."

Maria tilted her head, staring into his eyes. Her glare melted a fraction. "You mean it?"

"Of course. I want to start a family too."

She stood up, leaned down and gave him a kiss, then said, "I love you, Bobbie. I just want us to have a normal life."

Garcia placed his palm on her face and caressed her cheek, his mind racing through the events of the last year. His handler had promised him a big payout after it was all done. Retirement would be a snap.

29 Days to Zero Hour

Rome, Italy

FBI Agent Erica Blake jogged on the grimy, worn sidewalk, bypassing the pedestrians on their way to work. To her left, the Tiber River meandered and on her right, the avenue was packed with tiny autos and motor scooters. It was morning, but the summer heat was already building – her jogging outfit was drenched with sweat.

She loved the excitement of the city and had jumped at the opportunity to vacation here – her first real vacation in years. Dodging a shuffling, older man, she sprinted on the cobblestones of the road, then quickly ran back to the sidewalk as a Fiat blared its horn.

Picking up her pace, she sprinted past a cluster of Japanese tourists, cameras dangling from their necks.

Up ahead, a street vendor was selling pastries and the sweet aroma wafted by. She almost stopped, but didn't want to break her five-mile trek – she'd grab breakfast with Steve back at the hotel.

After jogging in place at the traffic light, she raced across the avenue when the light turned and made her way past the tree-lined park that led to the high-rise hotel. She stopped in front of it, caught her breath and walked in.

***

Erica found Steve in the bedroom, still asleep. The muscular, blond man was tangled in the sheets. Unlike her, he needed eight hours of sleep – she rarely slept more than two. Her curse, she called it, although it came in handy on stake-outs.

She headed into the bathroom, her thoughts turning to her odd, on-again, off-again relationship with her ex-husband, Steve McCord. A CIA agent, Steve had made a lousy spouse, but he was a great lover and they shared a passion for Rome. When she began planning this trip, she immediately thought of him.

Stripping out of her wet clothes, she turned on the light and studied herself. Not bad for a thirty-five year old – her curves and lean tone the same as in college. The gym and jogging saw to that. She pushed her long, black hair away from her pretty, sculpted face and noticed the wrinkles at the edge of her pale blue eyes. *Nothing stays the same,* she thought. She traced the slight scar on her cheek, the result of being grazed by a bullet years ago. She smiled and shook her head. Looks are fleeting, her mother had told her. Get an education, she had said, and make your own way in life. Advice Erica had taken to heart. But sometimes, Erica knew, she was too independent for her own good, a trademark that pissed off her bosses at the Bureau.

She pushed those thoughts aside and jumped in the shower, turning the tap to ice cold.

***

Wrapped in a white robe, she returned to the bedroom. Steve was still dozing and she rectified that by slapping his bare ass.

The man jumped up from the bed. "What the hell?" he mumbled.

"Time to get up, sleepyhead. It's nine already."

He rubbed his eyes, slid back into bed and pulled the sheet over his head. "Too early…."

She slapped his leg, leaving a red mark on it. "Get up. Time to have breakfast and screw."

Steve peeked from under the covers. "Didn't you get enough last night? I'm still sore."

Erica laughed. "I never get enough. You should know that by now."

He pulled the sheet completely off. "One of many things I love about you."

She let her robe fall open. "Probably the only thing."

"No it's not." His face got serious. "You're the one who wanted out of the marriage."

She nodded and went quiet.

His face brightened. "Tell you what, I'll order us some food from room-service."

Just then her cell phone buzzed. It was on the nightstand and she reached over, took the call and held the phone to her ear. She listened for a minute, said okay and hung up.

"Shit," she growled.

"Who was it?" he asked.

"Work. My boss. There's been a suspicious fire. Senator Carpenter, his wife and his bodyguard are dead."

"And?"

"They're giving me the case."

"You're on vacation, Erica. Why can't another agent handle it?"

She slumped on the bed. "Because I'm on vacation, that's why. I've mouthed off at my boss one too many times. This is payback."

"Asshole."

"Tell me about it."

Steve reached into her robe, began to caress her breast. "When do you have to go?"

"Now."

His hand wandered down her body and he touched her gently.

She lay back on the bed and pulled her robe completely open. "Maybe not *now*. But soon."

28 Days to Zero Hour

The Vice President's office
West Wing of the White House
Washington, D.C.

Vice President Taylor loosened his tie and leaned back in his chair. Things were going so well he decided to pour himself another drink. Reaching into his ornate wooden desk, he pulled out the bottle of Dewar's scotch and poured himself two fingers.

He held up the cut-glass tumbler, admiring the amber liquid, then sipped slowly, relishing the smooth burn of the liquor.

Putting the bottle and glass back in the drawer, he pressed the intercom on his desk. "Alice, show the General in," he said.

General Corvan stepped in the sound-proofed room and closed the door behind him. Taylor stood and the men shook hands.

"Have a seat, Corvan."

"Thank you, sir."

The general was a Marine four-star from the Pentagon and one of Taylor's most trusted allies. A tall, broad man with a regulation crew-cut, Corvan didn't look that bright, but Taylor knew the man was highly intelligent and always got things done.

The two men sat and the vice president leaned back in his wide executive chair, which had been custom-made to accommodate his overweight frame. Taylor smiled and said, "I called Garcia, after you gave me the news. He did a good job on the senator."

"I was hoping the operation could have been cleaner...." Corvan replied.

Taylor raised his palms. "Me too – but sometimes things get complicated."

"Yes, sir, they do."

"With Carpenter out of the way, we won't have a problem with the Senate Armed Services committee. They won't be sniffing around anymore. The rest of those guys are in my pocket."

"Yes, sir."

Taylor ran a hand over his bald pate. "Okay, then. How's the rest of BlackSnow proceeding?"

Corvan leaned forward in his seat. "Everything is on track, Mr. Vice President. The other generals are on board, as is one of the two admirals we need."

"So – Admiral Stanton still not in agreement?"

Corvan rubbed his jaw. "Not yet. I'm working on it."

Taylor's face turned red. "Damn, it. Get it done. We need those submarines."

The general pushed back in his seat and a frown crossed his face. "Yes, sir."

"Good. We still have time, but we need to lock down all the players."

Corvan nodded. "I'll take care of it."

Taylor glanced at the family photo on his desk – his wife and two sons. *I'm doing this for you*, he thought. *For your future.*

"Sir," the general asked, "what about the President?"

Taylor turned away from the photo and stared at the other man. "That jerk? He doesn't wipe his ass without checking with the Chinese first. Don't worry. President Wilson is clueless as to what we're planning." He rubbed his hands together. "I love my plan."

"Yes, sir."

"Anything else?"

"I've put all the details on this encrypted file," the general said, holding up a small flash drive. "I just need you to review it one last time and give me written confirmation."

Taylor studied Corvan closely, realizing the man was smart *and* wily. "My verbal okay isn't enough?"

"I'd prefer it in writing, in case things go south."

Taylor barked out a laugh. "A wise man. No problem. I'll read it and give you a letter today."

The general stood up. "Is there anything else, sir?"

"Want to join me for a drink before you go?"

"No thank you, sir. I don't drink."

"Very well. I'll call you later today."

The general saluted, did a crisp about-face and walked out of the office, closing the door behind him.

Taylor pulled out the bottle of scotch, poured himself another large drink and plugged the flash drive into the computer on his desk. He began reading as he sipped his drink:

Project Blacksnow
For the Vice President's Eyes Only

Project BlackSnow has been developed in order to free the United States from its crushing debt. Due to the massive national deficits the U.S. has run over the last twenty years, the country has had to borrow trillions of dollars. At first we borrowed from our citizens, but later had to rely on Japan and other countries to buy our Treasury bonds. After the Japanese nuclear reactor disaster in 2011, and the COVID-19 pandemic in 2020, the Japanese were unable to keep buying our Treasury bonds in large quantities.

The Chinese stepped in, and now hold over 89% of our debt. Because of this, America's foreign and even domestic policy has been dictated by the Chinese government for the last several years. BlackSnow has been developed to free our country from their domination. Although this plan does not strictly adhere to our Constitution, it is still felt that doing nothing is a much worse option. We must take action, if our nation is to survive.

Operation BlackSnow will take thirty days to complete. Two days ago, the plan was initiated. Seven days from today, the operation will be irreversible....

Taylor took another sip of his drink and savored the taste. Then he continued reading, knowing the best parts of the write-up were yet to come.

27 Days to Zero Hour

Fairfax, Virginia

Erica Blake drove her government-issue Ford Explorer through the open gate of the senator's estate and wound around the long driveway, the tires crunching on the gravel.

Pulling up to the front of the mansion, she surveyed what was left of the place. Yellow crime-scene tape dangled from the scorched brick walls and the nearby trees. Parts of the roof were charred and collapsed in places. As she got out of the SUV, the acrid smell of smoke filled her lungs.

Two Fairfax County police cruisers were parked in front, along with an unmarked sedan.

As she walked up the wide flagstone steps, a uniformed cop came out of the blackened front door under the portico.

"This is a crime scene, lady," the uniform said. "It's a restricted area."

She pulled her badge from her jacket, flashed it. "FBI. Looking for a Detective Gray."

He motioned with his head and stepped aside.

Climbing over the charred remains of the entryway, she stepped into what must have been the foyer. The burnt odor was even stronger here and she choked back a cough.

A wide marble staircase led up to the remains of the second level. The sky was visible through the gaping holes in the roof.

Glancing around, she spotted a slender man in a rumpled suit and walked over.

"I'm Erica Blake," she said, holding up her badge. "You Gray?"

The man gave her a hard look. "Glad you could make it, *Special* Agent."

"I was on vacation – they pulled me back to help you clean up this mess."

"Listen, sweetheart, I know the FBI has priority. But if you stay out of my way, you can follow me around. You might learn something."

Erica glared at him. "I'm not your damn sweetheart."

Gray's eyes widened, then a small smile spread on his face. "I've heard about you – you got quite a rep for being a bitch."

She stabbed a finger on his chest. "Call me a bitch again and I'll cut your balls off. Understood?"

He held up his palms. "Okay. Let's start over. We're both assigned to this case, so why don't we work together."

Erica shrugged. "Fine with me. As long as you know the ground rules. What do you have so far?"

The man pulled out a small notebook and started reading from it. "Senator Carpenter, his wife, and his bodyguard were shot. Multiple rounds. They were killed on the second floor, close to their bedrooms. The forensic techs say the same type of gun was used on all three. It appears the place was torched afterwards. An accelerant was used."

"The bodies?"

"At the morgue."

She nodded. "Signs of robbery?"

He waved a hand in the air. "Hard to tell. Most of the stuff is crispy."

"If I remember correctly, the senator had two kids."

"They were away."

"Lucky for them."

Gray closed the notebook. "If it was a simple robbery, not sure why they'd burn the place down."

Erica shrugged. "Maybe the guy was trying to cover up something...."

"Like what?"

She glanced around the foyer, mulled it over. "This is a fancy place, or was. Probably had extensive electronic surveillance. Cameras, alarms, motion detectors. How'd the perp get through without triggering the alarm and alerting the bodyguard?"

Gray shook his head. "Dunno."

"Looks like the perp knew what he was doing. A pro."

The cop gave her an appraising look. "You could be right, Blake."

"I know I'm right. The question is, was it an inside job? Did the help sell them out?"

Gray shrugged. "The Carpenter's didn't have any live-in staff. A maid and a grounds keeper came in several times a week."

"Interview them?"

"Yup. Nothing there."

"Do it again, Gray."

He was about to argue, but her cell phone buzzed. She took the call and held the phone to her ear.

She listened, made a face and said, "Okay."

Then she turned off the phone and handed Gray one of her cards. "Got to go. My boss needs me. But let me know what else you find – I'll talk to you later."

Gray took the card and put it in his rumpled jacket.

She turned, almost walked out of the house, then turned back and smiled. "I'm really not as big a bitch as people say."

The man nodded, but didn't look convinced.

***

Erica parked her SUV in the massive underground lot below the FBI building in D.C., then made her way through the security checkpoints and up to her cubicle on the fifth floor. The open cube was one of many that occupied the noisy bullpen. All were filled with agents, mostly male, who hunched over computers, their ears glued to phones. But she got so little sleep that this place was more of a home than the drab apartment she had nearby.

Booting up her laptop, she checked messages, grabbed a lukewarm cup of coffee from the break room, and headed up to the sixth floor. *No sense in postponing the inevitable.*

Special Agent Justin Temerius' office was one of a row of glass enclosed spaces that lined the north wall. She tapped on the glass door and went in, then slouched on the hard plastic visitor's chair that fronted his desk.

Crossing her arms, she said, "Wanted to see me?"

Temerius scowled at her. The man was in his fifties, with graying hair and a thick, salt-and-pepper mustache. He had a sallow complexion, as if he never got any sun. "Agent Blake. How good of you to come see me."

"If I could avoid it, I would."

His expression didn't change. "I wanted a progress report on the Carpenter case."

"Just got to the scene, but you called me away."

"I see. A pity." He brushed his mustache with his hand. "Pity about your vacation, too. Hated to cut that short – but duty calls. Couldn't be helped."

Her voice dropped to a whisper and she leaned forward in the chair. "You've got ten agents working for you. I guess they were all busy."

Temerius gave her an arrogant smile. "You're my best."

"I am the best damn agent you've got. But I won't kiss your ass and that's why you cut short my vacation."

He smiled again. "Not true. You're just being paranoid."

She noticed a letter opener on his desk, reached over and picked it up. "This thing isn't sharp, but I'm sure I could gouge your eyes with it."

A frown crossed his face and he pushed his chair back, obviously frightened by her threat. "Blake, don't do anything you'll regret."

She waved the opener in the air. "I regret this isn't a switchblade. They're more efficient." Then she dropped the opener on the desk and laughed. "Just kidding, boss. You know me, I'm a kidder."

The frown didn't leave his face. "You're dismissed. Just keep me informed."

Erica stood up. "No problem, Justin. But pull that vacation shit on me again, and I'll gut you like a fish. Comprende?"

The man nodded and she turned and left the office, a smile on her face.

***

She drove through the rural Fairfax County countryside, the twisting roads lined with oak trees. There were few homes, and they were on large properties that sat well back from the road. *It's a beautiful part of Virginia,* she thought. *I wish I could afford to live in this area. But on an agent's salary, that's never going to happen.*

Her phone buzzed and she unclipped it from her belt. It was Detective Gray.

"I'm just leaving the crime scene," Gray said, "where are you?"

"Headed there now," she replied, as she navigated the car around another turn.

"The M.E. called me. Said the final ballistics report came back. They were 9 mil slugs. One other thing – the accelerant used was most likely an incendiary grenade."

Erica mulled that over a moment. "That kind of ordnance isn't very common. Military source?

"Could be."

"Anything else?"

"Talked with the maid and groundskeeper again and also did a background check. They came up clean. Both have been with the Carpenters over five years. Their bank balances don't show anything out of the ordinary. I don't think there's anything there."

"Okay, Gray. I'm going to talk to some of the neighbors, see if they noticed anything suspicious."

She hung up and continued driving through the scenic countryside.

A mile from the senator's estate she spotted a large farmhouse, set well back from the road. *Probably one the closest neighbors,* she thought.

Pulling into the gravel driveway, she went past a stable and parked in front of the sprawling farmhouse. Unlike most of the new construction in the area, this house looked as if it'd been here a long time. *Old money.*

Climbing out, she pulled her badge and strode up the wooden steps to the front door.

An old woman opened the door, carrying a double-barreled shotgun. The woman was probably in her eighties, with gray hair pulled into a bun. "Saw you coming," she said. "Can I help you?"

Erica flashed her badge. "FBI. Special Agent Blake." She pointed at the shotgun. "Expecting trouble?"

The woman grinned. "Not really. But I don't get too many visitors. And after my husband passed away, I don't take chances."

"Smart. But you can put that down. I'm just interviewing some of the people in the area."

The woman leaned the gun inside the door. "Come in. It's not often I get to talk to an FBI agent. You remind me of my granddaughter."

They went inside and sat on Early-American style rocking chairs in the living room.

"I'm Telusa Smith," the lady said, as she began to rock in the chair. "My family's owned this place for over a hundred years." Her voice dropped. "Course, I'm the only one left, now."

"I see. I'm investigating the death of Senator Carpenter. His place was burned down the other day. You heard?"

"Of course. I may be old, but I watch TV. It's been all over the news." A glint came in her eyes. "I also use the internets…imagine that."

Erica nodded. "Yes, ma'am. Do you remember anything unusual that evening?"

Mrs. Smith stopped rocking. "Yes. My electricity went off. I remember it well, 'cause I was up reading. Couldn't sleep that night."

"I see. How long was it out?"

"Probably four, five hours. I called the power company right away and they said the area around here was having a blackout." Mrs. Smith's face brightened. "But they fixed it the next day."

"Okay. See anything else that night? Any strangers or something else odd?"

The woman began rocking again. "Nope."

Erica stood and handed Smith one of her cards. "Thank you for your time. You've been very helpful. If you think of anything else, my number's on the card."

A frown crossed the woman's face. "Leaving already? Why don't you stay awhile and I'll make us some tea. Would you like that?"

Erica smiled, feeling a little sad for the lonely woman. "Wish I could, ma'am. But I've got to continue canvassing."

Mrs. Smith nodded, holding the card tightly. "I'll be sure and call you, if anything else comes up."

Erica turned and walked out of the house, grateful she had stopped there. *That blackout,* she thought, *might not be a coincidence.*

26 Days to Zero Hour

Beijing, China

General Wu Chang rubbed his jaw as he waited in his spacious office thinking about the upcoming videoconference. As chief of staff of the armed forces of the People's Republic of China, he had many duties. But the task of communicating with the American president was one of the most important. A military man his whole life, Chang disliked this part of his job, but it was unavoidable. The Premier himself had assigned him the task.

Just then his pert assistant, Captain Lin, came in his office and said, "The President is on, sir." The young woman's shapely figure was obvious, despite her dowdy military uniform. She turned and quietly closed the door.

Chang glanced at his watch and waited a full five minutes. It was good to keep the man waiting. While he killed time, he looked down at his crisply pressed uniform and tidied up the numerous ribbons that were displayed on his chest.

Finally, he turned on the large monitor on his desk and the secure signal came to life.

The image of U.S. President Wilson appeared on the screen, sitting behind a desk in what Chang recognized was the Oval Office.

"Hello, General," the man said with a forced smile. "Good to see you again."

"Good to see you also, Mr. President," Chang replied in flawless but heavily accented English.

The general studied Wilson closely and noticed the subtle changes in his appearance over the last several years. His eyes looked sunken and his hair thinner. The suit he wore seemed a few sizes too big, as if the man had lost a lot of weight. The American president had aged considerably since taking office.

"Your assistant Lin said you needed to speak with me," Wilson said. "Something important, she said."

"Yes, Mr. President. We have been reviewing your request to purchase additional quantities of your Treasury bonds." He paused to let that sink in. "We are considering it."

A worried look came over Wilson's face. "Yes, we need that…in fact…the sooner the better."

"It is a large amount of money that you are borrowing, Mr. President. A significant amount. As usual, we expect something in return."

A slight twitch appeared on Wilson's left eye and he tried to blink it away. "What…what do you have in mind *this* time, General?"

Chang waited a moment before answering, then said, "Our space program is now in full swing and as your program lacks sufficient funds, we recommend you close NASA completely. We would like to access your rocket booster technology. We also want to have your space scientists come here, to work on our program. I am sure you will agree, Mr. President, it is a win-win situation."

The president loosened his tie. "But shutting NASA down…that would be a major setback for us."

"Mr. President, you really do not have the money to keep that program going. I am sure you realize that."

"But you've got to understand, the American people…will be angered by such a thing."

Chang leaned forward in his seat. "They would be more angry, Mr. President, if they did not receive their Social Security checks, or Medicare, welfare or food stamps. Now *that* would be tragic."

Wilson said nothing for a long time, but eventually his shoulders slumped and he nodded. "Yes, I can see your reasoning. I agree to your terms."

"Very good, Mr. President. I just have one more request."

Wilson's eyes bulged, but he said nothing.

Chang brushed a piece of lint off his immaculate uniform. "Mr. President, we ask that your naval 7th Fleet, which patrols the waters of the Pacific Ocean, in the future limit their patrols to the coastal areas of the United States."

"That's preposterous, General," the man said, alarm in his voice. "That would leave our allies, Japan, South Korea, and Australia, without U.S. support. Not to mention our state of Hawaii."

"Do not worry, Mr. President. Our naval fleet has grown over the last ten years. We would be glad to patrol the Pacific in your place. As for Hawaii, I have vacationed there many times. It is a wonderful place and we will protect it as if it were our own."

Wilson's face contorted with evident anger. Then he shook his head. "I can't agree to that, General."

Chang smiled. "Mr. President, be reasonable. We are close allies, are we not? We are your biggest creditor. We purchase the majority of your Treasury bonds. No one else wants them anymore. We are only trying to get a small return for our investment. Is that so unreasonable, sir?"

"Even if I were to agree, I would have to convince the Pentagon and Congress it was a good idea."

"Mr. President, we have sources that keep us apprised of your military situation. They tell us that unless you raise salaries for your troops, you will experience a high desertion rate. As it is, because of your budget problems, you have had to freeze military salaries for the last five years. What would happen if we do not finance your bonds? As for your Congress, they are more than aware of your country's massive debt. They also want to be re-elected. If their constituents do not receive the benefits promised by your generous entitlement programs, then they *will not* be re-elected. Remember what happened to your predecessor, President Cooper. He was a one-termer, because he tried to cut back on entitlements. Trust me, Mr. President. It will not be difficult for you to convince your Congress of the benefits of this deal."

Wilson's face blanched as beads of sweat formed on his forehead. His hands appeared to be shaking slightly, but he said nothing.

Chang smiled again, trying to soften the blow. "If you agree to our requests, we will purchase your Treasury bond allotment this time, and also purchase your allotment for the next six months. How does that sound, Mr. President?"

Wilson rubbed his forehead as if trying to shake off a bad headache. Eventually, he responded, his voice no more than a whisper. "I agree, General."

Chang clasped his hands in a steeple. "Excellent. Excellent. I will process the paperwork immediately. Thank you, Mr. President. We are pleased that the People's Republic of China and the United States of America are such close partners. Good day."

The general reached over and turned off the monitor, relieved the teleconference was over. He had accomplished his goal. The Premier would be pleased.

Chang sat back in his chair and waited, knowing his assistant would come into his office in a moment.

Minutes later Captain Lin came in, a tall glass in her hand. She closed the door behind her and locked it. Smiling demurely, she placed the drink on his desk, took off her uniform jacket and hung it on a coat hook. As usual, she was wearing a tight shirt under the jacket and her curves strained against the material.

Walking behind him, she began massaging his shoulders. He started to relax almost immediately. The touch of her delicate hands was soothing but also electrifying.

Reaching across the desk, he picked up the glass and sipped the Canadian whiskey, the harsh taste burning his throat.

"I listened in on the conversation, sir," she said as she continued the massage. "You were masterful."

"Thank you, Lin."

He had hand-picked this assistant over hundreds of applicants for the job and had never been disappointed. She was efficient and very discreet, something he was grateful for, since his wife of twenty years was a jealous and cold woman. But a man in his position could not afford a divorce. It would tarnish his reputation in the Communist Party. Instead he enjoyed the occasional tryst with Lin.

She kept massaging his shoulders while he sipped his drink.

When the glass was empty, she turned his seat around, so that he now faced her.

The demure smile still on her face, she slowly unbuttoned her shirt and unzipped her skirt. Then took off her underwear and let them drop to the floor.

Chang was breathing heavily now.

She carefully removed the thick eyeglasses from his face, folded them and set them on his desk. Then she sat on his lap and began to kiss him on the mouth. He groaned as she rubbed her naked body against him.

He leaned back in the chair as her hands unbuttoned his uniform. Moments later he savored the feel of her skilled hands on his bare skin.

She then straddled him and slowly lowered herself on him, the feeling so exquisite he almost exploded.

She put a finger to his lips. "Slow down," she whispered. "Try to make it last."

Closing his eyes, he took a couple of deep breaths.

But it was no use and he released, the sweet pain coming is a wild rush.

As he held her in his arms, he knew the passionate afternoon was far from over.

25 Days to Zero Hour

Zurich, Switzerland

Senator Megan Lewis waited in the bank director's outer office and gazed out the floor-to-ceiling windows at the mountains in the distance. As a two-term senator and head of the U.S. Senate Banking committee, she had been to Zurich many times and never tired of the scenic landscape.

Turning back to her notes, she gathered her thoughts for the upcoming meeting. She had met with Director Henry Mueller before, but always under more agreeable circumstances. Today's meeting would be difficult.

Moments later Mueller came out of his office and extended his hand. "Megan, always a pleasure." He was a tall, handsome man, with Nordic good looks.

He led her back to his sleek, massive office and they sat in a seating area that overlooked a lake. The room was furnished with ultra-modern chrome and black-leather furniture. Original Picasso and Van Gogh paintings hung on the walls.

"Coffee or tea?" he asked as he adjusted his Hermes silk tie.

"No thanks, Henry. I'm fine."

He nodded. "You said you had something urgent to discuss...."

Megan put her notebook on a side table and leaned forward in the leather seat. Not sure how to begin, she blurted out, "How's the family? Your kids must be in college by now."

Mueller frowned, apparently not sure where she was going with this. "Yes. My two girls are at the university – one of them graduates next year."

"Great, that's great. You must be very proud of them."

The man nodded, went quiet.

She glanced around the room, realized she'd better get on with it. "Henry, I'm sure you've been following the news about the U.S. economy?"

He choked back a laugh. "What part? I hear your movie and music industries are doing quite well."

She forced a smile. "Yes, that's a fact. No, I'm referring to our trade balance and our budget deficits."

Mueller shook his head slowly. "Very sad, what's happening. America used to be the leader of the free world. Now...."

"That's what I needed to discuss with you, Henry."

"I see."

"Your firm is the leading bank in Switzerland. You have close ties with the Swiss government. And you also have operating control of banks in Germany, England and the rest of Europe. I've done a lot of research. Your cash flow is tremendous and your balance sheet impeccable."

A small smile spread on his lips. "We have done good research, Megan."

She tucked her short blonde hair behind her ears. "On the other hand, the U.S. is running enormous deficits. Our national debt is out of control. We can barely pay the interest on the debt, let alone the principal. And we keep digging ourselves into a deeper hole every year. We finance the debt by issuing more and more Treasury bonds, but it's getting harder to find buyers." Her voice lowered. "The Chinese are financing much of our debt."

He nodded, a grim look crossing his face. "I'm aware of that. My sources tell me the Chinese are exerting significant control over your country."

"I'm afraid so. The President's hands are tied."

"Very sad, Megan. But how can I help?"

Her face brightened. "That's why I'm here. I have a proposal for you."

Mueller laughed. "You're a very attractive woman, but I'm happily married."

She smiled back. "Not that kind of proposal. Although that's an interesting thought. But it wouldn't work anyway, since I bat for the other team."

A puzzled look came over his face.

"I'm a lesbian."

"I didn't know."

"Not many people do. But since we've known each other a long time, I wanted to lay my cards on the table."

The man nodded.

"My proposal," she continued, "relates to our deficit and your ability to finance it."

He held his palms in front of him. "We do buy some of your Treasuries."

"Not many," she said. "I'm proposing you buy much more, and replace the Chinese as our largest creditor."

"You think we would be better financial partners?"

She leaned back in the chair. "I know you would. You Swiss like to make money. But you like to stay in the background. You wouldn't meddle in our affairs, like the Chinese do. You don't get involved with politics. During World War II, you remained neutral. Isn't that right?"

He rubbed his temple. "We...we did ignore the atrocities of Hitler. That's true. But tell me, Megan, what would we gain by buying more U.S. bonds? They're almost worthless."

She smiled sweetly. "Here's where my proposal gets interesting. Switzerland is a tiny country. How would you like to own large tracts of land in America?"

His eyes lit up. "What do you mean?"

"I've been working with congressional leaders and the President. If you agree to fund our debt, we would turn over Federal lands to you. Large parts of the national park system. Think of it – you could own pristine land next to Yellowstone and the Grand Canyon, and vast acreage in Montana and Utah."

Mueller's eyes widened, then a smile formed on his face. "You could do that?"

Megan nodded. "The President has authorized me to give you this." She reached in her notebook, pulled out a folded letter. Placing it on his desk, she said, "This is an initial proposal –we would have to work out the details, of course."

The man unfolded the letter and read it. "Amazing," he whispered. "Truly amazing. Your government must be desperate."

Megan sighed. "I'm afraid so."

Mueller leaned back in his chair, gave her a skeptical look. "But your citizens would certainly object. Americans are a proud people."

She nodded. "It's true, but our people are also greedy – they don't want to cut back on any government services. Our previous President tried that and he lost the next election."

Mueller went quiet for several moments, obviously in deep thought. Finally he sat forward in his chair. "I like it. This proposal gives Switzerland something we've never had. Vast territories."

"I agree, Henry. It's good for you and us. There's just one stipulation and it's an important one."

His eyebrows arched.

"We need assurances," she said, "that you would not interfere with our domestic or foreign policy."

Mueller smiled. "That will not be a problem."

"Good."

The man steepled his hands on his desk. "Of course, I have to get our board of directors to agree, along with the Swiss government."

She laughed. "We both know who runs this place. You."

"Ah, well, there is some truth to that. But, still, I have to convince a lot of people."

Megan reached into her notebook again, pulled out a second folded letter. "This is something to sweeten the deal." She handed him the letter and he began reading it.

"It's an agreement between our government and you personally, Henry. If this deal closes, we'll give you 5,000 acres of prime Wyoming land. And the best part of it, no one has to know but you." She smiled sweetly. "It would be our little secret."

Mueller looked up at her, a wide smile on his face. "You make it very tempting, Megan."

"That's my objective."

He nodded. "I will review your proposal and then meet with our board. I think they will be receptive. Then I'll have to convince...the others."

"Of course. How soon before you can let me know?"

"Several weeks, at a minimum. A month or two on the outside."

She forced a smile. "The sooner the better."

"Of course. By the way, would you like to have dinner with me tonight? We could talk in more detail...."

She stared at him. His eyes had a mischievous look that wasn't there before. "And dinner is all you have in mind? I thought you said you were a happily married man."

"I am. But you are a *very* attractive woman."

She chuckled, admiring his good looks. *It's not like I'm strictly a lesbian,* she mused. *I can go both ways, especially if it helps this deal.* "I'd love to have dinner with you, Henry."

He stood. "Excellent. I'll have my assistant set it up. I know this quiet little place overlooking the lake."

Megan stood and extended her hand. As they shook hands she studied his blue eyes. She had a good feeling about the deal. Maybe, just maybe, she could pull it off.

And if she did, the payoff could be immense. She was only in her forties and she had presidential ambitions. Something like this could pay big dividends in the future.

24 Days to Zero Hour

Washington, D.C.

Erica Blake stormed out of her boss's office in the FBI building, slamming the glass door on the way out. Once again Justin Temerius couldn't connect the dots. As she marched down the hall, her thoughts churned on the Carpenter case. There was something odd going on with the senator's death, and Temerius wouldn't accept it.

Skipping the elevator, she took the stairs, racing down the six flights to burn off her frustration. By the time she reached the parking garage in the basement, she was winded but less tense.

She found her Ford Explorer, got in and drove out of the garage, merging with the light nighttime traffic. Checking her watch, she realized why – it was past nine p.m. and the city's government workers had cleared out. They were already home in the nearby suburbs. She hadn't had dinner and almost stopped at her usual diner, but at the last minute decided to head straight home. The meeting with Temerius had given her heartburn and greasy food would make it worse.

Reaching her high-rise, she parked on the street and noticed a black Suburban SUV roll past slowly and take the next corner. She'd spotted a similar vehicle following her on the way over. She shook her head and chuckled. *Getting paranoid,* she thought. *There are a million of those things in the city.*

She entered the building, took the elevator to the third floor and let herself in the cramped, modest apartment. Her inexpensive furniture was from Ikea, and the walls were devoid of any personal items – no photos or art. Packing boxes, stacked in a corner of the living room, still sat unopened from when she'd moved in a year ago.

The place smelled of spoiled food and she checked her garbage bin in the kitchen. *Damn,* she thought. *Forgot to empty out the Italian take-out from yesterday.*

She was about to prepare a sandwich when her cell phone buzzed. Unclipping it off her belt, she glanced at the incoming call. Detective Gray. She held it to her ear as she slumped on the lumpy sofa in the living room.

"What do you have for me, Gray?"

"Well, hello to you too, Agent Blake. Thought we were on better terms."

"Sorry. Just met with the boss, you know how it is."

"Yeah. Been there. Listen, Erica, I ran down a couple of leads. This case is getting strange."

Her interest perked up. "Tell me."

"I talked to the power company a couple of times today. They gave me the runaround at first, then I threatened them with a subpoena. Finally they admitted what happened. The outage in Carpenter's area was caused by some type of EMP burst."

"An electromagnetic pulse? Thought those were caused by a nuclear explosion."

"That's what I thought too. But I was sniffing around, checked with one of my friends at the Pentagon – apparently the military has developed small, portable EMP devices. They create short bursts that knock out electricity. Black ops stuff."

"Damn, Gray – what the hell is this?"

"Dunno, but it's smelling like deep shit to me."

Erica rubbed her forehead, which was starting to pound from a headache. "When I met with Temerius, I told him about the military incendiary grenade. Told him I thought this was much bigger than a robbery gone wrong. But he wouldn't hear of it – said I should focus on the theft angle."

"Jesus. Well…like you said before, the guy's a jerk."

"That's a fact, Gray. But this new EMP stuff – he won't be able to ignore that. I'll check on the EMP stuff on my end. My ex-husband's a spook with the CIA – he'll be able to dig something up. In the meantime, why don't you go back to the scene, interview the neighbors again, see if anything else pops."

"You got it, Erica."

She hung up and put down the phone. Then she took off her blazer and unclipped the gun holster from her belt. After washing up, she went back to making dinner.

Opening the refrigerator, she looked at the meager contents on the shelves. A sad looking tomato, several containers of cold-cuts and a six-pack of Budweiser. Grabbing a bottle of beer and a package of ham, she started making herself a sandwich. Unfortunately all she had was stale bread, but it would have to do.

Sitting at her tiny dining table, she sipped from the beer as she absently chewed on the dry sandwich. Finishing a few minutes later, she snatched another longneck and sprawled on the sofa.

Grabbing her cell, she punched in numbers.

Moments later she heard Steve McCord's voice. "McCord here."

"Hey, it's me."

She heard him chuckle. "Hi, beautiful," he said. "How's D.C.?"

"It sucks. But you already know that. You still in Rome?"

"Yeah. It's a great morning. I'm having breakfast at that little trattoria by our hotel."

She took another sip of the Budweiser. "I'm jealous. I'd love to be there, doing nasty things to you right now."

McCord laughed. "Anytime, anywhere."

"Listen, hon, I'm working on the Carpenter case…."

"How's that going?"

She placed the beer bottle on the coffee table and sat up. "That's why I'm calling."

"I thought it was because you missed me."

"That too," she replied.

He chuckled. "Bullshit. What do you need?"

Just then there was an odd clicking sound on the phone and Steve's voice faded out for a moment. "You there?" she asked.

His voice came back. "Yeah. I'm here. The satellite signal must have kicked out."

"Guess so. Listen, there was a power blackout during the murders. Looks like an electromagnetic pulse was set off. The local detective on the case says the Pentagon's got some new portable device that can do that. Can you check it out?"

There was a pause on the other end, then he said, "Sure. Anything for you. I'll make some calls."

"Thanks. By the way, when are you coming home?"

"I'll be back in D.C. in a couple of days."

"Good. We'll get together. Maybe I'll fix us dinner."

He laughed. "You cook? No way. I'm not taking that big a chance."

"You bastard."

"Okay, Erica. Let's go out for dinner. The Palm?"

"Sure. But dessert at my place."

He laughed again. "I like you for dessert."

"Thought you would. See you." She turned off the call and took another sip of the beer.

Then she stretched out on the sofa, glanced at her watch. No way could she fall asleep now. As usual she was too wired.

Grabbing the remote, she turned on her small TV and surfed the channels. She found nothing interesting and eventually settled on one of the cable news outlets. Maybe that would help her fall asleep.

Listening idly, she rested with her eyes closed, the buzz from the beer making her lightheaded. Surprisingly, she fell into a fitful sleep.

She awoke with a start and gazed at her watch, which read 2 a.m. Realizing she'd slept over two hours, she knew she'd be awake the rest of the night.

Getting up, she went into the kitchen, grabbed another Budweiser and her Kindle and settled down at the dinette table to do some reading. Reading novels was one of the few ways she could pass the long stretches of sleepless nights.

She turned on the Kindle and began reading the mystery novel. She was halfway through it and was determined to finish it tonight.

Just then she heard a noise from outside her window and she got up and looked out. It was a quiet street, well-lit by several light poles along the road. Scanning the parked cars on the street, she noticed nothing unusual at first. Then she spotted it, a black Suburban, parked across from her building. It had heavily-tinted windows, so she couldn't see inside, but wisps of exhaust fume were coming from the tailpipe.

She didn't believe in coincidences. Un-holstering her Glock service weapon and tucking it in her waistband, she grabbed the flashlight in her kitchen and raced out of the apartment. She sprinted down the corridor, ducked into the stairwell, and quickly descended the three flights of stairs.

Rushing out of the building a moment later, she scanned the street.

But the black SUV was already gone.

23 Days to Zero Hour

20 miles west of Norfolk U.S. Naval Base
Virginia

Captain Bobbie Garcia stared out the side window of the unmarked Blackhawk helicopter as it skimmed over the rural, sparsely populated area. The chopper was the latest design in stealth technology and the sound from the rotors was muted, almost whisper-like. Garcia had picked it for that reason, since tonight's mission was more difficult than the last. Except for the vibration that shook the craft as it flew, he could swear the Blackhawk was a business helicopter instead of an efficient killing machine.

"It's up just ahead," the chopper pilot said over Garcia's headset.

"Copy that," the captain replied. Garcia looked back into the cargo compartment at the six heavily-armed men who sat across from him. Like him, the Special Forces team carried suppressed Heckler & Koch MP5 submachine guns and wore unmarked black uniforms and black helmets with night vision goggles.

"Okay guys," he spoke into his mike. "Almost there. Any questions?" They had rehearsed the operation several times and he wasn't expecting any. The men, all NCOs, shook their heads. Their expressions were stony.

Garcia had handpicked this team over the last year, swore them to secrecy and gave them specialized training in a facility located away from the other Special Forces units at Fort Bragg. His handler, the general, had appropriated the facility and Garcia and his men reported to him personally.

The captain looked out the window again, the ghostly green images of the tree line giving way to a large clearing by a curving rural road. Situated on the clearing was a sprawling, ranch-style house. Admiral Stanton's home. A widower, Stanton lived alone so Garcia hoped they could get in and out without any collateral damage.

The Blackhawk swooped down over the clearing just as one of the team unstrapped himself from the seat and slid open the side cargo door. A whoosh of air filled the cockpit and Garcia crossed himself. Feeling the adrenaline rush, his heart pounded in his chest.

"Let's go!" he yelled into his mike. The men scrambled to their feet, clutched the stubby MP5s and moved toward the door. Leading the way, the captain grabbed a handhold by the opening, stared out. The instant the chopper landed, he sprang out of the craft and sprinted toward the house, his combat boots making a sucking sound on the sodden ground. It had rained yesterday and the large grassy area of the backyard glistened with moisture.

They had landed a hundred yards from the house and the group fanned out as they ran forward. Halfway there, they stopped and took cover behind a row of bushes.

Scanning the home with his night-vision goggles, Garcia saw no light and no movement. It was 2:35 a.m. and the Admiral should be fast asleep.

Behind him the whisper of the chopper's rotor's died down and the night went quiet. All he heard was the drone of cicadas.

Garcia motioned to Master Sergeant Thomas and the man sprinted toward the house. Reaching it moments later, Thomas crouched by the side wall. His job was to cut the phone line, the power line and provide cover fire, if necessary.

Glancing at his watch, the captain counted off the minutes and then gave the signal to the rest of the team.

He ran forward, the MP5 in one hand.

The group spread out, surrounding the house, and in seconds were hugging the walls. Garcia quickly climbed the steps of the spacious wooden deck and crouched by the back door. Thomas was to his left and the man gave him a thumbs up.

Wasting no time, the captain glanced through a window into the house. Nothing moved in the darkened interior and he pulled the lock-pick toolkit that hung from his belt harness. Slinging the rifle over his shoulder, he selected one of the picks and worked on the lock for a moment. The tumbler gave way with a click and he turned the knob. Putting the tool away, he unslung the rifle.

He crouched in, trained his weapon in front of him and listened for any sounds.

It was quiet and he turned back, stepped outside a second and motioned to the others. Three of the men followed him back in the house.

Recalling the house diagrams his handler had provided, Garcia bypassed the kitchen to his right and followed the dark corridor on his left. The house had four bedrooms and Stanton's was at the end of this hallway. He headed there, while the others quietly opened doors, making sure the rest of the place was unoccupied.

Reaching the end, he pressed his ear against the closed door, heard nothing. Slowly turning the knob, he stepped inside.

A large lump lay on the king-size bed, covered by a light blanket. Garcia had been briefed on the admiral, knew the man was tall and overweight. He was sure the lump was Stanton.

He crouched near the sleeping man, verified the face. The admiral was an ugly man, with a large, hooked nose, pockmarked skin and bushy eyebrows. Clearly it was him. The man was wearing blue striped pajamas.

Taking a syringe from his vest, Garcia plunged it into the man's upper arm.

Stanton jerked awake, his big eyes bulging.

Garcia punched the man several times, the blows landing on the man's wide stomach, but the admiral fought back until a moment later the sedative kicked in. The admiral slumped back on the bed, unconscious.

Grasping a roll of duct tape clipped to his belt, he tore off a piece and slapped it on the admiral's mouth.

Just then Thomas came in the room, said, "Rest of the house is clear."

Garcia nodded, relieved. "Get a couple of the guys in here. We need to carry the fat bastard back to the chopper. Then grab one of the guy's suitcases, fill it with a week's worth of clothing and get Joey to start working on the cut cables. I want this place to look undisturbed."

"You got it, sir."

Before leaving, Garcia took the admiral's wallet, keys and cell phone, which lay on the nightstand.

***

Half an hour later the Blackhawk took off, the unconscious admiral stretched out on the floor in the back. As the ground receded below them, the dark house became a dot in the nighttime landscape.

Garcia was sitting in the co-pilot's seat and he turned his head to face the pilot. "How long before we reach the airfield?"

"No more than 20, Captain."

"Punch this thing. We're behind schedule."

Garcia was pressed into his seat as the helicopter picked up speed.

Ten minutes later the Blackhawk was hovering over an unmanned air field with only one landing strip. There was a small airport office building next to the runway, but the place was dark. A few small jets and twin-engine turboprops were parked off to one side in a fenced area. The place looked deserted.

At one end of landing strip, a Gulfstream jet waited with no lights on.

"There it is," Garcia said, pointing at the jet. "Land right by the plane."

The pilot pushed the joystick and the craft pitched forward. Seconds later it hovered again and touched down next to the black Gulfstream. Other than the tail numbers, the jet had no markings or logos.

Instantly, the side door of the jet opened and a ladder rolled out. Two uniformed men climbed out of the plane, their rifles at the ready. Garcia recognized them immediately – they were the rest of his team.

He unstrapped from his seat, grabbed his weapon and climbed out of the chopper. The sooner they got the admiral in the jet the better.

***

Las Vegas, Nevada

It was daylight when the Gulfstream landed on the remote airstrip ten miles north of Las Vegas. After touchdown, the jet taxied to the end of the runway and stopped. Garcia looked out the plane's window and saw nothing but empty desert, tall cactus and scraggly tumbleweeds. Mountains were visible in the distance.

He followed Sergeant Thomas out of the plane, and the rest of his team came out next, carrying Stanton down the steps. Scanning the area, Garcia noticed that next to the long, asphalt airstrip sat a gray Suburban with dark-tinted windows.

The men placed the admiral in the back of the SUV, along with the suitcase. When they were done, Garcia climbed in the passenger side front seat and closed the door.

The Suburban sped away, heading south.

***

The house is perfect for the job, Garcia thought when they drove up to the curb. The general had done well.

It was a small home, typical Las Vegas concrete-block design with a faded barrel-tile roof. And it sat away from the other houses in the scruffy, run-down neighborhood. Not far from the Strip, the area looked like an ideal hang-out for low-rent hookers, drifters and drug-addicts.

He climbed out of the car, gazed around. Not many people were out and they moved quickly away as soon as he spotted them. The guilty always run, he mused.

He motioned to Thomas, who went to the front door, unlocked it and went in. A minute later the man opened the single-car garage from the inside and the SUV slowly backed in, the large vehicle barely fitting in the narrow opening. The garage door closed and Garcia went in through the front door.

The place was a dump. Torn, dirty sofas were in the living room. Trash littered the floor. The scuffed walls were decorated with orange and yellow striped wallpaper.

His team stood in a semicircle in the kitchen, with the admiral lying on his back on the floor. The man was still unconscious and would be that way for several more hours.

Finding a chair by the dinette table, Garcia inspected it, brushed off dirt and sat down. Then he turned to Thomas. "All of us need to change out of these uniforms and into the civvies we brought. No sense in standing out. Then put Stanton in the bedroom and take the tape off his mouth. Take his clothes out of his suitcase and put them in the bedroom closet. After that, go find two prostitutes. And don't bring me skanky whores. I want lookers. Also, stop at one of the casinos, pick up some gambling chips."

The sergeant nodded and the men began to change into the casual civilian clothes they had brought. Then they carried the sedated man into the bedroom.

Thomas and another member of the team went into the garage and moments later Garcia heard the SUV pull away.

The captain changed into his civvies, put on disposable gloves, and sat back down on the chair. Then he folded his arms across his chest and leaned back in the wobbly chair.

All he could do now was wait.

***

An hour later Sergeant Thomas was back, trailed by two women in their mid-twenties. Both were busty, wore tight short-shorts and low-cut blouses that exposed bare midriffs. One of them was short and black, the other tall and blonde, but they were both good-looking. Only their eyes gave away their profession – they were way too weary for their age.

Garcia got up from the chair, studied the women closely as they walked up to him. One thing he knew for sure – in Vegas more than any other city, the whores were better looking.

"I'm Sugar," the black girl said, "and this is Lola," pointing to the blonde. "Heard you're looking for a good time." It was obvious Sugar was the leader of the two.

Garcia nodded. "That's a fact. My friend tell you what we want?"

Sugar laughed, glanced at the group of men in the room. "You're looking for a gang-bang. Fine with us. We give first-class service. But pulling a train costs extra."

"No problem. I've got plenty of cash."

She looked closely at the men's hands. "You guys are all wearing gloves. Is that some new kinky thing? Never seen that before."

"It's just something we like," Garcia replied.

She shrugged. "Like I said, we're not particular, as long as we get paid." She sidled up to him, put a hand on his shoulder and squeezed his bulging bicep. "What's your name, honey?"

"You can call me Bobbie."

She chuckled. "Bobbie. That's a sweet name for such a big, strong man like you."

"My wife says the same thing."

She rubbed his arm some more, then her voice turned business-like. "Let's get the money part out of the way first. Then we can have fun. It'll cost you a thousand. For each of us."

Garcia nodded, pulled out a thick wad of bills from his pocket. He counted out twenty one-hundred dollar bills and handed each woman her share of the money. "And if you're really good," he said, "I'll give you a big tip afterwards."

Her eyes sparkled. "I like you, Bobbie. You're my kind of guy."

The captain smiled, leaned down and rummaged through a canvas bag that sat on the floor by his feet. He pulled out a white, brick-shaped, cellophane-wrapped package. He held it up, showed it to the two women.

Sugar squealed. "Is that what I think it is?"

"It sure is," he replied, handing her the bag of pure cocaine.

The woman grabbed it, caressed the package like it was her first-born infant. "I never seen this much coke before."

Garcia smiled. "You two go in the bedroom, feel free to use as much as you want. My friend's in there, sleeping off a hangover. Just ignore him. I'll be in a few minutes."

Sugar's expression was ecstatic, as if she'd died and gone to heaven. "Take your time, Bobbie. Lola and me will have our own little party first. We'll be so hot and ready in five minutes that I'll have you coming before you know what hit you."

With that the woman took the other by the hand, and they rushed into the bedroom.

Garcia sat back down, glanced at his watch. He'd give them fifteen.

***

When Garcia and Thomas entered the bedroom, they found the blonde passed out on the floor by the bed. Also on the floor, kneeling, was Sugar. Both women were nude, their hands and faces coated with white powder.

The black woman was bent over the opened package of coke, its contents spilled over the dirty gray carpet.

She gazed up at him, her eyes glassy. "This is…good shit…Bobbie. The best…."

Garcia scanned the room quickly. The admiral's body, still dressed in the pajamas, was still inert, but he could tell the man was breathing.

Then he turned back to Sugar. "I told you you'd like it. Later, I'll let you take some of it home. How does that sound?"

"You're great...Bobbie," she said, slurring her words. "You know...that? Come on over here...let me polish...your knob...I got a mouth...that just won't quit...I'll suck you dry...bet the wifey...doesn't do that...anymore...." She laughed, leaned her head down and snorted more of the coke.

He walked up to her and squatted down so that when she turned her head back up he was facing her. The woman was a looker, with pendulous breasts and silky chocolate skin. *It's a pity*, he thought, *that I didn't meet you under different circumstances.*

She reached out and began to unbuckle his belt, but he grasped her hand, pushed it away. Surprise filled her eyes and he said, "I want to look at you first."

She must have thought that was funny because she began laughing uncontrollably.

"Be quiet, Sugar." He reached out with one hand and began to caress her face, staring intently into her large, dark-brown eyes. Then he gripped her jaw tightly.

With his other hand he pulled a combat knife from behind the small of his back and slashed her across the throat.

Blood spurted from her jugular and her eyes bulged wide. Still holding her face tightly, he watched as she struggled to pull away. But he was much too strong and she continued to bleed out. A moment later her bloody body slumped to the floor. Checking her pulse, he knew she was gone. By this time his shirt and gloves were smeared with blood.

Garcia got up and moved over to the blonde. Crouching down, he stabbed her in the abdomen several times, blood spurting on the carpet. The body spasmed and went still. He felt the side of her throat, knew she was dead.

Standing up, he turned to Thomas. "Strip the admiral, then spread the casino chips around the room."

While the sergeant took the pajamas off the man, Garcia pulled a snub-nosed .38 Special from his pocket. He screwed on a suppressor and walked over to the bed.

He stared down at the obese man, the admiral's pallid skin glistening from the cheap ceiling lamp. Garcia shook his head, disgusted at what he saw. The admiral had graduated from Annapolis, head of his class. He had been fit and trim back then. Shame he had let himself go. And shame he didn't embrace BlackSnow. It was going to cost him.

Garcia grabbed the man's inert right hand and closed it around the revolver's grip. Then placed the gun against the man's temple. He squeezed the trigger, the gun making a muted thumping sound. Stanton's head jerked the opposite way. A hole appeared in the temple and it began to ooze blood.

The captain unscrewed the suppressor, placed the gun back in Stanton's hand. He checked for a pulse and said, "It's done."

Grabbing the bloody knife, he placed it in the admiral's other hand, squeezed the fingers around the handle.

He stood back, looked at the scene, realized he needed to do a couple of other things. Picking up the half-used package of coke, he went around the room, spreading the contents on the floor and on the bed. Lastly, he took some of the white powder and pushed it up the admiral's nose and into his mouth. Then he spilled some of the coke on Stanton's naked chest and genitals. Satisfied, he threw the almost empty package on the floor.

Glancing at Thomas, he asked, "What am I forgetting?"

The sergeant thought a moment. "The wallet and his other stuff."

"Yeah, you're right." He pulled Stanton's wallet, keys and cell phone from his pockets. Taking the cash out of the wallet, he threw the money on the bed and on the floor. Then he placed the wallet, the keys and the phone inside the nightstand.

Garcia stood back, surveyed the room carefully and made sure everything had been staged correctly. "We're done."

Thomas smiled. "It should play out perfectly."

The captain nodded. "The general rented this house through a cut-out. For a month, so it may be weeks before the bodies are found. And when the LVPD find them, they'll realize it was something they've seen before. A drug-fueled sex party gone bad. Maybe the fat man was robbed by the whores or maybe he couldn't get it up, cause of the coke. Either way, he goes into a rage, stabs them, shoots himself, his brain fried from the drugs."

"In Vegas, gambling, hookers and drugs go hand-in-hand," Thomas said.

"That's a fact. In any case, the admiral's discredited and there'll be no suspicion that he was murdered. The Pentagon will be embarrassed, with one of their top brass going on a murder-and-suicide spree. They'll want to get this story off the front pages as soon as possible. And we get rid of a big roadblock for BlackSnow."

"Good plan, Captain. Bringing Stanton out here was brilliant."

"Yeah. I thought it was pretty slick."

Garcia took off his bloody gloves and shirt and stuffed them in a plastic sack that he had in the canvass bag. Taking out a fresh shirt and disposable gloves from the bag, he put them on. Then he said, "Go through the rest of the house, make sure we didn't leave anything behind. I'll check this room again, do the same thing."

Thomas nodded, turned and left.

Garcia scanned the scene one last time. He noticed Sugar's nude body was sprawled out on the floor, her legs wide apart. Thinking she ought to have some dignity in death, he pushed her legs together.

Staring at her open, lifeless eyes, he reached over and closed them with his finger.

Then he crossed himself, said a silent prayer asking for forgiveness, and left the room.

22 Days to Zero Hour

The Vice President's office
West Wing of the White House
Washington, D.C.

Vice President Taylor was at his desk sipping Dewar's when his assistant's voice came over the intercom. "General Corvan is here, sir," she said primly. "Needs to see you."

He gulped the rest of his drink and put the glass in a drawer. "Show him in, Alice."

Corvan came in, the two shook hands, and then sat down.

"Good news, General?"

"Yes, Mr. Vice President. Just got off the phone with Garcia. Our Stanton problem has been solved."

Taylor beamed. "Excellent. I'm glad that's behind us. Any collateral damage?"

"No, sir. Well, if you don't count the whores."

Taylor nodded. "I don't."

"The police will eventually find the bodies, but the captain's plan using Las Vegas should be very good cover."

The vice president leaned back in his chair and loosened his tie, then idly rubbed his stomach. "I'm glad you found Garcia. He's a keeper."

"I agree, sir. After this whole thing is over, I'll be giving him a special bonus."

"Good." He steepled his hands on the desk. "Now that you have my written authorization, are all the other contingencies for BlackSnow moving forward?"

"Yes, sir."

Taylor stared into the other man's eyes, looking for any signs of uncertainty. "You run into any problems, General?"

Corvan paused, was quiet a moment. "I have one minor concern, but I'm keeping it under control."

Taylor's face flushed. "What the hell is it?"

"The local police have been investigating the senator's death. As expected. But there was also an FBI agent assigned to the case, a woman named Blake. Erica Blake."

"Never heard of her."

"You wouldn't have, sir. She's not high up. I checked her background. Has a good record at the Bureau, but she's a hot-head. Doesn't get along with her superiors, has been transferred several times because of it."

"I see. So what's the problem?"

"She's been sniffing around. Picked up a possible military connection on the Carpenter case."

Taylor leaned forward in his chair. "You taking care of it? I don't want any screw-ups."

"Yes, sir. I have her under surveillance."

"What else, damn it?"

"I talked to the deputy director of the Bureau – a friend of mine. I've got it under control."

Taylor mulled that over a minute. "Okay. Stay on top of it."

"Yes, sir."

"The next phase of BlackSnow is coming up soon. Very soon. Are we ready?"

The general nodded. "Garcia's team has been rehearsing it for months. Everything's in place."

"Very good," he replied, as he rubbed his hands together. "I've been waiting for this for a long time."

"As have I, Mr. Vice President."

Taylor leaned back in the chair again, visualizing what was to come. A smile crossed his face.

The general cleared his throat. "Anything else, sir?"

The question brought Taylor back to the present. "No."

Corvan stood up, got ready to salute, but Taylor waved a hand in the air. "You can dispense with that from now on, at least in private. We're getting down to the wire here and we're becoming more like partners now."

The general smiled. "Thank you, sir."

***

The FBI Building
Washington, D.C.

Erica Blake went into Temerius' office and closed the door behind her. "I found the smoking gun," she said with a grin.

Her supervisor leaned back in his chair, a stony look on his face. "And what would that be?"

She sat on the forward edge of the visitor's chair. "Remember me telling you about the military connection?"

"This is on the Carpenter case?"

She gave him an incredulous look. "Of course. That's the most important thing I'm working on."

"Go on."

"Anyway," she said, "my ex's been digging into that side of it."

"The CIA guy, if I remember correctly."

She stopped and was about to mouth off at him for repeating the obvious. But she held her tongue for once, knowing she needed this guy on her side. "Yeah. That's right." She grinned again. "He found out that the EMP device that was used is top-secret, black-ops stuff. Brand-new, available only to specialized military units."

"I see," Temerius said as he brushed his mustache with one hand. The man went quiet, said nothing else.

"That's it? That's your reaction?" she asked, her voice rising. "This is a big break in the case. It means we're not dealing with a simple robbery. Not by a long shot."

Temerius folded his arms across his chest. "I'm glad you came to see me, Erica. I was just about to call you."

Her eyebrows shot up. "About?"

The man's face scrunched up, as if he knew her reaction would be negative. "I'm taking you off the Carpenter case."

Erica's jaw dropped. "You what?"

"Been giving it a lot of thought. I'm not sure you're the right agent for this."

"You've got to be kidding me!" she said, standing up. "I just got the biggest lead yet and you're taking me off? What are you, insane?"

"Sit down, Erica."

"I will not sit down." She leaned forward, planted her hands on his desk. Her voice dropping to a whisper, she added, "What's really going on here?"

The man uncrossed his arms, picked up a pen and began tapping it on the desk. "I'm re-assigning the case to Malone – give him the file."

"Malone's an asshole and you know it. He couldn't find a book in the library."

Temerius shook his head. "He's been in the Bureau a lot longer than you have."

"He also kisses your ass and doesn't make waves…."

The man held up his palms. "You may not agree with my decision, but it's done." He picked up a file from his desk and handed it to her. "I've got something else for you."

She ignored the file, leaned closer so her face was only inches from his. "I'm not taking this shit. I'm staying on the Carpenter case. I'll go over your head if I have to."

A thin smile crossed his face. "I've already talked with the deputy director. It's a done deal."

Her shoulders slumped and she sat on the chair. "You bastard."

"That may be, Erica. But I'm still your boss."

She wanted to punch him and wipe the smug look off his face. But instead she spoke in a low voice. "Why? Tell me what's really going on, Justin."

The man went quiet.

Moments later she shook her head slowly and picked up the file on his desk.

Without saying another word, she left the office.

***

Steve McCord's apartment
Washington, D.C.

Steve McCord unlocked the door and let himself in the well-appointed apartment. Switching on the lights and turning off the alarm, he carried his suitcase inside and slid it into a corner of the foyer. He was dead tired from the flight from Rome and unpacking would have to wait.

Taking off his suit jacket and shoulder holster, Steve placed them on a chair and headed to the bedroom. But as soon as he sprawled on the large bed, the door-bell buzzed.

"Damn," he muttered, getting up and going to the door. He opened it, was surprised to see who was there. She rarely came to his place.

"Just got home," he said, stifling a yawn. "Come on in."

Erica Blake stormed in and began to pace the spacious living room.

"What's wrong?" he said, alarmed by her actions and appearance. Her long black hair was disheveled and her blouse wasn't tucked into her pants suit. Unusual. Erica was one of the most well put together women he knew.

She stopped pacing and stared at him, her pale eyes blazing. "That bastard!"

He chuckled. "Which one?"

She continued pacing. "Temerius, that's who."

"Sit down, will you?"

"I can't. Been driving around the city for hours, trying to calm down."

"Hasn't worked," he said.

She halted and slumped on one of the expensive leather sofas.

"Want a drink?" he asked.

"What do you have? Budweiser?"

He shook his head. "Vodka, wine, and Heineken."

"Fine. I'll take the beer."

He went to the refrigerator and rummaged through the packed shelves. He grabbed a couple of bottles. Uncapping them, he handed her one and sat across from her on the opposite couch.

"So what's eating you?" he said after taking a sip.

She chugged the bottle, draining it in seconds. Then wiped her mouth with one hand. "Got more?"

He smiled, handed her his beer. "Tell me."

She took a deep swallow and set the bottle on the glass coffee table. "Temerius pulled me off the Carpenter case."

"Did I hear you right?"

"Hell, yeah," she said, her voice bitter.

Steve was shocked. "Did you give him the info I found out?"

She nodded. "Didn't matter to him. His mind was already made up."

"But that was a huge break in the case."

"Tell me about it." Picking up the beer, Erica drained it. Then she got up, went to the fridge and grabbed another. She stood by the open door as she guzzled the bottle. Finished with that one, she dropped it in the waste-basket, and rummaged through the fridge. "Damn," she said, "you don't have any more."

"Didn't know you were coming over. You rarely do. Otherwise I would have bought a case of Budweiser for you."

She turned from the fridge and glared at him. Then she glanced around the spacious, expensively furnished apartment. "I can't believe you CIA guys make so much more than us Bureau types. Every time I come here it pisses me off."

Steve smiled. "We could have stayed married."

She slammed the refrigerator door closed. "Yeah, there is that. But let's not rehash the past, okay?"

He nodded, as a familiar and sad feeling settled over him. He still loved her and wanted her back. But she was too independent for her own good. Pushing those thoughts aside, he stood up. "I'll get you a vodka."

She shrugged, sat back down on the sofa.

"Tell me more," he said as he mixed their drinks in the kitchen.

"It's weird, Steve. Justin just took me off the case, wouldn't say why."

"Who replaces you?"

"Malone."

He handed her the glass and sat across from her. He took a sip from his drink, pacing himself – he was so jet-lagged from the trip he knew if he drank too much he'd probably pass out. "I remember you telling me about him. He's –"

She held up a hand, made a face. "Don't get me started on *him*."

Steve laughed. "Okay, I won't." He paused, gave her a long look. "Why don't you run this up the ladder? Maybe the deputy director can help."

"Temerius beat me to it."

"Too bad, Erica. Look, I'm sorry this happened. You would've broken this case wide open."

"Tell me about it." She gulped her drink, emptied the contents. Finished, she held out the glass. "More."

"You sure? You've had a lot already."

Her eyes blazed. "I haven't had *nearly* enough."

He took the empty glass, mixed her another, came back and handed it to her. "So what's next?" he said as he sat back down.

"Temerius gave me some crappy case to replace it. A no-brainer I can do in my sleep." She took another sip. "But I'm not giving up on the senator's death."

"What do you mean?"

"I've been working with the local cop on the case – I'll keep in touch with him, work on this on the side. Something strange is happening and I'm going to find out."

"Is that wise? What if Temerius finds out what you're doing?"

She drained the glass, said, "I don't give a shit. I'll get even with him one day."

"You probably will."

"Count on it."

Erica thumped her empty glass on the table. "No more...shop talk," she declared, her words beginning to slur. A glint came into her pretty eyes. He knew what that meant.

He held up his palms. "I just got off a plane – I'm dead tired."

She stood up. "Sorry, buddy. No...excuses tonight...I need to get laid in the worst way."

He stood up and smiled. "You know I still love you."

"Yeah...I love you too...now, quit wasting time...."

He held out his hand and she took it. He led her into the bedroom, but her walk was unsteady, and she leaned against him to keep from falling over.

When they reached the bed, she steadied herself on the headboard and took off her jacket. Then she crawled on the bed, turned and lay on her back.

He was about to take off his shirt when he heard a slight snore.

Looking back, he saw she was fast asleep.

Sitting next to her on the bed, he softly caressed the faint scar on her cheek. *God, I love you,* he mused.

Getting up, he crossed the room and turned off the lights. Closing the door behind him, he headed for the spare bedroom.

***

Steve woke with a start. He was lying in bed on his back, the bedroom dim, when he felt a soft hand caress his bare chest.

Startled, he almost went for his gun. Then he realized it was Erica, her nude body snuggling up to him.

"How are you feeling?" he asked. "You had a lot to drink."

"Just needed a couple of hours of sleep," she replied, her hand massaging his abdomen.

"What time is it?"

She chuckled. "Time to screw."

"Have I ever told you that you use that word way too much?"

"Constantly."

He laughed. "You're a piece of work, Erica Blake."

She put a finger to his lips. "Did I ever tell you that you talk too much?"

"Constantly."

She laughed at that, then slid her hand across his chest and then headed lower, grasping him firmly. "Look what we have here."

He groaned from her touch and pulled her body closer to his.

"I love you, Erica," he said, his breathing heavy now.

She continued her ministrations and said, "Talk is cheap. Prove it."

Steve rolled on his side and gave her a kiss. She put her arms around him, kissed him back hungrily.

Spreading her legs apart with his hand, he then straddled her.

She let out a throaty laugh. "Come on in, cowboy, the water's fine."

As he thrust inside her, she let out a low moan.

Rocking over her slowly, he let the moment build. He wanted to postpone the ecstasy as long as possible.

21 Days to Zero Hour

Los Angeles, California

Bobbie Garcia peered through the binoculars, caught a glimpse of the man as he went into the Chinese Consulate. Garcia was in an unmarked black cargo van with heavily-tinted windows. At the wheel next to him sat Sergeant Thomas. They were parked across the street from the consulate, which was located west of downtown LA, near Wilshire Boulevard.

"It's him," Garcia said, placing the binos on the dash.

"You sure, sir?" Thomas asked.

"Yeah. He's wearing civvies today instead of the uniform, but it's definitely him. Army Lieutenant Jing Zhao, of the People's Republic of China." His handler had briefed him thoroughly on Zhao. The man was a military attaché to the consulate and possibly a Chinese spy. The perfect candidate. Unfortunately Zhao lived in a secure Chinese government compound in LA, so access to him was limited.

"How do you want to play this?"

Garcia glanced at his watch. "If he's on schedule, he'll be in there an hour, two at the most. So we just wait."

"Yes, sir." Thomas began tapping the steering wheel with his fingers.

"Nervous, Sergeant?"

"No, sir...actually, yes. The next couple of days are going to be difficult."

"Relax. We've rehearsed it many times." Garcia paused. "Trust me, it'll be fine," he added with more confidence than he felt. He would never admit it to his NCO, but this part of the op had him more than a little spooked.

"Okay, guys," Garcia said into the mike of his headset. "We'll be sitting here for a while, so get comfortable." In response, there was a chorus of 'yes, sirs' from the men in the cargo compartment of the van. A metal partition separated the front cab from the rear and the small window at the center of the panel was closed.

The captain stretched his legs, but kept his eyes glued to the entrance of the consulate. Car traffic was heavy on the busy avenue, but the van was custom-made and its high sitting position gave a clear view of the building.

***

At noon Lieutenant Zhao strode out of the consulate building, went through the front gate, and descended the wide steps to the sidewalk. He began to walk north. The man carried a satchel under his arm, and tugged at his suit, as if he wasn't comfortable in the garment.

Garcia turned to Thomas. "Let's go." Then he spoke into the mike. "Get ready guys."

The van took off, merged with the heavy flow of traffic and followed as Zhao crossed the next block. The man walked into a multi-story parking garage, and Garcia lost sight of him for a moment.

"Step on it, Sergeant. We can't lose him."

Tires squealing, the van went through the garage entrance and up a ramp. The building was full of parked cars and Garcia craned his neck to find the Asian man.

He spotted him climbing into a blue Jeep Wrangler. The vehicle was parked nose out by one of the large concrete supports. "There!" he said. "Block his car."

The van shot forward, screeching to a halt moments later. It stopped right in front of the Jeep.

Garcia banged on the metal partition and yelled into the mike, "Go! Go!"

His adrenaline pumping, he scrambled out of the van, scanned the inside of the parking garage. There were no people about on this level and he breathed a sigh of relief.

At the same time four of his men burst out of the back of the van and surrounded the Jeep. Like Garcia and Thomas, the four wore civilian clothing.

Zhao leaned on the horn, the loud blast echoing in the parking garage.

Garcia stood in front of the Jeep, held up a badge. "This is the police," he said loudly. "Step out of the car, sir."

The Chinese man looked confused, then worried, but a second later he climbed out. "What is this about? I have done nothing wrong."

"Just a routine check, sir. Please put your hands on the hood and spread your legs."

"I'm with the Chinese consulate," the man protested. "I have diplomatic immunity."

By this time, Garcia's team had surrounded Zhao and drawn their weapons.

"I apologize, sir," Garcia said, his tone calm. "I'm sure we can clear this up in no time. I just need to see your ID."

Zhao seemed to relax a bit. "It is in my jacket. I will get it for you."

"Don't move, sir. I'll get it out for you." As he approached the Chinese man, Garcia reached into his own pants pocket and pulled out a syringe. Two of his men grabbed Zhao by the arms, while a third slapped duct tape on his mouth.

Garcia rushed forward, plunged the needle into the man's arm and moments later the man ceased struggling. His body collapsed to the ground.

"Carry him into the van," the captain said. "Joey, get his keys and follow us in the Jeep."

"Yes, sir."

The group hurriedly lifted the body and carried it into the vehicle, just before a family emerged from the elevator at the end.

Garcia climbed in and the van raced off, the tires squealing all the way to the exit.

***

Pushing aside a corner of the vertical blinds, Garcia peered through the binoculars at the plaza below. It was dusk and light was beginning to give way to night. From his vantage point on the twentieth floor of the steel-and-glass office building, the rectangular grassy area was clearly visible. The plaza was ready for the next day, with American flags and colorful bunting arrayed behind the temporary podium that had been assembled. Among the police officers who were setting up barricades, he spotted four of his team. As part of the plan, his men were assisting with security. His gaze shifted up, toward the roofs of the other office towers that bordered the plaza. Secret Service sharpshooters were already there, setting up.

Garcia glanced left, saw Thomas was almost finished assembling the Chinese-made high-powered sniper's rifle. Like the captain, Thomas was wearing Marine fatigues and disposable gloves. An official lanyard dangled from the sergeant's neck, the anti-terrorism security clearance clearly displayed. The general had done a lot of work to make this possible, including the clearances and rifle.

Garcia let the binos dangle from his neck, then sat down on one of the metal chairs. They were in an unoccupied office, filled with half-assembled cubicles and stacks of metal chairs. Vacancy rates were at all-time high in LA due to the depressed economy, and places like this were a dime-a-dozen.

"All done," Thomas said, standing up. The large rifle sat in a clear area of the floor, a heavy tripod supporting the barrel.

Garcia got up, walked over and crouched by the gun. He caressed the finely-tooled steel, admired the large, precision scope. "It's a beauty, alright."

"Almost as good as our stuff."

Garcia nodded. "Pretty soon, their weapons will be better. You ready for tomorrow, Sergeant?"

"I need to work on the sighting, but yeah, I'm ready, sir."

"Good." He glanced at his watch for the thousandth time. "All we have to do now is wait."

20 Days to Zero Hour

The Vice President's office
West Wing of the White House
Washington, D.C.

Vice President Taylor had just finished reading the latest budget proposal from Congress when he heard a knock at his door.

His assistant, Alice, came in the room. "Sir, you wanted me to remind you. The President will be giving his speech soon." In her late fifties, the matronly woman was prim but also very efficient.

"Yes. Thank you, Alice."

She went to the wall-cabinet, opened it and turned on the large TV. Then she handed him the remote. "Will there be anything else, sir?"

"No, Alice."

She left the room and he switched the channel to ZNN News.

The image on the screen showed a large plaza filled with a crowd of spectators. Uniformed police were everywhere and barricades kept the public well away from the podium. Dozens of American flags decorated the area. Behind the podium, the mayor of Los Angeles was speaking and standing to his left were President Wilson and the governor of California.

The image on the screen changed to a blonde female reporter standing off to one side of the plaza. "The Mayor is continuing with his remarks," she said in a perky voice. "After his speech, the Governor will address the crowd, and lastly the President will speak. It's an important event today, commemorating the new economic stimulus package that has been granted to the state of California." She paused, her cheery demeanor dimming a bit. "As you know, the state is beset with a massive budget deficit, and this new package will alleviate that...."

Taylor muted the sound.

But he watched intently, not wanting to miss a moment of the event.

***

Los Angeles, California

Bobbie Garcia watched as two of his men carried the still unconscious Zhao into the office and placed his inert body a few feet from the tall windows. As before the blinds were still closed.

One of the Marines tore off the duct tape from the Asian man's mouth, then took off the binds on the hands and feet.

In the center of the office, by the windows, Sergeant Thomas lay on the floor, cradling the large sniper's rifle. The rifle was pointed out the window. A small hole had been cut on the blinds and the glass, giving Thomas a clear view of the plaza below.

Garcia peeked out the window, scanned the area again with his binoculars. The mayor was still talking. The man had a penchant for long speeches and he was proving it again today.

Turning away from the windows, he crouched by Zhao. Then Garcia removed a small pill from his own pocket. He pried open the man's mouth and carefully inserted the pill by the back molars. Using both hands, he clamped Zhao's jaw shut, heard a snap. The cyanide pill had cracked, he knew.

He waited a moment, then checked the man's pulse. There was none.

Standing up, he studied the body, his thoughts racing over all the details. He wanted to make sure he wasn't forgetting anything. Earlier, they had wrapped Zhao's hands on the rifle's barrel, stock, scope and even the high-powered rounds. When the event was investigated, it would be clear that the Chinese man was the culprit. And to avoid capture and questioning, he had committed suicide. *It's a good plan*, he thought. He and his men just had to clear out of the office quickly after the event. Then, during the panic and bedlam that would ensue, they would rush out of the building and help the police and Secret Service secure the area.

Garcia walked over to where Thomas was crouched. The sergeant was fiddling with the scope.

"You ready?" Garcia asked.

Thomas looked up. "Yes, sir."

"Shouldn't be long now."

Garcia stepped to the windows, peeked out again. The governor was beginning his remarks.

He glanced at his watch, then back out the window. His heart was thudding in his chest.

***

Washington, D.C.

Erica Blake was sitting on her couch in her apartment, idly watching news and munching on a sandwich. It was noon and she had decided to come home for lunch, skipping the cafeteria at the FBI building. She took another bite and washed it down with a sip of Pepsi. Leaning back on the couch, she set the bottle down and picked up the remote. Switching from the local news, she turned on ZNN. They were covering some type of event where President Wilson was speaking. The president droned on and she was about to switch channels when the man winced, then crumpled to the ground.

Sitting up quickly, her gaze was transfixed to the screen. Men in dark suits rushed to the podium. She watched as these Secret Service agents formed a protective cordon around the president's body. Their guns drawn, the men looked up and away, their mirrored sunglasses reflecting the bright sunlight.

While several of the agents hurriedly carried the body away, screaming erupted from the crowd. People scattered, pushing and shoving their way out of the plaza.

A woman's voice came over the images. "Something has happened to the President," she said in an agitated voice. "He appears to have fallen during his speech. We're checking on his status." She paused a moment, then continued, "One of our sources tells us that it appears the President has been shot...."

Erica leaned forward on the couch, not believing what she heard. She picked up the remote, changed to Fox News.

After watching for a minute, she realized with a sinking feeling that it was true. The president had been shot and badly wounded. It was unclear if the assassination attempt was fatal.

19 Days to Zero Hour

Zurich, Switzerland

Senator Megan Lewis's head was pounding from a massive headache. She rested on her back, naked, on the bed of her luxury hotel suite, her thoughts racing over the recent events. Mentally worn out, she hadn't been able to get up and dress this morning.

She rubbed her temples, her brain still trying the process what had happened.

Yesterday morning she had been ecstatic – Director Mueller had informed her that the deal she proposed had been approved by his board of directors. The other approvals would take place, he said, faster than anticipated.

Then later in the day she had learned the other news. President Wilson had been assassinated in LA, his corpse rushed back to Washington D.C. Vice President Taylor had been quickly sworn in as the new president.

After the initial shock of the news wore off, her mind went into overdrive. *What kind of impact does it have for me personally?* Megan had been close to Wilson and was able to influence his decision making. She had been the architect of the Swiss deal. But now that Wilson was dead, would the new president support it? Her thoughts turned to Matt Taylor. She despised the man, recalling the many arguments they'd had over the years. Her past rocky relationship with him didn't bode well. He would block her at every turn. Probably sink her own presidential ambitions.

She kept massaging her temples, but it was no use – the damn headache wouldn't go away. Rolling off the bed reluctantly, she shuffled to the bathroom and took three aspirins, washing them down with tap water.

She was about to get in the shower when the phone in her room rang.

Picking up the receiver, she heard a familiar voice on the other end. It was FBI agent Erica Blake.

"Erica," the senator said, a smile coming to her lips. "Haven't heard from you in ages. How the hell are you?"

"Sorry I haven't kept in touch, Senator. But you know how it is."

"Yeah, I know. How'd you find me?"

"I called your office, Senator. They gave me your hotel."

"So," Megan said, as she leaned her bare bottom against the bathroom sink. "Is this a social call or business?"

"Business, I'm afraid."

"Too bad." Megan recalled their last meeting, how pleasant that had turned out. "So what's up?"

"I was assigned to investigate Senator Carpenter's recent death. I found out some unusual things, then I was taken off the case."

"I see. What did you find out?"

"I'd rather not say over the phone, Senator. I'd like to meet in person."

"Okay. I'll be back in Washington today. We can meet then."

"I'd appreciate that."

"I'll be tired from the trip when I get in, so I'll be going directly home. Why don't you meet me there? I'll call you when I land."

***

Bethesda, Maryland

Erica Blake climbed the steps leading to the portico of the stately home. You could tell the place was expensive, but at the same time it wasn't showy. Erica remembered something from the senator's past – before going into politics, the woman had founded a high-tech company, then sold it to Microsoft for a sizeable amount.

Erica rang the bell and waited.

A thin woman wearing a maid's uniform opened the door. "You must be Miss Blake. The senator is expecting you."

She was led into a large study, its walls lined with custom bookcases filled with old, probably rare books. The room was furnished with understated, but expensive leather couches that rested on Persian rugs. A marble fireplace dominated the far wall.

Before she had a chance to sit down, Senator Megan Lewis walked in the room.

"There you are," Lewis said, giving her a mischievous smile. "You look lovely as ever."

"Thank you, Senator. Kind of you to say that."

They shook hands and sat down on opposite couches.

She studied Lewis closely. The good-looking woman was wearing a casual, blue jumpsuit and her short blonde hair was still damp, as if she'd just come out of the shower.

"How was your trip?" Erica asked.

Lewis beamed. "Very successful." Then her smile faded. "But after the tragedy here, maybe less so."

"The assassination is still hard to believe," Erica said.

"As is Taylor's new position. That bastard and I are less than friends...."

Erica nodded. In her past meetings with Lewis, the senator had made no secret of her dislike for the man. "Well, maybe you two can patch things up, Senator. Every day is a new day."

Lewis gave her a skeptical look. "We'll see." She leaned back on the couch, crossed her legs. "You wanted to see me? Something about Senator Carpenter?"

Erica leaned forward. "During my investigation, I found a connection between the killer and high-grade military equipment. Black-ops stuff newly developed. Only available to U.S. government types."

"I see. How good are your sources?"

"The best. My ex, the spook, found it."

Lewis smiled. "How is that dear man?"

Erica chuckled. "He's very useful, in the right circumstances."

The senator laughed, gave her a wink. "He's a hunk. I bet he is useful."

Erica recalled her last meeting with the senator, when after a long night of drinking, she had succumbed to the woman's charms. Though pleasant, the new experience was one she wanted to avoid in the future.

"Yes, Senator. Anyway, after I got this and several other leads, the FBI took me off the case."

Lewis's smile faded. "Why?"

"My boss wouldn't say."

"Curious."

"I thought so. I was mad as hell at the time, still am really. But I've calmed down a bit and I'm still working on the case, on my own."

Lewis nodded. "Good girl. I'd probably be doing the same in your shoes. So. You wanted to see me so that I can help you in some way?"

"Yes, Senator. Something odd is happening and I suspect people in the Bureau are covering it up. I went over my boss's head, talked with the deputy director. He clammed up, told me to get out of his office."

The senator gave her a sly grin. "I'm somewhat of a barracuda – I may be able to find out what's going on. Senator Carpenter was a good friend of mine and I took his death hard."

"Yes, ma'am. There's something else."

The woman arched her eyebrows. "What?"

"I have no facts, just a feeling," Erica continued. "What if Carpenter's death and the President's are linked in some way?"

Lewis's voice turned hard. "Do you have any proof?"

"No, ma'am. I just find it too coincidental – two high-level deaths in such a short period of time."

The senator nodded and a thoughtful look came over her face. "I see your point. Keep digging, and let me know the minute you have anything. I'll be glad to help you anyway I can."

"Thank you, ma'am."

Lewis stood up, came over and sat next to Erica. "You can dispense with the ma'am stuff. We've known each other too long for that. Would you like a drink?"

Erica didn't reply at first, her mind recalling their last meeting. Against her better judgment, she said. "Just one. Then I have to go."

"Of course," the woman replied, as she rang a small bell that was on the ornate wooden coffee table. "What would you like?"

"Beer's fine, ma'am, I mean Megan."

The maid came in the room, took the drink order and left. She was back in a minute, placing a heavy tumbler in front of the senator, and a glass and a bottle of Sam Adams in front of her.

Lewis picked up her glass and took a sip. "So, tell me what's going on with your personal life. Any new men? Anything serious?"

Erica glanced at the beer bottle, fought the temptation to pick it up. "New men – yes. But nothing serious. Seems like I always go back to McCord. Strange, huh?"

The senator put down her drink, placed a hand on Erica's leg. The FBI agent was wearing long slacks, but the touch still gave her a tingling feeling.

"No, Erica. It's not strange at all. I always say people gravitate to what's most comfortable."

"You're probably right, Megan."

"The beer's getting warm, dear. Why don't you have some? It'll relax you, take the edge off."

The senator's hand moved closer to Erica's inner thigh and a sensual thrill shot through her. Erica stood up abruptly and began to pace the room. Then she stopped and stared at the woman.

"What happened last time, Senator…."

Lewis smiled. "Did you like it?"

"I never had sex with a woman before that."

"But did you like it?"

"Yes."

"Then what's the problem, dear?"

Confused, Erica grabbed the beer bottle and gulped the contents. She drained it in seconds, set it back down. "I'm sorry, Senator. I'm just not comfortable with the idea."

Lewis smiled. "Give it time. I won't rush you again. When you're ready, let me know."

Erica folded her arms in front of her. "Can I still count on your help?"

"Of course. I want to find out the truth as much as you do."

Erica uncrossed her arms and extended her hand to shake. Lewis took it with both of hers, held it.

"We'll get to the bottom of this, Erica. Trust me, if there's a cover-up, we'll find it."

Erica stared into the other woman's eyes, saw the steely determination there. She was glad she had set up this meeting.

"Thank you, Senator. I'll show myself out."

18 Days to Zero Hour

Beijing, China

General Wu Chang was nervous. He was sitting alone in his office, tapping his thick eyeglasses on the desk. An infantry veteran, he was used to battle and war. But this was different. Much different.

His role as the primary contact with the American president had been altered, maybe forever. The assassination of Wilson had seen to that. And now the new president, Taylor, wasn't returning his calls. Furious at first, Chang eventually calmed down. Taylor was a different man and would have to be handled differently. But in the end, the new U.S. President would have to crawl back to him, hat in hand. The Americans were desperate and urgently needed Chinese financial support.

A small smile crossed his lips as he visualized this, but a moment later he frowned. There was the other problem. A possibly bigger problem.

Chang's spies in the American State Department had told him there was evidence the assassination had been perpetrated by the Chinese government. This alarmed the general, the Premier, and the high-ranking members of the Politburo. The idea was unthinkable. It was also false. The last thing China wanted was to stir up anger in the United States.

But what worried Chang most was the disappearance of a military attaché at the Chinese consulate in Los Angeles, the same city where the assassination took place.

He picked up the phone, spoke with Lin. "Find Colonel Deng," he said. "I want to see him immediately."

***

Colonel Deng stood in front of him, his body ramrod straight. The man was short and wiry, and his military uniform was freshly pressed.

"At ease, Colonel," Chang said.

Deng's body visibly relaxed.

The general leaned back in his chair. "Tell me about the military attaché. What have you found out?"

"Yes, General. His name is Lieutenant Jing Zhao. He has been assigned to our Los Angeles consulate for a year. In addition to being a military attaché, he works for the MSS, our spy agency. He has an exemplary military record with several commendations, so it is unlikely he defected."

"I see. Our people have been searching for him?"

"Yes, sir. We've been looking for him since he disappeared. We've checked with the American police, the hospitals, and the morgue. He's vanished."

"What about his personal belongings? His bank accounts?"

"His clothes and personal effects are all still in his apartment, General. His vehicle is missing. As far as his bank accounts and credit cards, there have been no withdrawals or activity for days."

Chang mulled this over a minute, took off his glasses and wearily rubbed his eyes. Then he placed the eyeglasses on the desk, leaned forward in his chair. "Keep looking, Colonel. This has the highest priority. If you find anything, contact me immediately."

"Yes, General."

"Dismissed."

The man saluted, turned and left the office.

A sinking feeling settled in Chang's stomach. Zhao's disappearance was an ominous sign.

***

Los Angeles, California

Steve McCord looked across the grassy plaza, which was now ringed with crime-scene tape and police barricades. The area was swarming with police, FBI, Secret Service, and forensic lab techs. To his left, the podium still stood, although the flags had been taken away.

Although not assigned to the assassination case since the CIA had no in-country jurisdiction, Steve had nevertheless talked his boss into letting him come out here. Steve was an astute problem solver and if he were to help with the case, it would make the Agency look good.

Striding over to the podium, he looked up at the surrounding office towers. From the case reports and from the frenzied activity at its entrance, he knew the shots had been fired from the building directly across from him. The high-rise looked no different than the others. It had the same bland, steel-and-glass boxy shape that filled this city.

The shots had been fired from an empty office on the twentieth floor of the building. A hole had been cut in the window. The corpse of the assassin had been found soon after the shooting, but details about the man were being kept secret. Pending further investigation, only the Secret Service and a few higher-ups in the FBI knew his identity.

Steve glanced around the buildings again, scanning the roofs. Something bothered him, but he couldn't pin it down.

He headed toward the entrance of the building, hoping to learn more. You could tell a lot by seeing the scene from the killer's vantage point.

17 Days to Zero Hour

The Oval Office
The White House
Washington, D.C.

President Matt Taylor stared out the three, tall windows, and then turned back to the large, oval office. He stood behind and admired the historic wooden desk named the *Resolute*. The desk had been built from the timbers of the *HMS Resolute*, a British naval ship. Queen Victoria had given the desk as a gift to President Rutherford Hayes in 1880. It had been used by many presidents, including Kennedy, Reagan, Bush, Obama, Trump, Cooper, and his own predecessor, Wilson.

Taylor caressed the ornate wood of the desk, savoring the moment. Now it was all his. He glanced up at the rest of the room, at the beautiful, historic furnishings. It was all his.

He'd waited a long time for this. Had sat in this room talking with Wilson, while visualizing this very moment. A smile crossed his lips.

Taylor glanced down at his ample mid-section, and buttoned the jacket of his custom-made suit. Shaking his head slowly, he swore to himself he would lose weight. He only had one year left of his predecessor's term, so an election was just around the corner. The last fat president was Taft, and that was a long time ago. Americans loved to eat, he mused, but they disliked the idea of an obese president.

Taylor's reverie was broken by a knock at the door.

His assistant Alice stuck her head in. "Excuse me, Mr. President. They're ready for you in the Situation Room."

***

Taylor walked into the large conference room and immediately everyone stood up. He went to the head of the table and sat down. "Please," he said, "have a seat."

The men and women of the Cabinet, and the military chiefs, all sat down.

He surveyed the room quickly, scanning the familiar faces. This was his first meeting as president in this famous room, and he wanted to savor the moment. Almost all of the participants here were holdovers from Wilson's team. He had made only one change. To his right sat General Corvan, who replaced the previous White House Chief of Staff.

"Let me begin," Taylor said, "by thanking everyone one here for their tireless work over the last few days. I know most of you have been working 24/7, ensuring a smooth transition during this time of national crisis." He paused, put on his most sincere expression. "I also want to express my humility for the great responsibility that has been transferred to me. I only wish to serve this great country with the same high level of integrity that President Wilson did. My prayers and condolences are with the president's grieving family."

Taylor paused and breathed a sigh of relief. It was difficult praising his predecessor, but necessary.

He spread his hands flat on the conference table. "I want to promise each and every one of you that I will do everything in my power to find out the truth about the assassination." His voice rising, he added. "I will not rest until his death is avenged."

Turning to Corvan, he said, "General, can you bring us up to speed on the investigation?"

"Yes, Mr. President. I've been talking with the Attorney General, and he has the latest information."

Taylor turned to the tall, black man to his right. "Okay, Mr. Harwood, fill us in."

"Yes, sir," Harwood replied. "First off, what I'm going to say is classified information and highly confidential. It should not leave this room, until you, Mr. President, deem it to be appropriate." Taylor nodded and Harwood continued. "The FBI and the Secret Service have taken the lead on the investigation and they have made tremendous progress, considering how recently the assassination took place."

"Go on, Harwood," Taylor said impatiently. "Let's save the kudos for later."

"Of course, Mr. President. The assassin was a Chinese man named Zhao, a Chinese military officer to be exact –"

There was a chorus of astonished expressions from the group, and Taylor held up a hand. "Please, let the man talk."

"The FBI's best current hypothesis," Harwood continued, "is that the assassin was a Chinese government operative. The type of sniper rifle he used is only available to top-military. Unfortunately, the killer committed suicide after the shooting. He swallowed a cyanide capsule, probably to avoid capture and questioning. By the way, we traced the cyanide to a plant in Shanghai, China."

His tone skeptical, Taylor asked, "How reliable are your sources?"

"Very sure, Mr. President. The deputy director of the FBI is personally in charge of the investigation. He has assured me that Bureau labs have confirmed this information."

Taylor nodded. His voice was grave as he said, "But what would the Chinese gain by killing Wilson?"

"I don't know, sir. Maybe they wanted to destabilize our country. We know they're itching to be the predominant power in the world. In any case, I've got all our people in the Justice Department working on that exact question."

"Good work, Harwood. You are to be commended for your quick analysis. Keep me fully briefed as more details come in."

Harwood smiled, said, "Yes, sir."

The president turned back to the group and leaned forward in his chair. "Until this investigation is complete, I want to keep this meeting confidential. This information is too explosive to release without all the facts."

Everyone in the room nodded their assent.

He put his hands flat on the table. "That will be all, ladies and gentlemen. We'll reconvene soon. General Corvan, please stay, will you?"

The meeting room emptied out except for the two men.

A smug smile crossed Taylor's face. "That went well, don't you think?"

"Excellent, Mr. President. What do you want me to do next?"

Taylor stared at the general. "That's obvious. Leak the Chinese connection to the press."

16 Days to Zero Hour

Aboard the USS Nevada
U.S. Navy Trident nuclear submarine
100 miles west of San Diego
The Pacific Ocean

Commander Roger Lamont was in his quarters working on his laptop when he heard a rap at his hatch door. "Come in," he said as he looked up.

Lieutenant Michael Johnson came in the small room, closed the hatch behind him.

"What is it, Lieutenant?"

"Sir," Johnson said, "we're getting close to the Demarcation Line. I thought you should know."

Lamont knew he was referring to the Presidential Directive Wilson had issued, which limited the U.S. Navy to coastal waters. He gritted his teeth and he could feel his blood pressure rising. "Yes, Lieutenant. I'm aware of that." He motioned to his computer. "I just received an encrypted message from the Pentagon. We've been given new orders. Our sub is exempt from the Directive. We're sailing west."

Johnson looked confused. "But what about the agreement with the Chinese?"

"Screw the Chinese. We have a new president now. As I understand it, he's 'modifying' the agreement."

"Yes, sir."

"Take us down to a depth of 10,000 feet, then we go west at a heading of 273 degrees, full speed."

"What's our destination, Commander?"

"I'll let you know."

***

Zurich, Switzerland

Director Henry Mueller sipped coffee in his office as he read the bold headline across the front page of the newspaper. *American President may have been assassinated by the Chinese*, it read.

Finishing the article, he sat back in his chair and gazed out the window at the lake below. A queasy feeling settled in the pit of his stomach. The picturesque scenery outside didn't calm him, as it usually did.

Picking up his phone, he said, "Get me Senator Lewis — she's back in Washington." Replacing the receiver, he waited for his assistant to locate the woman.

Twenty minutes later his phone rang and he picked it up.

"Henry," Lewis said, "I'm glad you called." Her usual cheery voice sounded strained.

"I've been reading the news, Megan. The assassination...I'm sorry for the loss of your president. I know you two were good friends."

"It's tragic," she replied. "I'll miss him."

"Megan, I know things must be difficult right now, and that a lot is up in the air. But my board of directors has asked me how this affects our deal. As I told you, they agreed to it and would like to proceed."

"As would I. But it was all negotiated with Wilson. Now that he's gone...."

"Is the deal dead then?" he pressed. The thought of owning 5,000 pristine acres in Wyoming now seemed elusive.

"No. Absolutely not," she replied, but there wasn't much confidence in her voice. "I just need to get President Taylor involved. I'm sure he'll recognize what an excellent solution this is."

"I see. I'm assuming this may take some time?"

"I'm afraid so, Henry. Things in D.C. have to settle down. So much has happened."

"I understand."

"I'll call you next week – after I have a chance to meet with the president."

"Of course. If I can do anything to expedite the matter, let me know."

Mueller replaced the receiver and sipped his coffee, now cold.

***

Los Angeles, California

Steve McCord stared out the office windows where the shots had been fired. It was his third visit up here and he now realized something was terribly wrong.

The grassy plaza below was still ringed with crime-scene tape and barricades, but there were less police in the area. The remaining people on the ground looked like FBI techs and Secret Service types.

There were several techs still in the office he was in, scouring the place for trace evidence.

He glanced out at the other office towers, specifically at the roofs of the buildings.

There was no way the Secret Service stationed there on the day of the shooting could have missed it. The assassin had only made a small hole in the window, but it still didn't track. *They're too well trained,* he thought. *It doesn't smell right. It's either incompetence or something much worse.*

Keeping his thoughts to himself, he walked past the techs and headed out of the office.

Moments later he was back on the sidewalk in front of office building.

Deciding that his cell phone might not be the best idea considering what he suspected, he scanned the area in both directions for a pay phone. A rarity nowadays, he finally found one four blocks away.

Dialing her number, he waited for her to pick up.

"Blake," she said.

"Hi, beautiful," he replied.

"Hey, Steve. You still in LA?"

"Yeah. Listen, something strange is going on."

"Like what?"

"Something's not right."

"Spill it."

"Can you get to a pay phone, Erica? I'm calling from one now. I'd rather not talk over this line. Here's the number."

"Call you back in five, Steve."

He hung up and waited for her call. The pay phone rang seven minutes later and he picked it up.

"Okay, this better be good," she said, out of breath. "I just ran six blocks to find this damn thing."

He laughed. "The exercise will do you good. Keep your pretty ass in shape."

"You're not going to touch my ass anytime soon, if you don't start talking."

"Okay," he replied, chuckling. Then he turned serious. "Like I was saying, something's not right. The assassin fired from an office building across from the plaza. The Secret Service sharpshooters who were posted on the nearby buildings would have spotted him."

"Maybe they screwed up and missed him, Steve. I read the crime-scene report you sent me. The hole the shooter made in the window was small."

"It's possible, but unlikely. Those guys are well trained. And there's another thing."

"What?"

"The Service would have canvassed the area thoroughly before the event. They would have searched any empty offices in the nearby buildings."

"You're right, Steve. So you think somebody on the inside is involved?"

"I'd put money on it."

"What do we do?"

"I'm going to run it up my chain of command at the Agency, see what happens. But I've got to be careful. If this is a conspiracy, there's no way to know how far up it goes."

"Okay, Steve. I can't talk to anyone at the Bureau about it. Not many people I trust there. But I'll share it with someone I do trust."

"Who's that?"

"I'd rather not say."

"I understand, Erica. I'm heading back to D.C. tomorrow. See you soon."

***

Special Operations
Marine Corps Detachment
Training Facility, Building 14
Fort Bragg, North Carolina

Bobbie Garcia looked at his computer screen and smiled. The wire transfer had just gone into his secret Cayman bank account, effectively doubling his previous balance. Retirement from the Marines was much closer now. And in 16 days, when everything was all over, the amount would quadruple. That was the deal the general had promised him and the general had never let him down.

Garcia studied the numbers closely, reflecting on how the rest of his life would unfold. A sweet job in private security work, with one of the black-ops organizations the Pentagon kept on retainer. His wife Maria would be happy then. They'd have two kids, maybe more. Then a dark thought crossed his mind. *She can never find out. Maria can never know where the money came from.* Raised Roman Catholic with a strict sense of right and wrong, her view of him would be shattered if she found out. Then a solution popped in his head. *Once I get the new job in private security work, I'll tell her I received bonuses from it.* Satisfied with that, he closed the file and turned off the laptop.

He glanced around his cramped office in Building 14, the facility the general had appropriated for his team. The office furnishings were basic, with plain metal desks, metal folding chairs, and ubiquitous military green paint on the walls. But the place had one important distinction. It was in a separate area, well away from the other Special Forces units such as Delta, SEALs, and Green Berets housed at Fort Bragg. Although all Special Forces teams were secret, black-ops, need-to-know units, Garcia's team was the only one that didn't go through the normal chain-of-command. They reported directly to the general. Garcia's team was officially part of MARSOC, the U.S. Marine Corps Special Operations Command, which is headquartered in Camp Lejeune, North Carolina. But his specific team had been assigned to work at Ft. Bragg on the top-secret BlackSnow operation.

There was a knock at the door and Sergeant Thomas stepped in the room. The man had a wide smile on his face.

"I'm guessing you saw your bank account?" Garcia asked.

"Yes, sir."

"Sweet, huh?"

"Very."

"Have a seat, Sergeant."

Thomas sat, and Garcia leaned forward in his chair and folded his hands on the desk.

"Sergeant, the team has done well over the last couple of weeks. Extremely well. We've accomplished all of our objectives. Notify the men they can take tomorrow off. We've got more to do and I want them fresh." He paused, then said. "That includes you too, Sergeant. Take tomorrow off."

"Thank you, sir. How about you? You going back home?"

"No, Sergeant. I've got something else that needs to be done."

***

Garcia peered through the binoculars at the large home. The general had been very specific with his instructions on this task. Observe only, nothing else. It seemed odd to Garcia, considering how much damage his team had already inflicted. But he didn't question it. He was a Marine, and Marines followed orders.

15 Days to Zero Hour

The Oval Office
The White House
Washington, D.C.

President Taylor sat behind his desk and adjusted his tie, while a female assistant touched up his makeup. Two television cameras had been set up ten feet in front of his desk, along with a teleprompter. Floodlights lit up the room, the glare bothering his eyes and making him perspire. He felt beads of sweat on his forehead and the assistant quickly dabbed them away.

His stomach churned as he went over the speech in his head. This would be his first nationwide address as president, and he didn't want to blow it. The election was only a year away and he had to make a good impression.

Off to one side of the room stood several members of the Cabinet, along with General Corvan. He gave them a quick glance, then looked down at his custom-made suit, which was buttoned at the waist. The jacket felt tight, though he'd paid a ton of money for it. Finally he decided to unbutton it. Momentarily relieved, he swore to himself again he would lose weight.

The producer standing by one of the cameras started a countdown with his fingers as the makeup girl hurried away.

The countdown went to zero and the producer gave him the signal to begin.

"My fellow Americans," Taylor began his voice somber, "our nation has suffered a deep tragedy. As you all know, my esteemed predecessor, President Wilson was assassinated. Our country mourns for him and our prayers and thoughts are with his family." He paused for effect, then continued. "My only wish is to serve this great country with the same high level of integrity and distinction as President Wilson."

Taylor spread his hands on the desk. "I wanted to speak with you today for several reasons. First, I wanted to assure you that our great democracy continues without interruption. I have retained all of President William's Cabinet members in order to insure a smooth transition. There will be no disruption of government services. Social Security, Medicare, Medicaid, food stamps, housing and welfare programs will all continue as before." He paused again, wanting to make sure that sunk in – people who received government assistance always voted.

He clasped his hands in front of him. "I also wanted to speak with you about a second matter. As you may have read in the papers, or watched on the news, there has been much speculation regarding the person who assassinated President Wilson. The killer's corpse was found at the scene. The man obviously committed suicide after the killing, not wanting to be captured alive."

"There have been many rumors about this man," he continued, "and I'd like to put those rumors to rest. The Justice Department, the FBI and the Secret Service have just concluded an in-depth investigation, and I'd like to share that information with you. As American citizens, you are entitled to know the truth."

Taylor leaned forward in his chair for emphasis. "The assassin's name is, or was, Jing Zhao. He was a lieutenant in the army of the People's Republic of China. Officially, he was a military attaché, stationed at the Chinese consulate in Los Angeles. More ominously, he was also a spy, working for China's infamous MSS. This organization, the Ministry of State Security, is the Chinese government's largest and most active foreign intelligence agency. Additionally, we have determined that the weapon he used to assassinate our president was a high-tech sniper's rifle, available to only to select Chinese black-ops units. We have traced the bullets used to a factory in Shanghai, China. Further, we have been able to ascertain that this killer used secret information obtained by the Chinese consulate in Los Angeles in order to plan and execute this horrific act. The Chinese government hacked the website of our Secret Service in order to find specific information about the president's visit."

Taylor voice took on a hard edge. "From these and other still classified details, we have concluded that the Chinese government instigated and perpetrated the assassination of President Wilson. It's no secret that the Chinese want to become the pre-eminent power in the world, and they chose this shocking act as a way to destabilize our country."

He lowered his voice so that it was no more than a hoarse whisper. "My fellow Americans, I want to assure you that I will not rest until we have avenged this cowardly act. I know you will agree with me on this. Much like the Japanese attack on Pearl Harbor, this act will go down in infamy. As Commander-in-Chief, I have just issued orders raising the military readiness of our armed services and have raised our nuclear capability to DEFCON 2. We do not expect another treacherous Chinese action, but we will be prepared if one were to take place. As we move forward over the next days and weeks, rest assured that the safety and security of every American will guide my actions. Thank you, good day, and God bless America."

The TV cameras blinked off and Taylor reclined in his chair, took out a handkerchief and mopped his brow.

"Turn off those damn lights," he yelled, and a moment later the floodlights went dark.

The Cabinet members came over to his desk, and one by one congratulated Taylor on the speech. He ignored them, stared at Corvan. "What did you think, General?"

"It was flawless, Mr. President. It struck the perfect tone of statesmanship, humility, and outrage."

Taylor nodded, then stood up, loosened his tie and took off his jacket, which he placed on the wingback of his chair. "Damn, it's hot in here. Somebody, get me a glass of water."

Alice hurried out of the room for the water, while the Cabinet members moved away from his desk, but lingered, talking among themselves by the cameras.

"What's next, Mr. President?" Corvan whispered.

Taylor continued to mop his brow. "I go upstairs to my private quarters," the president replied, his voice barely audible. "And get drunk."

***

Fairfax, Virginia

Erica Blake leaned against her Explorer, crossed her arms and waited. She was parked in a rural park about five miles from the Fairfax County police offices. Night was falling and there were few people remaining in the park. Most were packing gear in their cars, obviously ready to head home. The park lights that lined the roads were beginning to glow.

The maintenance workers must have just mowed, she thought, because the aroma of cut grass hung in the air. It was a warm evening, with no breeze. Erica was hot and she removed her blazer and placed it on the hood of her SUV. Glancing at her watch, she realized with irritation that he was late.

Ten minutes later a car's headlights swung around the bend and an unmarked Chevy Impala pulled into the parking lot and stopped next to her SUV.

Detective Gray climbed out of the car and the two shook hands. She noticed he was wearing the same rumpled suit he always wore.

"How's the case going?" she asked.

"It's not," he responded, his face grim. "They took me off the Carpenter case. Gave it to another detective. To a guy that's retiring next month."

Erica shook her head slowly. "Figures. No question now there's a cover-up going on."

"My thought exactly."

She leaned back against her SUV, trying to determine if she could trust this man. But the fact he'd been taken off the Carpenter case spoke volumes.

Finally, she said, "My ex's been in LA, poking around the site of the assassination."

"The spook?"

Erica smiled. "Yeah, that's him. He's not officially on the case, 'cause the CIA can't get involved with domestic matters...."

Gray chuckled. "So what's he doing there?"

She shrugged. "You know how that goes. Anyway, he says there's a good chance it was an inside job. Thinks there was collusion between the killer and the Secret Service."

Gray's jaw dropped. "Shit...you kidding me?"

"No. I don't want to get into the details, but take my word for it, this info is solid. Steve's never been wrong before. He wasn't the perfect husband, that's for sure, but he's a hell of an agent."

Gray was quiet for a time. Then he said, "I watched the president's speech today. He said the Chinese government did it."

"Yeah. I saw it too. I don't know what to think. But something doesn't jive."

The detective rubbed his jaw. "What are you going to do?"

"I can't sit on this info, especially since there's also the cover-up of the senator's death. Too much is happening, too fast. I have a feeling it's all connected, somehow."

"Be careful, Erica. Sounds like some powerful people are involved."

She laughed. "They already took me off the Carpenter case. What else could they do to me?"

He didn't laugh back, his expression stony. "Just be careful, will you?"

She held out her hand and they shook. "Careful is my middle name."

They got back in their vehicles and Erica fired up her Explorer. Then she headed out of the park and in a few minutes was back on the state road.

An hour later she was in Bethesda and soon after she eased her SUV unto the long driveway of the senator's stately home.

As before, the thin maid answered the door and showed Erica to the same large, book-filled study.

She sat on the expensive couch to wait.

Moments later Senator Megan Lewis walked in the room, dressed in a casual pants suit, her blonde hair pulled into a ponytail.

The senator beamed. "What a lovely surprise, Erica." The woman sat down on the opposite couch and crossed her legs.

"Sorry I didn't call for an appointment, Senator. But I needed to speak with you as soon as possible."

Lewis waved a hand in the air, gave her a mischievous grin. "We're old friends. You can drop by anytime."

"Thank you, ma'am."

Lewis turned serious. "What do you have on your mind? The Carpenter case?"

Erica leaned forward on the couch. "That…and something else. Last time we met, I told you I had a strange feeling about the president's assassination. I thought there may have been a connection between the two deaths."

"You found it?"

"Not exactly. But I do have information regarding the assassination. Steve's been in LA looking into it. What he found is troubling. Very troubling."

A perplexed look crossed Lewis's face. "In what way? In his speech today, Taylor said the investigation was complete. Although I can't stand the bastard, I have to give him credit. He actually sounded presidential."

Erica rubbed the scar on her cheek. "Steve feels the Secret Service may be complicit in the assassination."

Lewis uncrossed her legs and stood up. "Are you crazy?"

Erica held her palms in front of her. "Please, Senator, hear me out."

The color had drained from Lewis's face, but she sat back down. Then she rang the bell that was on the coffee table. The maid entered the room and the senator ordered two white wines.

The maid came back with the drinks a minute later, placed them on the coffee table and left the room.

"Go on," Lewis said.

"Yes, ma'am. Steve was out there for several days, studied the crime-scene area. He says there's no way the Secret Service could have missed the assassin's location."

The senator looked skeptical. "I know Steve's a hunk and probably a stallion in bed. Sure that's not clouding your judgment?"

Erica's face turned red, but she didn't respond, instead waited until her anger dissipated.

"This has nothing to do with that, ma'am. If Steve says there's something going on, I believe him."

Lewis smiled. "Okay, I can see you've got the hots for him. But you're right, I've seen his CIA file – he's a good agent. Plenty of commendations. If he saw something that smells, he's probably right. The problem I have is that the president has just announced to the whole damn world that the Chinese are behind it. What do you say to that?"

"I don't know what to say, ma'am. Except that something's wrong. I think there's a cover-up."

"That's a serious charge, young lady. You've got no evidence. Just speculation."

"I know, Senator. I also know that there have been two high level deaths in a matter of weeks and they may be connected."

Lewis picked up her glass and sipped the wine. She was quiet a moment, then said, "There may be three. The press didn't really talk about it much, but a four-star Navy admiral died in Las Vegas recently. His body was found with two dead hookers. The LVPD chalked it up to a murder-suicide. Lots of drugs involved. Anyway, the Pentagon was able to keep it low-key."

Erica's heart began to pound. "There. You see? This may be a lot bigger than we both realize."

Lewis finished her glass of wine. "Maybe. Maybe so. I've got to say, it does seem to have a bad smell." She put the glass on the table. "I want you to leave this matter with me. I'm going to dig into it. I've got a lot of contacts in Washington. If there's something here, I'll find it."

Erica grinned. "Thank you, ma'am. I'm glad you're on my side."

"Thank you for coming to me. By the way, didn't I say you could dispense with that 'ma'am' crap? Makes me feel old."

"Sorry, ma'am...I mean Megan."

"That's better." The senator leaned back on the couch, crossed her legs. She glanced at her watch. "Listen dear, it's getting late. Why don't you spend the night here? I can put you in one of my guest bedrooms." She smiled and added, "Or you can share mine."

Erica gave this some thought. Surprisingly, she found the idea oddly appealing, but finally decided against it. "Thank you, Megan. But I need to get back home. Hope you understand."

Lewis continued to smile. "I do understand. But I'm not giving up on you. Not by a long shot."

***

Bobbie Garcia peered through the night vision goggles, saw the woman exit the home and get back in the Ford Explorer. Garcia's black SUV was parked across the street and from that vantage point, he could clearly make out the woman's identity. She was the meddlesome FBI agent, Blake.

The Explorer wound around the long driveway and eased into the light Bethesda traffic. He lost sight of her in seconds, but that didn't matter. His target was inside the house.

But the general had been very specific. Just observe. Take no action, at least not yet.

***

Erica Blake reached the end of the street, took a right and slowly circled around the block. She had spotted the parked SUV when she left the senator's house. It was a Suburban with dark-tinted windows, similar to the one she had seen prowling around her apartment a week ago. She didn't believe in coincidences and decided to check it out.

She parked her vehicle on a perpendicular street, grabbed her compact Nikon from the glove compartment and walked to the corner, careful to stay out of the line of sight of the Suburban. The vehicle was still there, and from the wisps of smoke coming from the exhaust, she could tell it was idling. Although the street lamps gave off decent light, the windows of the Suburban were almost black and it was impossible to make out who was inside. Nevertheless, she focused the camera lens on the vehicle and snapped a few photos. Maybe the tags would provide a clue.

She was about to approach the SUV when a stream of police cars, lights flashing and sirens blaring, roared past her on the street. They were heading east, toward downtown Bethesda.

After the black-and-whites moved through, she spotted the Suburban pull into traffic, heading west.

Sprinting back to her Explorer, she quickly got in, drove back to the senator's street and stepped on the gas, the tires squealing as she weaved in and out of traffic after the Suburban.

Minutes later she realized the vehicle must have turned into one of the side streets, because the Suburban had vanished.

***

Beijing, China

General Wu Chang was livid, his hands clenched into fists. He was in his office, staring at the three TV monitors that sat on a long credenza behind his desk. The TVs were tuned to live satellite feeds of three American news broadcasts: ZNN, Fox and CBS. Chinese subtitles scrolled at the bottom of the screens, but since his English was flawless, he listened rather than read the commentary. All of the news broadcasts were showing variations of the same story – massive anti-Chinese demonstrations had broken out across the United States. The images were coming from different cities: New York, LA, Chicago, Miami, Kansas City. Spontaneous, flag-waving marches had begun hours after the president's address, and were now turning into angry mobs. The Chinese consulate in Los Angeles had been surrounded by a large, rock-throwing crowd, and the LAPD had sent in SWAT teams to break it up.

His recalled President Taylor's speech and his face turned beet red. *The bastard had lied.* Chang knew for a fact his government was not involved. It was bad enough that the president had never returned his calls, and now this. *Damn him,* he thought. *What the hell is he trying to do?*

The general muted the sound on the TVs. Then he loosened his military tie and unbuttoned the top button of his freshly starched uniform shirt. This was a disaster. His dream of one day ascending to the head of the Politburo was evaporating with each passing minute. The Premier was calling him every half hour, demanding an explanation. But he had none. The American's actions baffled him. What was the man's motive?

He stabbed the intercom button, brusquely said, "Get me a drink!"

A moment later, Captain Lin came in the room and placed a large tumbler on his desk.

The young woman was well aware of the current events and her eyes were wide with fear. "Can I get you anything else, General?" she said in a low voice.

He glared at her, picked up the glass and took a long pull.

"Would you like a massage, General? That always relaxes you."

"Get the hell out of my office!" he growled.

Lin drew back as if he'd slapped her and she quickly left the room, closing the door behind her.

Chang went back to staring at the TVs, surfing through the other American channels, ABC, NBC and the rest of the alphabet soup, but the scenes they showed were all depressingly the same.

The intercom flashed on his desk and Lin's nervous voice came on. "Sir – "

"What the hell do you want? I told you to leave me alone!"

"I'm sorry, General. It's the Premier. He just called. Needs to see you immediately."

That made him pause and he willed himself to calm down. "Thank you, Lin. Let him know I'll leave now."

***

The tall, ornate, double-door was flanked by two uniformed soldiers, carrying their rifles at parade rest.

"I'm here to see the Premier," Chang said to one of the guards.

"He's expecting you, General." The guard said, as he opened one of the doors and stepped aside.

Chang went into the massive office. Large Chinese tapestries and historical oil paintings hung from the walls. At the far end of the chamber was an ornate wooden desk, flanked with flags of the People's Republic of China. Floor-to-ceiling windows showed a view of the congressional buildings and beyond, downtown Beijing. Behind the desk sat Premier Tse. Tse was a big man, but the office was so large he was dwarfed by the room.

The general had been to the premier's office many times, but usually under much better circumstances. Chang strode through the vast office, his boots clicking on the intricate in-laid marble tiles. Moments later he approached the desk and stood at attention.

"Premier," he said. "You wanted to see me."

Tse glanced up from his desk, a grim look on his face. "At ease, General."

Chang relaxed his body a fraction, but said nothing.

"I've been watching the American news," the premier said.

"As have I, sir –"

"Do not interrupt me, General."

"Yes, sir," he responded, his stomach churning.

"Chang, years ago I personally assigned you the responsibility of handling the American relationship. And you have performed admirably. Until now. What do you have to say for yourself?"

"Premier, the recent developments in the U.S. are baffling. The new president is not acting rationally. As you know, there is no basis for his accusations."

"That is true, Chang. But what is his motivation? Is it possible the investigation into the assassination is flawed? Or is it an intentional deception?"

"I've asked myself the same questions, sir. It's possible President Taylor is thinking about the upcoming election and wants to increase his popularity."

"Don't the Americans desperately need us to fund their debt?"

"Yes, Premier. They are financially bankrupt."

Tse tapped his pen on the desk for a time and looked pensive, but remained quiet. Eventually he said, "General, you will continue to head our American communication efforts. You still know more about them than anyone else. Work our network of spies in the U.S. State Department and elsewhere. Get to the bottom of this."

"Yes, Premier."

"And one other thing, General. If you fail in resolving this problem, the consequences to you personally will be severe."

Chang had been around Chinese politics long enough to know this meant more than a demotion. His life was at stake.

He saluted crisply. "Yes, Premier. You can be assured I will correct the situation."

***

Chang was back at his office, furiously thinking about his next steps. He was not at all confident about his promise to the premier, but at least he'd bought himself some time.

He pressed on the intercom. "Hold my calls, Lin. I don't want to be disturbed."

"Yes, General," she replied.

Turning to his computer, he tapped in the secret number to a secure line at the U.S. State Department. Minutes later, the woman's face lit up the screen.

14 Days to Zero Hour

Washington, D.C.

Erica Blake was sitting at her desk doing paperwork at the FBI building when she decided to call. She tapped Steve's number on the cell phone and waited for him to pick up. Yesterday she had thrown away her regular cell phone, replaced it with an untraceable 'burner' cell.

When he answered, she said, "Got anything on that license plate number?"

She heard a chuckle from the other end. "What, no foreplay first?" he said. "At least say hello, how are you."

"Sorry, Steve. This mess has me really wired."

"I can tell. Okay, here's the scoop. The reason you couldn't trace that government plate is because it was issued to a government agency that doesn't exist. It's a dummy cut-out, a drop-box agency that certain classified groups use to prevent people from tracking them."

"Classified how? Like the National Security Agency?"

"Could be Erica, or DoD Intelligence. Even the CIA uses it sometimes."

"Why would spooks or the Department of Defense be monitoring Senator Lewis?"

"Don't know."

"Okay. Maybe this is all connected to Carpenter's murder. Lewis has been sniffing around."

"Maybe, Erica. Listen, here's another wrinkle. I was able to trace the plate another way. The Suburban is registered in the state of North Carolina."

"So?"

"You know what's located in North Carolina?"

"Enough with the suspense, Steve. Just tell me, damn it."

"Okay, beautiful. I can tell you're in no mood for games. Fort Bragg is located there."

"Like I said, so?"

"Bragg isn't just a military base. It's also where the country's Special Forces are headquartered."

Erica mulled this over a moment. "There may be a connection – the equipment used in the Carpenter killing was military-grade black ops."

"Bingo."

Her mood lifted and she smiled to herself. "Thanks, Steve. We may be getting somewhere now. You'll keep digging?"

"Of course. How about dinner tonight?"

Her mood brightened some more. "You got it. Call you later."

She hung up, put the phone down, and went back to her paperwork.

Just then her desk phone buzzed and she picked it up eagerly, thinking it was Steve again. But it was her boss, Justin Temerius, demanding to see her immediately. Her mood soured instantly.

Turning off her computer, she slid on her blazer and headed to the elevator.

***

Erica knew immediately something was wrong. Two stony-faced, dark-suited agents were stationed outside Temerius's office, and through the glass walls she saw a third one standing to one side of her boss, who was sitting behind his desk.

When she approached the office, one of the agents by the door opened it and stepped aside. He followed her as she walked in and he took a position in the corner of the room.

Temerius had a somber look on his pasty white face. He pointed to the visitor's chair, said, "Have a seat, Erica."

"What is this, a wake?" she said sarcastically as she sat down.

"This is no time for one of your jokes, Erica."

She shrugged, then leaned forward in the chair. "What's this about?"

Her boss tapped on a large manila envelope on his desk. "Before I show you this, I have a couple of questions for you."

She was about to mouth off at him, but bit her lip instead. With witnesses around, she had to be careful. "Okay. Shoot."

The hint of a smile crossed his face. "I gave you a direct order to stay away from the Carpenter case. Isn't that right?"

"Yeah. So?"

"Isn't it also a fact that I took you off that case and assigned it to another agent?"

She didn't like where this was going and simply nodded.

"I didn't hear your response, Erica. Didn't I take you off that case?"

"Yeah."

"Didn't you turn over your case file to the other agent?"

"Yes, damn it. So what?"

He opened the manila envelope, took out a sheaf of black and white photographs, and with a smirk slid them on the desk toward her.

Her stomach began to churn as she picked up one of the 8 by 10s, studied it closely. It was a grainy photo, obviously taken with a long lens, showing two vehicles parked in a desolate park. A man and a woman were standing next to each other, talking. The photo was stamped with the day and time. She put down the first photo, picked up the next, a close-up which clearly showed her talking with Detective Gray. She glanced at the other pictures, which confirmed a variety of details, such as the vehicle makes and license plates.

Erica threw the photos back on the desk, stared at Temerius, but said nothing.

"You disobeyed a direct order, Erica. You continued working on the case, well after you were taken off of it."

She shrugged. "What are you going to do, shoot me?"

His face hardened. "No. I'm going to do the next best thing. I'm terminating your employment with the FBI."

Her jaw dropped. "You can't, you bastard. You can't do that."

The smirk was back. "I can and I have. I've already reviewed this with the deputy director. I have his blessing." He reached into his desk, took out a white envelope and pushed it on the desk toward her. "The details are all here."

She ignored the envelope, her eyes boring into his.

Her hands clenched into fists and her face turned beet red. Then she rose slowly from the chair and planted her fists on his desk. Her heart pounding in her chest, she said, "I'll appeal. You won't get away with this, you son of a bitch."

"Appeal away," he replied. "The process takes months, even years. And with your background of insubordination, you won't win."

She almost reared back and punched him, but saw the agents in the room take a step toward her.

"Don't do anything rash," Temerius said. "I'd hate to arrest you for assault."

She stood up straight, tried to calm her raging anger.

Temerius gave her a cold smile. "I'll need your gun and your badge." He paused, and a moment later added, "And your vehicle keys too – the Explorer is government property."

She set her face into a stony mask and slowly took out the Glock, the badge and keys and let them drop to the floor.

He stood up and shook his head slowly. "Defiant to the bitter end. That's your downfall, Erica. Your Achilles heel."

"My downfall was working for a piece of shit like you."

His mouth pressed into a thin line. "These agents will take you back to your desk. You will pack all of your personal belongings and they will escort you out of the building. If you decide to appeal this dismissal, you can do so online. Do not return to this building unless you are requested to do so. Is that clear, Erica?"

She gave him an enigmatic smile. Then she hit him with a solid uppercut, the punch knocking him off his feet.

***

Secretary of State Audrey Cruz turned off the computer screen and leaned back in her seat. She was in her spacious office at the State Department, mulling over the call she'd just concluded.

Between bites of a stale doughnut, she sipped coffee. The call disturbed her on several levels. First, she hadn't liked his brusque tone and secondly, hadn't appreciated his hint of a threat. She swiveled her chair, looked out at the D.C. skyline. It was a bright, sunny day outside but her mood was dark.

Years ago, her arrangement with the general had seemed like a win-win. She received hefty quarterly wire transfers to her private Swiss bank account. All she had to do was keep her Chinese 'contact' informed of U.S. foreign policy. It had worked like clockwork for a long time, but now things had soured. The general had become very demanding, trying to pry more and more information from her. But now that Taylor was president, many of her sources had dried up. Taylor was a different animal, inscrutable. And she wasn't buying the Chinese involvement in the Wilson assassination. The Chinese were too clever for that. They had nothing to gain and everything to lose.

Audrey drained the last of her coffee and picked up the phone. She had one good source left. She hated to use her friend, but her options were limited.

***

Bethesda, Maryland

Senator Megan Lewis stood in front of the mirror in her bedroom and slowly combed her hair. Finished, she touched up her lipstick and was about to sit down and read for a while when she heard a rap at her door.

"Your guest is here, Senator," her maid said, her voice muffled by the closed door.

"Right down," Megan replied as she took a last look at her appearance. Satisfied with her hair and the way she filled out her low-cut black dress, she headed out of the room.

Moments later she found Audrey Cruz seated in the study, sipping a glass of wine. A vintage bottle of Sauvignon Blanc sat on the coffee table.

Megan bent down, gave the woman a kiss on the mouth and said, "Audrey. I'm so glad you called. I've been thinking about you." She sat next to the woman, picked up her glass of wine and took a sip.

Cruz smiled. "You look great, Megan."

"As do you, dear." She studied the other woman. The secretary of state was tall, with long, raven hair and sculpted good looks. She was wearing a stylish, body-hugging gray jumpsuit. The two women had shared many delicious times in each other's arms and Megan was looking forward to more.

"How are things at State?" Lewis asked.

Cruz waived a hand in the air. "With everything that's happened, it's hard to tell."

"I know," Megan replied. "Now that Wilson is gone, nothing's quite the same."

The secretary drained her glass, set it down. "Taylor's a bastard. If he gets elected next year, I'll be out at State." Her voice had a hard edge to it.

"You think?"

"I know it for a fact. We never got along."

Megan nodded. "I know that feeling. Taylor and I are like cats and dogs when we're around each other. I had a deal cooking with Wilson...don't know if Taylor will go for it...."

"A deal? What kind of deal?"

Megan paused, not sure if she should share the information with her friend. "It's confidential...you understand."

Cruz placed a hand on Megan's cheek, then leaned over and kissed the senator on the mouth. Megan felt a thrill and pulled the woman closer. As their tongues intertwined, Megan felt the other woman caressing her breasts.

Minutes later the senator pulled away, took another sip of her wine. Her face was flushed and she was breathing heavily.

A playful smile crossed Cruz's lips. "Just like old times."

Megan smiled back, picked up the bottle of expensive wine and refilled the glasses. "Our time together has always been special."

Cruz's eyes twinkled. "Tell me about this deal of yours. I'm curious."

Megan shrugged. "Sure, why not. We're good friends." She sipped the wine, then proceeded to tell Cruz the deal she'd made with Henry Mueller, the Swiss banker. She left out the sexual interlude she'd had with him, but other than that, told her everything else.

The secretary's eyes went wide. "Wow. That's some deal."

"Yeah, that's a fact."

"Did he go for it?"

"He did, as did his board of directors. But now with Wilson gone...I don't know what's going to happen."

"Have you talked with Taylor?"

Megan pursed her lips. "Called his office several times, to set up an appointment. The new chief of staff, Corvan, gave me the runaround, said the president's too busy. I've been a pain in Taylor's side for a long time, so I'm not holding my breath."

Cruz looked pensive. "I see."

The senator drank more wine and leaned back on the couch. Just then the maid knocked on the door and peered in the room. "Dinner is ready, Senator."

Megan glanced at Cruz. "You hungry, Audrey?"

"I'm hungry. But not for food."

Megan turned to the maid. "Put the dinner in the warming oven. We'll be upstairs for a while."

The maid nodded. "Yes, ma'am."

Megan stood and led Cruz up the stairs and into her bedroom.

A half-hour later, Megan lay on her back, nude, with an equally naked Cruz grinding on top of her. The senator had already come once, thanks to Cruz's voracious mouth, which had begun working on her minutes after the two women undressed.

Megan cupped the other woman's breasts with her hands, felt the intense thrill as Cruz rubbed her glistening body ferociously against her. Their bodies rocked in unison, building toward a joint release. The bedroom smelled of incense candles, expensive perfume and sex, and the senator breathed deep, wanting to remember the moment with all her senses.

"Don't...stop." Megan whispered urgently.

Cruz said nothing in response, only increased the tempo, continuing to grind even harder.

Megan knew she was almost there, her fingernails digging into Cruz's flawless breasts, almost cutting the skin.

She saw Cruz squeeze her eyes shut, heard her groan, and felt the woman's body tense, just as her own pent-up pleasure exploded. Megan gritted her teeth as the bliss cascaded through her in a long series of waves.

Cruz collapsed into her arms and Megan held her tightly.

They lay like that for a time, their ragged breathing eventually slowing to normal. Neither spoke, the only sound in the room coming from the antique clock on the mantle above the fireplace.

Cruz rolled off of her to lie on her back. "Just like old times," she said.

Megan turned on her side, stared at the beautiful woman next to her. She reached over with her hand caressed Cruz's face. "You're the best friend I have, Audrey."

Cruz's covered Megan's hand with her own, and the two women looked into each other's eyes.

Then a sly grin crossed Cruz's face. "I'm not done with you yet."

Megan laughed and pulled the other woman towards her. "Dinner can wait," she murmured.

***

Bobby Garcia was tired. Tired of sitting in the Suburban and tired of this assignment. Watching the senator's comings and goings was becoming a bore. He would have assigned it to one of his men, but the general had been very specific. He wanted Garcia to do it.

He glanced at his watch, then peered through the night-vision goggles at the stately home across the street. The senator's visitor was still inside, her BMW sedan parked in the driveway. He had recognized the woman – she was Audrey Cruz, the secretary of state.

Sipping his now cold coffee, his thoughts drifted to his wife, Maria. He wished he were home now, snuggled up to her watching something on TV, instead of sitting in the SUV wishing the time away. But his mood brightened as he remembered the countdown of BlackSnow. Only two weeks left.

The whirring sound of the vehicle's air conditioner brought him back to the present.

The home's portico lights came on and he spotted Cruz walking down the front steps and climbing into her car. Moments later the BMW was back on the street, merging with the rest of the traffic.

But Garcia stayed put, continuing to monitor the house. The portico lights turned off and he crossed his arms and settled back in the seat.

13 Days to Zero Hour

Washington, D.C.

Erica Blake leaned against the cell's concrete wall. She was in jail, in a temporary holding area for the recently arrested. The FBI had charged her with assault and turned her over to MPDC, the district's local police force.

Erica glanced at the other women in the cell, mostly sleazy-looking women – low-rent hookers, drifters and junkies with arms sporting fresh tracks. The women sat, muttering or groaning, on the long benches by the wall. She had inspected the bench earlier – it was coated with a foul-smelling, greasy substance she couldn't identify. She chose to stand instead.

The room reeked of urine, feces, vomit, and foul body odor, and was stifling hot. If there was AC in the place, she couldn't tell. Fluorescent, bluish-cast lights flickered overhead.

Staring through the bars at the far end of the cell, she thought about the events of the last day. It was stupid, she knew, to have punched Temerius. But it had felt good, really good, in spite of the pain in her hand. Like the credit-card commercial says, it was priceless.

But now she had to pay the price. She glanced at her wrist to look at the time, quickly remembered they had taken her watch during processing, along with her belt, blazer, money and everything else in her pockets.

A burly black woman came up to her, said, "What you looking at, sister?" The voice was low and menacing. The woman, dressed in a torn, white t-shirt and jeans, had tattoos on both arms and on her neck. Her black hair was close-cropped and the word 'butch' came to Erica's mind.

"Minding my own business," Erica replied, her tone neutral.

"My name's T'wana, and I run this place."

Erica gave her a cold smile, glanced around the room. "Nothing to be proud of. This place is a shit-hole."

T'wana closed the space between them and jabbed her finger on Erica's chest. "You dissing me? I want some respect. You hear, white girl?"

Erica's voice dropped to a whisper. "Take your hand off of me."

The woman sneered. "Or what? Pretty white girl like you, I could have a lot of fun with you, once I break you in." The woman let out a harsh laugh.

The other inmates by now had all stood up, formed a semi-circle around the two.

Erica took a step back from T'wana and the woman smiled. "Thought as much. You got a yellow stripe down your back."

Erica closed her fist and punched the woman's solar plexus. As T'wana staggered back, Erica spun her body into a roundhouse kick, her foot landing with a thud on the woman's face. T'wana dropped to the floor.

The other inmates whooped and hollered, obviously not close friends of their cellmate.

Erica crouched by the black woman, stared at her bloody nose and felt her pulse. T'wana was unconscious, but would be okay in a while.

"It's all over, girls," she said to the others as she stood up. "You can go back to knitting, or whatever else you do in here."

The group broke up and Erica went back to leaning on the wall.

Two hours later a clanging noise outside the cell startled her and she saw a uniformed correctional officer approach the cell door, while a second one stood guard next to him, his hand touching the gun in his holster. The first one unlocked the door, swung it open, pointed to her and said, "Blake. You're coming with us. Your bail's been posted."

The guards led her through narrow concrete corridors and back up to the discharge area. There, a rotund, grouchy officer gave her a large envelope with her personal belongings. "Follow me," he said, and led her through the last cell door and into a sparse waiting room.

"Wait here," the officer said. "I'll call, let them know upstairs you're ready to go."

She sat at one of the metal tables and a few minutes later a door opened at the end of the room. Steve McCord walked in, wearing a gray, pin-stripe suit and tie.

Erica stood up, walked up to him and gave him a hug. "You're a sight for sore eyes," she said.

He hugged her back for a moment, then pulled away. "You smell like crap, Erica."

She laughed. "Thanks for noticing."

He laughed back, gave her another hug.

It felt good to be in his arms. "Thanks for getting me out of here."

"What are ex-husbands for?"

An hour later, the two of them were sitting in his apartment's living room, sipping coffee. Erica had taken a long, hot shower, which had washed away the foul odor that had permeated her hair and body. Then she had thrown on some of Steve's casual clothes, a polo shirt and a pair of shorts that were way too big for her, but would have to do.

Sitting on the couch across from her, he said, "So. What are you going to do now?"

"I finish my coffee."

"I meant after that, Erica."

"Well, let's see. I no longer have a job. And I need to hire an attorney for when my assault charge goes to court. Other than that, things are peachy."

He shook his head. "This is no times for jokes."

"That's the damn truth."

He leaned back in the seat, said, "I know a good criminal attorney, and if you need help financially, I can help."

She sipped more of the coffee. "Thanks. But I've got some money saved."

He nodded. "What are you going to do for employment?"

"I'll appeal the termination."

"And if that fails...."

"Jesus," she said sarcastically, "don't be such an optimist."

"Sorry. I just know if the deputy director approved it, it's going to be tough."

"I know."

His face brightened. "Get out of government work. I hear the private security business is booming."

"I've now got a criminal record, Steve. Unless I get that thrown out, I won't be able to do anything but be a mall cop."

He nodded, went quiet.

"Got anything to drink besides coffee?" she asked.

"I've got Heineken and Chivas. What's your poison?"

"I'll take the scotch. I need the hard stuff. I want to fry my brain."

He shrugged. "You sure? You've been through a lot. Maybe you should stick to beer, so you can pace yourself."

"Get the damn scotch, will you? I'm in no mood for games."

***

Beijing, China

General Chang terminated the secure call and turned off his computer. Then he stood up and began to pace his office. His contact at the U.S. State Department had just given him some stunning news regarding a pending deal the Americans were planning with the Swiss.

He had dealt with the woman for years and knew her information had been reliable in the past. If this deal went through, it was a game changer. His own position would be superfluous. As it was, the premier had already told him his life was at stake.

He stopped pacing and sat back down at his desk. Trying to sort through the implications, he came up with several scenarios. The deal apparently depended on what the new president, Taylor, decided. The odious man had yet to return his calls.

Chang decided he would not share this latest information with the premier. At least not yet. He had to be sure.

***

The Oval Office
The White House
Washington, D.C.

President Taylor was signing Executive Orders when his intercom buzzed. "General Corvan is here," he heard Alice say over the speaker.

"Show him in," he replied, and put aside the orders.

Corvan came in, nodded and sat down in front of the desk.

"How are things, General?"

"Proceeding as planned, Mr. President."

Taylor ran a hand over his bald head. "Watched the news a little while ago — the anti-Chinese demonstrations are widespread. Still going strong in our mayor cities."

Corvan smiled. "Yes, sir."

"I'd like to ratchet it up a notch – let's go ahead with the next phase of the operation."

"Yes, Mr. President. I'll notify Garcia."

"Good. What else is happening?"

"Sir, Senator Lewis keeps calling. Like I told you before, she wants a meeting, says it's urgent."

Taylor's face scrunched up as if he'd swallowed a sour lemon. "That bitch. When I was VP, she couldn't stand to look at me, but now…."

"Yes, sir. I understand. But she's an influential senator, has a lot of friends on Capitol Hill."

Taylor rubbed his jaw, went quiet. After a time he said, "Okay. Set it up for later today. I guess if I want to get elected next year, I need all the friends I can get."

"Yes, sir."

***

Senator Megan Lewis was shown into the Oval Office by the president's assistant.

"The president will be right with you, Senator," Alice said. "Please have a seat."

Alice left the room and Lewis took a chair in front of the large wooden desk.

Glancing around the beautifully appointed Oval Office, Megan once again admired the historical details of the place. Many have held this office, she thought, and one day, God willing, I will too.

Her reverie was broken as President Taylor walked in the room, approached her and held out his hand. She stood and the two shook.

"It's good to see you," the man said with a forced smile. "Please have a seat."

"Thank you, Mr. President."

She waited until he had sat at his desk before she took her own seat.

"And thank you, Mr. President, for giving me the opportunity to meet with you."

He waved that away. "No problem."

She studied the man closely, and was, as always, repulsed by his demeanor. It was obvious he hated dealing with her and had only agreed to meet because of the up-coming election.

"My chief-of-staff tells me you had something urgent to discuss?"

"Yes, sir."

"Go ahead, then."

"Mr. President, before the assassination —"

Taylor frowned and interrupted her. "A tragic event in our nation's history."

"Yes, sir. As I was saying, President Wilson and I had been working on a resolution to our debt crisis...."

"Really?"

"Yes, sir. We devised a plan that would fund our overspending and borrowing."

Taylor gave her an icy glare. "You're aware that Wilson had pretty much capitulated to Chinese demands, in exchange for their underwriting our debt?"

"Yes, Mr. President. And he was miserable about it. The poor man aged considerably over the last couple of years."

"He was weak, Megan. Admit it."

She didn't want to argue with Taylor, but she still felt loyal to Wilson's memory. "He was doing the best he could, under the circumstances."

Taylor shrugged and said in a cold voice, "Doesn't matter now. He's gone."

She nodded. "Yes, sir. As I was saying, we came up with a plan that would have the Swiss buy our Treasury bonds, instead of the Chinese. We felt the Swiss would not interfere with U.S. foreign or domestic policy."

An incredulous look crossed his face. "The Swiss? Those bastards barely sniff at our bonds."

She reached in her briefcase, took out an envelope and placed it on the desk. "We offered them a very attractive proposal. The details are all in there. You should be aware that the Swiss have agreed to it. Of course, now it's up to you. You would have to approve it."

Taylor opened the envelope, took out the document and began reading.

A few minutes later he looked at her. "Interesting. But you're making the assumption that the Swiss would not interfere with our affairs like the Chinese have."

"It's in the agreement, Mr. President."

"I saw that. But once they taste the power they have over us, who's to say they won't renege on that part of it?"

"I know their chief banker well, sir. He's an honest man."

"You're naïve, Megan."

Her face turned red, but she bit her tongue, knowing she had to keep her emotions in check. She took a deep breath. "Mr. President, I think this is workable solution for our country. We're in a big hole and we desperately need to climb out. This plan does that."

The president leaned back in his chair, became pensive.

"Okay, Megan. I'll read this thoroughly and review it with my advisors. I'm not making any promises, but I will consider it."

She nodded. "Thank you, Mr. President."

***

Aboard the USS Nevada
U.S. Navy Trident nuclear submarine
60 miles south of Hawaii
The Pacific Ocean

Commander Roger Lamont smiled as he turned off his laptop. He had just received a new encrypted message from the Pentagon. Using a notepad, he wrote down the new coordinates.

Standing up, he went to the phone, which was mounted on the wall of his cramped quarters, and punched in a call.

When Lieutenant Johnson picked up on the other end, he said, "Lieutenant, come to my quarters. I've got a new heading to give you."

There was a pause on the other end. "Sir, is it just for us?"

"No. This involves all the Trident subs in the Pacific."

"Yes, sir," the Lieutenant responded in a somber voice.

***

Special Operations
Marine Corps Detachment
Training Facility, Building 14
Fort Bragg, North Carolina

Sergeant Thomas was in his office when his cell phone buzzed. He unclipped the phone from his belt clip and took the call.

Captain Garcia's voice came over the phone. "Sergeant, I'm still in Washington, but I just got the orders. The next phase is a go. Get the guys ready. Take the jet. I'll meet you out there."

"Yes, Captain," Thomas responded.

The call was disconnected and the sergeant replaced the phone back on the clip.

He packed his laptop computer in his ready bag and went into the training area, which was a cavernous, warehouse space with high ceilings. The team was in a corner of the room, cleaning their weapons. "Pack it up guys!" he yelled across the room, the sound echoing. "It's a go!"

The group hurriedly began to stuff their gear into large duffel bags.

Half an hour later they were on their way. The small, unmarked jet sped down the runway and lifted off the airfield.

Thomas stared out the co-pilot's seat window as the sprawling military base below receded from view. He was looking forward to the next phase. The team hadn't seen any action in days and he was itching for something to do.

12 Days to Zero Hour

Los Angeles, California

Bobbie Garcia got out of the gray Toyota Camry he had rented earlier under one of his aliases. He grabbed his backpack from the trunk, took out several small containers and slipped them in his pockets. Then he put on the backpack and glanced around the half-full parking garage.

A minute later a black Ford cargo van pulled into one of the empty slots a few cars down. His team began to climb out of the vehicle. Like Garcia, they were dressed in casual clothes – jeans, golf shirts and T-shirts in muted colors, so as not to stand out. Two of the men had backpacks. Several of them also carried hand-made signs with anti-Chinese slogans.

Sergeant Thomas broke from the group, walked over to him.

"The men ready, Sergeant?"

"Yes, sir. We're good to go."

Garcia nodded.

He strode down the aisle toward the stairs, the group following behind.

Ten minutes later Garcia stopped on the sidewalk a block from the Chinese consulate to survey the scene. A large group of demonstrators were pacing in front of the building, carrying signs and chanting. The crowd was a mixed assortment of people – business types in blazers, soccer moms, homeless men, and young college students, the last group being the most vocal. For the most part, the demonstration appeared peaceful, though several uniformed LAPD officers stood right by the front gate, ready to diffuse trouble before it started.

It was a brutally hot day in LA, the sun beating down from a cloudless sky. Garcia brushed perspiration from his forehead and inhaled the city's peculiar odor of smog, asphalt and car exhaust.

Garcia scanned the sidewalk on both sides of the street and spotted his men, who had now blended in with the protesters.

Marching closer to the crowd, he saw Thomas and gave him the go-ahead sign.

Moments later Garcia heard loud shouting and saw a scuffle break out as several in the crowd surged forward. A woman screamed, as a sign was thrown at the gate. Then a flurry of rocks flew, hitting the façade of the building. Glass shattered and he noticed one of the cops go down to the ground. Several of his men began to lob small black objects.

Rushing forward, he pushed through the mêlée, the crowd all around him.

He heard an explosion and saw the wrought iron gate blow open. His men went into the courtyard, followed by the younger members of the crowd. The older protesters stayed back, obviously fearing the mounting violence.

Garcia followed the rioters into the courtyard, grabbed an incendiary grenade from his pocket, pulled the pin, and lobbed it at a consulate window. The device shattered the glass and exploded immediately, the burst of flames visible from the courtyard.

To his left he spotted Thomas doing the same.

Uniformed Chinese guards opened the wide front door of the consulate and pointed AK-47 rifles at the unruly crowd, but seemed reluctant to fire.

Shots rang out and one of the guards crumpled to the ground.

Garcia pulled his compact Berretta semi-automatic from a pocket and fired point-blank, hitting a second guard in the forehead, bringing him down.

The Chinese began firing indiscriminately and several of the protesters fell in the courtyard, wounded. Garcia fired again, as did the rest of his men and in moments the guards were either dead, wounded or had retreated inside the building.

A large fire erupted from inside the consulate, the flames licking out the windows and the open front door.

Garcia emptied his automatic and stuck the gun in his waistband. Then he hugged the wall by the door, which was now bullet-ridden and partially on fire. Three of his men took cover behind the stone pillars on the portico and continued firing into the consulate.

He took off his backpack, pulled out the rest of the incendiary grenades, and while his men continued to provide cover fire, he lobbed the explosives into the building.

As the grenades went off, he glanced back into the courtyard. The area was chaotic, with dead and wounded guards and protesters littering the square. He spotted the bleeding bodies of two of his men on the ground, unmoving. He cursed to himself, grieving for the dead, but realizing there was no other way.

Just then Garcia felt an intense heat and saw the brilliant flash of an explosion from inside the consulate. The multiple grenades had worked.

In the distance he heard the wail of police sirens and he motioned to his men. I was time to get the hell out.

***

Garcia sipped a Coke while he surfed the channels, looking for news. He was in a seedy room of a gritty motel that had seen better days. The place was located in a run-down part of East Los Angeles, a perfect place to lay low for a while. He sat on the foul-smelling, lumpy mattress, his back to the wall, and stared at the small TV. He was so focused on finding news about the riot that he barely noticed the decrepit décor.

Surfing past the daytime wasteland of talk shows, infomercials and soap operas, he finally found Fox News. An attractive brunette was the reporter and he turned up the volume.

"The scene here at the Chinese consulate is chaotic," the woman said into the mike. She was standing on the sidewalk across the street from the building. The camera's wide-angle shot showed the avenue blocked off from traffic by police barricades. The area was filled with fire trucks, black-and-white cruisers, SWAT trucks and ambulances, their flashing lights blending together in a strobe-light effect. Uniformed firemen, police and EMT personnel rushed about, while numerous local TV camera crews were setting up outside the crime-scene tape areas. Plumes of black smoke rose from the consulate itself. Its façade, which was visible beyond the shattered gate, was a mixture of soot, charred wooden trim, and blackened stone.

"According to the fire marshal," she continued, "the blaze in the consulate has been extinguished, but damage to the building is extensive. For those of you just joining us, the fire broke out during an anti-Chinese demonstration protesting the assassination of President Wilson." She paused, lowered her voice. "As I mentioned earlier, estimates are now that a total of twenty-three people have died here." She paused again, held one hand to her earpiece and then continued. "We've just learned of a shocking new development. Of the twenty-three dead, fifteen were American protesters, shot by Chinese guards as they tried to quell the riot."

Garcia shook his head slowly and sipped the now-warm Coke. He knew that of the dead, three were his men. Silently, he said a prayer for them and for the American protesters.

***

Aboard the yacht Solstice
Cruising the Mediterranean Sea
Ten miles south of Monte Carlo

Henry Mueller reclined on the chaise lounge at the rear deck of his ninety-foot yacht, watching the news streaming on his iPad.

Looking up from the device, he glanced over at his wife, who was asleep next to him on her chaise. They had been married for many years, but he still admired her Nordic good looks. Her voluptuous body was barely covered by a tiny bikini.

The steward brought him a fresh martini and set it on a side table. Taking a sip of the drink, Mueller went back to the news broadcast. The scene had shifted from the flooding in Bangladesh to a breaking story from the United States. A fire had decimated the Chinese consulate in Los Angeles, with a number of deaths reported. He watched intently – he was apprehensive about anything that could affect the pending American deal.

Just then the satellite phone on the table rang. He picked it up and heard the voice of Megan Lewis on the other end.

His wife woke with a start and asked who it was.

Mueller covered the receiver, said, "Senator Lewis from the States."

His wife grimaced, closed her eyes and went back to sleep.

"Megan, good to hear from you," he said.

"Likewise, Henry."

"Senator, funny you should call now – I was just watching this tragic event in Los Angeles."

"Yes, the fire is tragic. But not totally unexpected. The protests here are spreading. The American people are furious."

"Understandable, Megan, in light of what happened."

"If it's true."

"What do you mean?"

"There's some evidence the Chinese may not have been behind the assassination."

"But…I watched your new president…he sounded so certain."

"I'd rather not talk too much about this, Henry, over this line."

"Yes, I agree. When are you coming back to Zurich?"

"Soon. I met with Taylor recently. Reviewed our deal with him. I'm hopeful, but at the same time, I can't guarantee anything."

"Of course. But my board keeps asking…."

"I want this as much as you do, Henry."

"Yes." Mueller glanced at his wife, who appeared to be fast asleep. Nevertheless, he lowered his voice to no more than a whisper. "Maybe we could have dinner again, when you return?"

She let out a throaty laugh. "That's an excellent idea. You were a special treat."

"Thank you for saying that, Senator. Goodbye."

He replaced the phone back on its cradle and noticed his wife had awakened.

"What was that about?" she asked in French, her tone clearly annoyed.

"Business, dear," he replied, in the same language. "That deal I told you about before."

Her eyes turned into slits. "Make sure it's just business, Henry. If I find out it's more than that, there'll be hell to pay. Remember, divorces are expensive. Very expensive."

***

Washington, D.C.

Erica Blake strode down the aisle of the worn, sad-looking cars, checking the prices marked on the windshields. This was the third used-car lot she'd been to this morning and after a few minutes realized the pickings weren't any better here. But since the Bureau had taken away her SUV and she hated borrowing Steve's car for more than a few days, she was a motivated buyer.

Just then a salesman popped out of the small office, a phony smile plastered on his face. The mustachioed man wore a pink pin-stripe shirt, a blue tie and blue suspenders. His jet-black hair looked odd, as if he were wearing a wig.

"How you doing, Miss," he said, his voice fast and loud. Already she knew she wouldn't like this guy.

"Looking for a car?" he asked.

"No. I'm shopping for potatoes."

He gave her an odd look, then laughed. "Yeah. Stupid question. Well you came to the right place."

"Why is that?"

"Because we got the best used cars in D.C., at the lowest prices."

"Save it, buddy. I've heard it all before."

He appeared surprised at her tone. "Okay. I see you're a sophisticated buyer." He pointed to the neon sign over the office, which read, *Honest Tony's Carland!*

"I'm Tony Toluca," he said, as he stuck out his hand. "What's your name?"

They shook and she noticed he had a limp handshake. Another bad tell. "Erica Blake."

"Erica. That's a pretty name for a pretty lady."

She reached out with one hand, grabbed his tie and yanked him forward. "Listen, Tony. I'm here to buy a car, not here to listen to bullshit. Are we clear?" She let go of his tie, and he stepped back from her.

"Sure…sure…I understand," he stammered. He took out a blue handkerchief and mopped his moist brow.

She crossed her arms in front of her. "I'm looking for reliable transportation. A car that won't break down as soon as I drive off this sorry lot."

He pointed to the late-model Jaguar sedan she had driven into the lot. "You're used to fancy wheels, Miss. I've got a couple of used cars that are somewhat comparable, just a lot older."

She shrugged. "The Jag belongs to a friend of mine. I don't need anything fancy."

"Okay. What's your budget?"

She told him and he nodded.

"That's not much," he said, "but I've got something that may fit the bill."

"Let's see it, Tony."

He led her back to a corner of the lot, pointed to a Ford Taurus sedan with faded green paint. There were dents on the doors and hood.

"Looks like a piece of crap, Tony."

He gave her a brilliant smile. "Looks can be deceiving. I just got this one in, had it checked out. It runs good, even if it looks tired. And it's within your budget."

She walked around the car, noticed the balding tires and the small crack on one of the side windows. She opened the driver's side door and unlocked the hood. Walking back to the front of the vehicle, she lifted the hood, inspected the engine compartment carefully. Surprisingly, the engine was clean and appeared well-kept. She slammed the hood shut, got in the car and sat in the front seat. The seats and dash were worn, and smelled of stale cigarettes.

She rolled down the window and said, "Keys?"

Toluca stuck his hand in one of his bulging pockets, took out a bunch of keys, selected one and handed it to her. "Go ahead and start it. This baby runs like a dream."

She grabbed the key and fired up the engine. The car started immediately, and she gave it gas. The motor sounded strong.

"Take it out for a spin, Erica. You'll see."

She nodded, put the car in gear and rolled out of the lot. She came back ten minutes later and climbed out of the car.

"Not bad, Tony. It runs well."

"I told you you'd love it."

She gave him a hard look. "I don't love it, but it'll do. Put on a new set of tires, and get rid of the cigarette smell inside, and I'll take it."

His smiled another one of his wide, phony smiles. "Done."

"One other thing, Tony. It's over-priced by four-hundred bucks. Cut the price and we've got a deal."

She saw his smile vanish and he swallowed hard. "I don't know, Erica...."

"I'll pay cash."

The smile came back, but tentatively, as if he was worried she'd have more demands. "Okay," he said, "you've got a deal."

***

Steve McCord had just returned to his apartment after a long day at Langley, when he heard a knock at his door.

Approaching the door, he peered through the peephole. Two bulky men in dark suits and ties stood outside. They were holding up badges.

"Mr. McCord," he heard one of them say, "We're Federal officers. We need to speak with you, please."

Steve opened the door. "What's this about?"

The taller of the two men held his badge so Steve could read it clearly. It looked authentic and it identified the man as an NSA agent.

"What's the National Security Agency want with me?"

"I'm agent Logan and this agent Saunders," the taller one said. "Can we come in?"

Steve shrugged, stepped aside and the two men came in. He closed the door after them. "Okay, what's this about? You know I'm with Central Intelligence."

"Yes, sir," Logan said. "We know who you are."

"So?"

"Mr. McCord," the man said, "you've had several conversations with your superiors recently regarding the assassination of President Wilson."

"What business is that of yours? But, yes, I was discussing the findings of my visit to the crime-scene in LA."

"Sir, do you know that the CIA is prohibited from engaging in domestic matters?"

Steve grimaced. "Of course. But my visit there was with the full knowledge and support by my supervisor. Our intent was to assist the FBI and Secret Service in their investigation, nothing more. And in fact, the information I found was shared with those agencies and they appeared to be grateful for the assist."

Logan shook his head. "The investigation into the president's assassination has been escalated. It has now been assigned to the NSA."

Steve cocked his head. "Whatever. It's hard to keep up with all the bullshit in Washington."

Logan pulled a folded sheet of paper from his suit pocket and handed it to Steve. "This is a FISA court warrant for your detention, sir. You'll have to come with us."

Steve felt like punching the bastard, but instead took a deep breath. Grabbing the sheet, he read it carefully. He had never actually seen a Foreign Intelligence Surveillance warrant, but this appeared very real. The warrants were issued by a secret federal court, Steve knew. The court had been created when the Patriot Act was enacted in 2001 after the terrorist attacks on September 11th. The Act had been renamed the USA Freedom Act in 2015, but was called the Patriot Act by most people.

Seething, he threw the warrant at Logan. "This is bullshit! I'm a CIA agent. There's no way this'll stand up. I'm calling my supervisor right now."

The document bounced off Logan's chest and dropped to the floor. The man picked it up, folded it and stuck it in his pocket. "That won't be possible, sir. He's also being served with a similar warrant."

Steve stuck his hands on his hips. "You guys are unbelievable! There's no way I'm coming with you."

"This is a legally binding warrant, Mr. McCord. After we've questioned you, you may elect to retain an attorney, if that's your wish."

"Listen, I'm not going anywhere with you goons. I've been in Central Intelligence long enough to know that once I'm in one of your 'rendition centers', I'll never get out. Now, get the hell out of my house!"

Then everything happened in an instant.

Logan pulled a gun from a shoulder holster, leveled it at Steve, and fired.

Steve felt an immense pressure on his chest and a second later blacked out.

***

Steve was startled awake by the splash of ice-cold water on his face.

Glancing around, he knew instantly he was in big trouble. He was strapped to a metal chair, his hands and feet bound with plastic binds so tight they almost cut his skin. The room was small, dark and dank. A cellar of some type with concrete walls, no windows and a dim, bare light bulb hanging from the ceiling. The place stank of bleach and rancid odors he couldn't identify.

Agent Logan stood in front of him, holding an empty bucket. The man had shed his suit and tie and had a smug look on his face. "Glad you're awake, McCord," he said, placing the bucket in a sink that was off to one side. Steve saw the other agent, Saunders, standing silently in a corner, his arms folded in front of him.

"Where the hell am I?" Steve shouted.

Logan laughed. "We ask the questions here, my friend."

Steve scanned the room again, looking for any way to escape. But found none.

"Lucky for you, McCord, the gun I used on you was a stunner. I could have shot you for real." He laughed, but there was no humor in it. "You were resisting arrest. Isn't that right, Saunders?"

The other man nodded, said nothing.

Logan smirked. "Saunders is the quiet type. But he has unique skills. Ones he may have to use on you, if you don't tell us what we want to know."

Steve's heart was thudding in his chest. Things looked grim. "I want a lawyer."

"We'll see. But first things first. Now, who did you talk to about the assassination, besides your boss?"

"Just him."

Logan grabbed a pair of black leather gloves that were lying on a nearby table, slowly slipped them on. Then he walked in front of Steve and backhanded him across the face. The sharp blow stung and his lip began to bleed.

"Who else, McCord?"

Steve took a deep breath. "Nobody."

"Why don't I believe you?"

"Because you're an asshole?"

"You're going to make me mad," the NSA agent said.

Logan hit him with an uppercut, the punch sending Steve, still bound to the chair, toppling to the floor.

Saunders came over, righted the chair and went back to his corner.

Steve was dizzy and felt a tooth loose in his mouth. He spit it out, the bloody incisor landing on the floor. The metallic taste of blood filled his mouth.

Logan grunted. "Serves you right, McCord, for mouthing off." He paused, took a step back. "Make it easy on yourself – tell us and you can go back to doing whatever you CIA types do. How's that sound?"

"Kiss my ass, Logan."

"You're going to regret that." He pulled off the blood-stained gloves and threw them in a trash container. "I'll let Saunders take a crack at you."

"I'm not talking, no matter what you do."

A sinister grin spread on Logan's face. "We'll see about that."

Logan stepped aside and Saunders rolled a small table in front of Steve.

Grabbing a metal briefcase from the floor, Saunders set it on the table. Without saying a word, the man opened the case and turned it so Steve could see the inside. Steve's heart sank when he saw the contents.

Neatly arranged in the case were rows of what appeared to be very sharp dental instruments. Among the dentist tools were chisels, picks, drills, surgical scissors and a heavy-duty forceps. The spotless, stainless-steel tools gleamed from the overhead light.

"You're such a tough guy," Logan said, "that we're going to skip the water boarding. We're going right to the fun stuff."

Silently, Saunders picked up the forceps. A wicked smile crossed his face.

11 Days to Zero Hour

Aboard Air Force One
Flying at 41,000 feet over central Kansas

President Taylor leaned back in the leather seat and stared out the plane's windows. The scene outside was turbulent – an angry gray sky was illuminated by flashes of lightning, with storm clouds swirling below.

In the conference room with him were General Corvan and Treasury Secretary Mike Longstreet. Longstreet was going through a monotonous Power Point presentation regarding the country's massive debt problem. Taylor was only half-listening. He had heard the grim predictions many times before and was frankly sick of them. Longstreet was not part of BlackSnow, another reason the president tended to brush him off.

Taylor turned back to the secretary, held up a hand. "Okay, Mike. That'll be enough for today."

"But, Mr. President," Longstreet said, "we have a deadline coming up. If we don't–"

Taylor slapped a hand on the table. "I said enough. We'll pick this up tomorrow."

"Yes, sir." The secretary turned off the projector and shuffled his reports into a stack. Standing up, Longstreet nodded to both men and left the room, closing the door behind him.

Taylor leaned forward in his seat and said, "That man is exhausting. After the election, he's gone."

Corvan nodded. "Yes, sir."

"Okay, General, bring me up to date on BlackSnow."

"Things are going exactly as planned, Mr. President. The Chinese consulate assignment went like clockwork."

"I agree. Better than planned, in my opinion. The Chinese guards shot innocent civilians. Americans are really fired up."

"Yes, sir. The demonstrations are spreading everywhere."

"Good. Now let's go over the other preparations."

Corvan pulled a sheaf of paper from inside his uniform jacket and slid it across the table. "The Tridents are getting into position," he said. "This shows you where they are right now."

The president scanned the sheet, noted the location of the submarine fleet. "Excellent. So everything is coming together."

Corvan rubbed his jaw. "Yes, sir. We do have a couple of other issues, but I'm dealing with them."

Taylor's hands formed into fists. "Problems, General? I don't want *anything* to interfere with this operation. We're too close now for anything to go wrong. Tell me, God damn it."

"Cody Preston has been working on this, sir. I'd like for him to go through it."

"Okay, get him in here."

The general picked up the phone on the table and spoke for a moment.

A minute later Cody Preston walked in the room, closed the door behind him and sat down. The NSA director was a tall, lean man with a large, hooked nose and sunken eyes. He had been director of the National Security Agency for three years.

"We were just discussing the issues you've been working on," Corvan said to Preston. "Why don't you bring us up to date?"

"Of course," Preston said, placing his hands flat on the table. "Mr. President, we recently learned that a Central Intelligence agent by the name of McCord has been out in LA, sniffing around the assassination's location."

Taylor's face flushed red. "What? What the hell does the CIA have to do with this?"

"Apparently, sir, this agent was conducting an independent inquiry. He reported back to his boss at Langley that there was possible collusion between the Secret Service and the assassin."

"How in the hell did he come up with that? Our security on this has been air-tight."

"Don't know, sir. I dug into his personal file – he's a pretty smart guy. Maybe he just figured it out on his own."

Taylor bolted out of his seat and glared down at Preston. "So what the hell are you doing about it? If this shit gets out, it'll jeopardize our whole operation!"

The NSA director pushed his chair back a bit. "Yes, sir. Of course, sir. I have it under control."

"How?"

"Two of my men picked him up yesterday and put him in custody. His boss has also been detained."

The president gave him a withering stare. "So they're under wraps?"

"Yes, Mr. President. They're in a secure location. We're questioning McCord now, using aggressive interrogation techniques –"

Taylor held up a hand. "I don't need to know the details."

"Yes, sir. We're trying to ascertain if he told anyone else beside his boss."

"And?"

"Too soon to tell. We're still working on him."

"Get to the bottom of this, Preston. And whatever you do, don't release those two."

"Of course, sir."

"There's one other issue," Corvan interjected.

Taylor slumped onto his seat, a grim expression on his face. "Well?"

Preston folded his hands in a steeple. "A few days ago, we picked up a coded transmission from our State Department to Beijing, China. A secret call was made. The call was encrypted, but one of our NSA wiretaps picked it up and we were able to decipher parts of it."

"What the hell?" Taylor exclaimed. "Who was it at State?"

"We don't know, yet," Preston replied. "We're still working on that."

The president scowled at him. "Find out. Now! We can't have that kind of shit going on. We're too close now."

"Yes, Mr. President."

Taylor shook his head slowly. "Any more bad news?"

Corvan leaned forward in his seat. "No, sir. That's all of it."

"Okay, gentlemen, that'll be all. We'll review this again tomorrow, when we're back in Washington."

***

U.S. Senate Chamber
Washington, D.C.

Senator Megan Lewis huddled with two other Republican senators, devising a strategy to block the upcoming bill. The Democrats were trying to ram through another massive stimulus package, regardless of the cost. She was determined to stop them.

The three stood at one side of the Senate well, while other small groups of lawmakers talked in clusters around the room. The hum of their muffled but urgent conversations filled the chamber.

Just then Megan's aide Lisa came up to her and handed her a note. The senator read it, glanced at her watch. The vote was in two hours, time enough for her to take care of this.

Excusing herself from the other two senators, she followed her aide out of the chamber. They took the private underground subway that connected the U.S. Capitol to the Hart Senate Office Building. A few minutes later they were in the senator's office.

Sitting behind her desk, Lewis glared up at the young assistant, who remained standing. Lisa was a thin, plain-looking young woman with a sallow complexion. She always wore her hair in a bun and favored all-black suits.

"This better be good, Lisa. I've got an important vote coming up. Your note said something urgent came up?"

"Yes, ma'am," Lisa replied primly. "You wanted me to notify you if something broke on the Wilson matter."

Megan's interest picked up immediately. "Yes. Tell me."

"One of our sources at the Justice Department just called," Lisa said. Over the years, Megan had developed an extensive network of 'friends' at the various government agencies, and they gave her a heads-up on issues of interest to her. Megan reciprocated, making her a powerful force to deal with in Washington circles.

The senator lowered her voice. "No need to mention who. The walls have ears. Just tell me what they said."

"Yes, ma'am." The young woman scanned her notes, then looked back at the senator.

"Something strange is happening at Central Intelligence," Lisa continued. "The National Security Agency has detained two agents from the CIA. They were served with FISA warrants."

Megan's jaw dropped. "Those are used to fight terrorism. What the hell is going on?"

Lisa shook her head. "Our source said the details are murky. He only found out because his girlfriend works at Langley. Anyway, it's become a real turf war."

Megan nodded. "I can imagine."

"There's more, Senator. It appears the whole thing started when a CIA operative investigated the president's assassination."

"What's the agent's name?"

"Steve McCord."

Megan bolted off her seat. "Damn. I know him. He's the ex-husband of a friend of mine. Where are they holding him?"

Lisa shook her head. "Unknown. He could be anywhere. There are NSA rendition centers all around the world."

The senator slumped back in her seat, her mind racing. "Maybe Erica's right," she murmured to herself. "Maybe there is a conspiracy."

Lisa stepped forward, as if straining to hear. "What was that, ma'am?"

Meagan glanced up. "Nothing."

She noted the time on the wall clock. "I've got to go back to the chamber. But I want you to keep working on this. Call our source at the Pentagon. See if he's heard anything."

"Yes, ma'am."

The senator stood up and strode out of the office. As she walked down the corridor, she tried to focus on the upcoming vote. But her thoughts kept coming back to the NSA action. Something bad was happening, that was for sure. She just hoped she could use the situation, whatever it was, to her advantage. Maybe, just maybe, she could still further her presidential ambitions.

***

The Palm Restaurant
Washington, D.C.

Erica Blake pulled the Taurus into the parking lot of the upscale restaurant and parked by the valet station. She climbed out and tugged down the hem of her clingy black dress. Erica rarely wore dresses, but Steve had insisted. When he asked her out to lunch a couple of days ago, he said he had something important to discuss. He insisted she wear something special. Against her better judgment, she finally relented and wore the cocktail dress. Now she was paying the price.

One of the valets came over and gave her a ticket stub. The young man scrutinized the shabby-looking Taurus as he took the keys.

"Park it in a safe spot," she said, sarcasm dripping from her voice. "This car is priceless."

He gave her a perplexed look, got in and drove away.

Erica went into the restaurant and approached the maître d' station. She had never been here before because she couldn't afford it. But she knew the place was a hangout for the D.C. elite.

"I'm Erica Blake," she told the officious-looking man in the tuxedo. "The reservation is under McCord. Steve McCord. Is he here yet?"

The man glanced down at his book. "No, Miss. He hasn't come in yet. Would you like to wait in our bar?"

"Sure," she replied.

She went into the crowded bar area, which was filled with well-dressed patrons, mostly men. Sleek, glass-topped tables were clustered in the front, with a long, teak bar along the wall. Drawings of famous celebrities hung on the walls.

She found an empty stool at the bar, sat, and signaled the bartender.

"Budweiser," she said loudly, trying to be heard over the noisy conversations in the room.

"Would you like a glass with that?" he asked.

She glared. "Just bring me the beer, will you?"

He nodded, moved away.

Pulling her cell phone out of her compact purse, she dialed Steve's number. She had called him several times, but it had been going to voicemail. Hearing the recording again, she turned off the phone.

The man seated on the stool next to her leaned over. He was wearing a pin-stripe suit and cloying, probably expensive, cologne.

"Buy you a drink, honey?" he asked, his words slightly slurred.

"Screw off, buster."

A confused look crossed his face. "You're not a working girl?"

"I'm not a pro, if that's what you're thinking."

He held up his palms. "Sorry, honey. We get a lot of that here."

She tugged at the spaghetti straps of her dress, which had slipped off her shoulders. "Get lost, buddy."

He picked up his drink, stood, and moved to another stool.

The bartender come over and put the Budweiser in front of her.

She took a sip from the bottle. It was her first drink of the day and the familiar taste was refreshing. Then she took a long pull of the Budweiser and put the bottle down.

Glancing at her watch, she realized Steve was thirty minutes late. Impatient, she cursed to herself. She dialed his number again, got the same recording.

Erica signaled the waiter for another beer.

A minute later he set the bottle down and moved away. Draining it in seconds, she wiped her mouth with her hand.

She was about to order a third when her cell phone buzzed. Picking it off the bar, she took the call.

She recognized the voice immediately. "Erica," Senator Lewis said, "I'm glad I caught you."

Erica got off the stool, went to a quieter area of the room. "Hi. What's up, Senator?"

"I've got some bad news for you."

Erica strained to hear over the loud, boozy conversations all around her. "What?"

"It's about McCord."

"Steve? What going on?"

"He's been arrested by the NSA."

"What the hell?"

"It's hard to believe, I know. Some trumped-up terrorism charge."

Erica pressed the phone to her ear, not sure she'd heard the woman right. "Terrorism?"

"Look, Erica. I think this is connected to his trip to LA, if you get my drift."

"Oh?"

"Yeah. It's that. The subject you mentioned, I think it's true."

Erica's brain processed the information, then realized what Lewis was talking about. The president's assassination. The possible cover-up. "I understand, Senator."

"Good. Now listen. If they arrested Steve, you may not be safe."

"What do you mean?"

"Erica, I think you're in danger. You've got to get out of town until things cool down."

"Senator, where's Steve?"

"Don't know. I've got my sources trying to find out."

"I've got to get to him, post his bail."

"It may not be that simple, Erica."

"What do you mean?"

"He could be in rendition."

Her heart sank when she heard the words. While at the Bureau, she'd heard whispers about this happening after the enactment of the Patriot Act. Steve could be incarcerated anywhere, not just in the United States. And the interrogation methods used were – she stopped her mind from going there.

"What should I do, Senator?"

"Go to some place safe. Do you have any family, out-of-state?"

"No. My parents passed away and I don't have any brothers or sisters."

"I see. Then just pick anyplace away from D.C."

"There is one place."

"Don't say where, just go."

"Yes, Senator."

"One other thing. Get rid of your cell phone. Get a burner. Hopefully they won't be able to track you that way."

"I already did that, a couple of days ago."

"Get a new one. The NSA is involved now, and they've got sophisticated tracking systems. Call me when you get settled. I may have more information about Steve then."

"Okay."

"Good luck, Erica. We're both going to need it."

The call clicked off and she put the phone back in her purse.

Still dazed by the news, Erica left restaurant.

While she waited for the valet to bring her car around, she spotted a trash bin and threw in her cell phone.

Moments later she was back in the Taurus, speeding home. On the way she made two stops. She filled her tank at a corner Shell, then bought a new burner cell phone at a Wal-Mart.

Parking on the street, she went into her apartment building. She skipped the elevator and raced up the stairs.

Once inside, she paused a moment, trying to decide what to do first.

Going to her bedroom, she pulled an empty suitcase from her closet and threw it on the bed. Then began stuffing it with a week's worth of clothes. Slamming it shut, she went to the small lock box beneath the bed.

From it she retrieved a wad of cash, her passport and her personal weapon. The handgun was a Smith & Wesson .38 caliber revolver with a two-inch barrel.

Realizing she was still dressed in the uncomfortable cocktail dress, she unzipped it and let it drop to the floor. Kicking off her high-heeled shoes, she grabbed a pair of jeans and sneakers and put them on. Lastly, she found a gray polo shirt and threw it on, leaving the shirt tail out.

Slipping the gun into her waistband, she then stuffed the cash and passport into her pockets. After a last look around, she grabbed the suitcase and headed out of the bedroom.

There was a knock at her door and she peered through the peephole. Two men in black suits were standing in the corridor.

There was another knock, this time louder.

"Who is it?" she asked.

"Miss Blake," came the muffled reply, "we're Federal officers. We need to speak with you, please."

"I'm not dressed," she lied. "Give me a moment while I put something on."

"Of course."

Dropping the suitcase to the floor, she sprinted back to the bedroom. Quickly sliding open the window, she climbed out to the fire escape. Descending the metal stairs two at a time, she reached the end and dropped the last ten feet to the sidewalk.

Running to her car, she got in, slamming the door shut behind her. She cranked the engine, but then heard a knock on her side window.

A bulky man in a black suit and opaque sunglasses stood there, holding a badge in front of him. With a sinking feeling she realized they had sent more than two men for her.

"Erica Blake," he said loudly, "I'm a Federal agent. Please step out of the car." He drew his gun, pointed it at the ground.

Out of the corner of her eye she spotted two more men in suits climbing out of a parked SUV.

"No problem, sir," she replied. "I'll just turn off my car."

"Okay, but no sudden moves."

Her heart thudding in her chest, she made a split decision.

In a blur of motion she slid the transmission lever into drive, took off the parking brake and cranked the wheel hard left. Then she stomped on the accelerator pedal. The car roared out of the spot, but not before clipping the Nissan parked in front of her. She felt her car shudder from the impact and heard the crunch of metal.

The Taurus veered left as she sped away, almost out of control. She spun the wheel right to avoid the oncoming traffic.

Stomping the gas pedal with her foot, she raced down the street, the tires squealing all the way.

She heard men shouting, then the clatter of automatic weapons. The back windshield of her car imploded, the glass shards showering her head.

Cursing, she swerved the wheel hard right, took the next corner. The car was going so fast two of the wheels came off the pavement as she took the turn.

Then she stepped on the gas again, weaving in and out of traffic, desperately looking for a place to ditch the car. The men had gotten a good look at her Taurus and would issue a BOLO in minutes.

Several blocks later she spotted an empty, grassy lot between two buildings.

Slamming on her brakes, she steered the car into the area, dodging the pedestrians on the sidewalk. Driving the car through to the alley behind one of the buildings, she cut right, scraped the wall as she slammed on the brakes again. The car screeched to a halt and she climbed out. But she left the engine running, with the key in the ignition. If she was lucky, someone would steal the damn thing.

Erica sprinted down the alley and after several blocks, found a street with run-down retail shops. She spotted what she was looking for moments later.

Going into the scruffy, second-hand shop, she quickly grabbed a baseball cap, a black windbreaker and sunglasses from the shelves. She paid cash, tucked her long hair under the cap, and put on the jacket and glasses.

She glanced at herself in a cracked mirror on the wall. It wasn't a great disguise, but would have to do. Then she left the shop and walked quickly away, but not too fast to avoid suspicion.

An hour later she was at the Greyhound bus terminal.

Winded from her trek, she stood in line to buy a ticket. Scanning the routes on the reader board, she picked the one that had the earliest departure time. Paying cash, she walked toward the boarding area.

She only had to wait a few minutes then she climbed on the bus. Grabbing a seat behind a Hispanic-looking couple speaking Spanish, she settled on the cramped seat and tried to stretch her legs as best she could. It was hot in the bus, as if the A/C was broken. And the seat smelled of garlic from the empty take-out bag on the floor.

Warily looking out the window as the bus pulled away from the terminal, she breathed a sigh of relief. But the feeling was temporary, she realized. *Those men back there are pros.*

***

Washington, D.C.

Bobbie Garcia was in his home office when his cell phone buzzed. He immediately answered the call.

"It's me," he heard the general say. The connection sounded weak and a bit garbled.

"Is this a secure line, sir?" Garcia asked. "It doesn't sound right."

"Yes, Captain. I'm calling from Air Force One. We just got a break on the leak at the State Department. Make this your highest priority. We want this dealt with immediately. I'm e-mailing you the details after I hang up."

"Yes, sir."

The line went dead and he put the phone back on the desk.

A minute later an encrypted e-mail popped up on his screen. He opened the attachment and read it thoroughly. Rereading it again to make sure he memorized it, he then deleted the e-mail.

Thinking it over a few minutes, he decided to tackle this one by himself. The fewer people involved the better.

He turned off the computer and went to the kitchen. He made himself a sandwich, which he ate standing up. He washed it down with a Pepsi. Then he went to the bedroom, picked out a dark suit, tie and a starched, button-down white shirt. Dressing quickly, he looked closely at himself in the bathroom mirror, satisfied that he appeared official.

Then he grabbed his go-bag from the floor and headed out of the apartment.

Four hours later he was on K Street, following the BMW sedan as it wound its way out of D.C. and into nearby Virginia. It was six in the evening and traffic was still heavy.

He kept his Suburban two cars back, but it didn't really seem to matter, because the woman driving the Beemer had been on her cell the whole time. Although she seemed oblivious to the traffic around her, he still kept a safe distance back.

According to the mission specs, she lived in an upscale townhome in an exclusive area of Virginia, not far from D.C. The route she was taking would bring her directly home.

He would have liked to have more time to prep, but the general had been very specific. It had to be taken care of today.

Half-hour later, the BMW took a left off the main road and onto a quiet side street. Elegant four-story townhomes lined both sides of the road. The upscale homes were in the Federal style, with large, symmetrical windows. Three-car garages made up the lower level of each townhouse.

The Beemer pulled unto the driveway of one of the homes. The door to one of its garages opened and the car slid in. A moment later the garage door closed and he saw lights going in the house.

Driving past the home slowly, he scouted the area. He went to the end of the street, circled at the cul-de-sac and went back to the woman's home, where he pulled into the driveway.

Glancing in the rear-view mirror, he adjusted his tie and combed his hair. Then he climbed out of the SUV and walked up the stairs to the front door.

He pulled a badge from his suit pocket and rang the bell.

"Yes?" a woman's muffled voice came through the closed door.

"Secretary Cruz," Garcia said, "I'm Special Agent Sanchez with the FBI. I need to speak with you." He was sure she was looking at him through a viewer on the door, so he held up his forged badge.

The door opened and the woman stood there, wearing a stylish, blue pantsuit. The secretary of state was a stunning woman who looked better in person than in the news clips.

"You're with the FBI? What's this about?" she asked, concern in her voice.

He handed her his badge and a business card that matched it. She looked at the badge closely, handed it back, but kept the card.

"Madam Secretary, I'm sorry, but I have some bad news for you."

Her eyebrows arched. "What?"

"Your niece, Samantha, has been kidnapped. The FBI has been given the lead on the case. As I understand it, you and her mother Estella are very close. She's asked for your help in getting her daughter released."

Cruz's eyes went wide. "My God! I can't believe this. Of course, I'll do anything to help."

"Very good, Miss Cruz. We have Estella at a safe house – I'd like to take you there now."

"Do I have time to let my office know where I'll be?"

"No, there's no time. You can call when we get to the safe house."

"Of course. I'll just get my purse."

The woman went into the house and was back a moment later clutching her Louis Vuitton purse.

"Do you want me to follow you in my car?" she asked.

"No, we'll go in my vehicle – it'll be quicker that way."

She nodded and followed him to the Suburban. They both got in, and he pulled out of the driveway and sped away.

Twenty minutes later, the SUV got off the state road and wound its way for another mile through the suburban Virginia area. The homes were modest, but set on large pieces of property. Garcia slowed the Suburban and turned into the gravel driveway of a large, ranch-style home on a wooded lot. Built probably in the '60s, the non-descript brick home was plain-looking with faded white trim. But it was set well away from the neighbors, the reason the general had purchased it specifically for these types of operations.

"We're here," he said as he drove on the driveway, the tires crunching on the gravel. "This is our safe house."

Cruz peered at the house. "Where's the rest of the cars?" she asked. "I thought there would be a lot of other agents here."

"They're parked in the back."

She nodded, but apprehension clouded her face. "The house is dark. You sure this is the right place, agent Sanchez?"

"Yes, Secretary," he replied in an even tone. He could tell the woman was getting suspicious.

Pressing the garage door remote button, he eased the large SUV into the garage as soon as it opened. The fluorescent lighting of the garage cast a bluish glow inside the vehicle.

Cruz pulled a cell phone from her purse, turned it on. "I need to call my office," she said in a shrill voice. She began to stab numbers on the phone.

He grabbed the phone away, and with his other hand struck her on the face with a closed fist. Her head snapped back, hitting the closed side window with a thud. The whites of her eyes showed and she slumped on the seat, unconscious.

Using the remote, Garcia closed the garage, climbed out of the Suburban and went into the house, putting on the lights. He came back, lifted Cruz out of the car and carried her into one of the bedrooms. After dropping her on the bed, he methodically took off all her clothes and bound her legs and arms to the bed posts. For a moment he admired her curves and flawless skin, then pushed those thoughts aside. He had no intention of sexually assaulting her, but knew she would feel much more vulnerable nude.

Pulling up a chair next to the bed, he sat down and waited for her to regain consciousness.

A while later, her eye lids fluttered and she groaned.

Then her eyes snapped open and her head jerked left to right, taking in the scene.

"What the hell is this, Sanchez?" She pulled against the straps, straining to break free. "I demand you release me, immediately!"

"Don't pull against the straps too hard, Miss Cruz. You'll only end up cutting yourself."

Her eyes burned with hate. "Who the hell are you? You're no FBI agent, that's for damn sure."

"You're right about that, ma'am."

"What do you want? Are you going to rape me?"

"Can I call you Audrey? Miss Cruz sounds so formal, don't you think?"

She struggled against the straps some more, but finally gave up, her face contorted in pain. "Shit...shit. I should have known you were a phony. Damn. You'll never get away with this. I'm the Secretary of State. They're probably already looking for me." Then she began cursing at the top of top of her voice, the yelling carrying throughout the house.

"This house is sound-proofed," Garcia said. "None of the neighbors can hear anything. Can I call you Audrey?"

She grunted. "Call me whatever you want. You've got the upper hand here."

"That's true, Audrey. I do."

"I've got money. Lots of money. Whatever you want. I'll write you a check. Better yet, I've got cash and jewelry back at my house."

"That's not what I want, Audrey."

A bewildered look crossed her face. "What *do* you want? Do you want sex? No problem. Just take off these straps and we can —"

Garcia held up a hand, interrupting her. "That's not what I want."

"What then?"

"I just need answers to a few questions."

"Questions? You kidnap me to ask me questions? What kind of sick bastard are you?"

"I'm just a guy doing a job."

Her eyes darted around the room as if looking for some way to escape. After a moment her shoulders slumped and she said. "What's your real name?"

"Bobbie."

She nodded. "Who do you work for, Bobbie?"

"That's not important."

"Okay. If I answer your questions, you'll let me go?"

"Of course."

He stood up and grabbed a folded bed sheet that was lying on the top of the bureau. Opening the sheet, he covered her body up to her neck. "Is that better, Audrey?"

"Yes, thank you."

"Would you like some water or a soda?" he asked.

"Yes. Water's good."

He went to the kitchen, grabbed a glass and filled it from the tap. He returned, tipped the glass to the woman's lips as she drank greedily.

Putting the empty glass on the night table, he sat back down.

"Feel better, Audrey?"

She nodded. "Let's get this over with. What do you want to know?"

"You recently had a secret conversation with someone in Beijing, China. From the details we have, the call originated from a government building there."

Her eyes went wide. "I...no...."

"Don't deny it. The NSA picked it up. The call was scrambled, but those guys are good."

"Listen, Bobby, there's been some mistake. I didn't have any conversation like that. You've got to believe me."

Garcia crossed his arms in front of him. "I don't want to hurt you, Audrey. You're a beautiful woman and I'd hate to scar your face."

Her lower lip trembled and her body edged away from him. "Please...."

Standing, he took off his suit jacket and draped it over the chair. Next he loosened his tie and rolled up his shirtsleeves. Reaching behind his back, he pulled a combat knife from his waistband and held it up to the light. The sharp, stainless-steel blade gleamed from the overhead light. Crossing the room, he turned on the CD player on the bureau. Classical music came out of the speakers.

Turning back to her, he walked to the bed slowly, letting the anticipation build.

Finally he sat next to her on the bed, caressed the sharp edge of the blade against the soft skin of her face.

Terror filled her eyes and she began screaming. Her bowels loosened and he smelled the putrid stench as it filled the room.

"Tell me the truth," he whispered, "and nothing bad will happen to you. Lie to me and...." He punctured her cheek with the point of the blade and rivulets of blood dribbled down her face. She screamed and flinched away.

"Please, Audrey. I don't want to hurt you."

"Yes, yes!" she cried out, her breath ragged. "It's true. I was talking with General Chang."

"Now we're getting somewhere. Who's he?"

"He's head of their armed forces."

"Why were you talking to him?"

"We have a deal. I give him U.S. foreign policy information and he pays me. A lot."

"You're doing well, Audrey. Now I want you to tell me exactly what you said and what he said. Word for word."

"You won't cut me anymore?"

"That's right. I won't. Now talk. And don't leave anything out, or you'll regret it. Understand?"

She nodded her head vigorously and began talking.

Ten minutes later she was done.

"That wasn't so hard, was it Audrey?"

She shook her head, but her eyes were still wide with fear.

Putting the knife back in his waistband, he stood up. "I'll get a bandage for your face and give you something for the pain. Then, after you've had a chance to rest, I'll drive you back home. Okay?"

She nodded, said nothing.

Garcia opened a drawer in the bureau and took out a first-aid kit. He also took a hypodermic needle that was in the drawer and placed both items on the bed next to the woman.

Carefully, he cleaned the wound on her cheek and applied a bandage. He picked up the hypodermic, said, "This will help you relax. The needle will sting a bit, but you'll feel much better in no time."

He rubbed her shoulder with a swab of alcohol and gingerly applied the shot, trying to be as gentle as possible.

Moments later her eyes got a dreamy look and she closed them. A minute later she was fast asleep.

He breathed a sigh of relief. He would have hated to hurt her more. He didn't mind killing, but torture repulsed him.

Then he went to the living room and made two calls.

The first one was to the general, filling him in on the details of the interrogation.

The second was to his contact at the National Security Agency. Their guys would be coming here to pick up Cruz and take her to an undisclosed location. She was no longer his problem.

10 Days to Zero Hour

Beijing, China

General Chang sipped whiskey as he reviewed reports in his office. It was mid-day and his stomach was growling with hunger. But lunch would have to wait. With everything going on with the Americans, he had been neglecting his other military duties. Reviewing the status reports on Chinese tank readiness along the Russian-Chinese border was important and he vowed to finish it today.

The intercom on his desk buzzed and he heard Captain Lin's voice. "Sir, the President of the United States is calling on the video link. Should I put him through?"

Chang's heart began to race. He'd been calling the man for weeks and had yet to hear back. But now he was calling back. A good sign. Maybe things could get back to the 'old normal'.

He swept the reports to one side of his desk. "Yes, Lin, put him through." He glanced down at his crisply starched uniform and adjusted the military ribbons on his jacket. Then he turned on the secure line monitor.

The monitor came to life and seconds later President Taylor's face filled the screen. Although he had seen the U.S. leader in many news clips, it was never in such a tight close-up. The man's heavy jowls hung from his corpulent face.

"Mr. President," the general said, "I am glad you called."

"General Chang," the president replied, his voice warm and soothing. "I have to apologize for not getting back to you sooner. As you can imagine, things here in Washington have been hectic, to say the least."

"Understandable, Mr. President." Chang wanted to scream at the man, but knew diplomacy was a much better approach.

"General, now that I've been in office a few weeks, I've had a chance to review the records of your discussions with President Wilson."

"I see." Chang didn't know what was coming next. He was expecting the worst.

"Although Wilson and I didn't always agree on everything, I have to admit the transactions you two negotiated were beneficial to the United States."

The general breathed a sigh of relief. Maybe there was hope yet for his own future in Chinese politics. "That is good to hear, Mr. President."

Taylor smiled broadly. "My first name is Matt. Why don't you call me that from now on in private? As a sign of our special relationship."

"That would be excellent, Mr. President, I mean Matt. Please call me Wu."

"Very good, Wu." The American paused, glanced down at his desk as if reading something, then looked at Chang again. "Before you bring it up, I'd like to address the issue of the assassination. I know that must be a sore spot with you and your people."

Chang hands formed into fists and he took a deep breath to release his anger. "Yes. I wanted to talk about that."

A contrite look crossed the president's face. "Wu, I want to extend the Chinese government a sincere apology. Right after the assassination, a rushed investigation was conducted and a horrific mistake was made. Things in Washington were chaotic then and a lot of misinformation was flying around. The investigating team incorrectly identified the assassin as a Chinese man. A new, more in-depth investigation is taking place. It now appears the killing was committed by an al-Qaeda terrorist. We will be releasing this new information to the public as soon as we have confirmed all the facts."

"That is very good news, Matt. However, the Chinese reputation has been damaged by your original statement. We have lost face."

"And once again, I apologize for that. Be assured that all of the original investigators have been fired. Further, they have been prohibited from any future employment by our government."

"I applaud your efforts, Matt. This will be welcome news to our premier. When do you think you will announce the al-Qaeda terrorist suspect? The sooner the better, from our perspective."

The American smiled again. "I am positive the inquiry will be complete in two weeks, probably less. I will go on national TV and address the nation. I will also give my apology publically to the Chinese government then. I hope that is satisfactory?"

"Yes, Matt."

"Excellent. I hope we can continue our mutually beneficial arrangement in the future. I look forward to personally working with you."

"That is good, sir. I also look forward to it."

"Goodbye, Wu."

The screen went dark and Chang turned off the monitor.

Ecstatic from the call, his life looked a lot brighter now.

After taking a long pull from his glass of whiskey, he pressed the intercom. "Lin, call the Premier. Tell him I need to meet with as soon as possible."

Half-hour later Chang stood ramrod straight in front of Premier Tse. Tse was sitting behind his desk in his office, a grim look on his face.

"You have some news?" Tse asked, his tone harsh.

"Yes, sir. I just received a call from the American President. The man apologized profusely for not returning my calls. And he also gave me very good news."

"I'm not a mind reader, General. Spit it out!"

"Yes, Premier. The Americans made a tragic mistake in their investigation. They now realize that no Chinese operatives were involved in the assassination."

Tse's jaw dropped. "A mistake? How is that possible?"

"Taylor says that with all the confusion after the event, their agents overlooked vital information. He was very apologetic, sir."

"We as a nation have lost face."

"Yes, Premier. But the President will apologize publically to us in a nationally televised address."

"When?"

"He believes the new investigation will be completed in a matter of weeks. At that time he will go on TV."

Tse's face seemed to relax. "I see." He motioned with one hand. "Have a seat, General."

Chang, enormously relieved by the premier's change in tone, sat in one of the ornately-upholstered wingchairs. "Thank you, sir."

"So, Chang, you believe Taylor is being honest with us?"

"Yes, Premier. I could tell by his tone and attitude. It was clear he wanted to resume our 'special relationship'."

Tse nodded. "The man is finally realizing they need us more than we need them."

"I agree. They are in a deep hole, one that gets deeper by the day."

The premier barked out a harsh laugh. "That is a good analogy, General. We definitely have them by their short hairs." He leaned back in his chair, turned his head and glanced out the tall windows. The sky was overcast in Beijing, signaling the coming rain. Then he turned back to Chang. "Keep Taylor on a short leash. Once he makes his public apology, I want to start getting more concessions from the Americans. For every single Yuan they borrow, I want something in return." A wicked smile crossed his face. "I want to bleed them dry."

"Yes, sir."

"Keep me up-to-date, General, as you get additional details. Good work. You are to be congratulated for turning the situation around."

Chang stood, saluted, and left the office, feeling a lot better than when he'd come in.

Back in his own office later, the general paced the room, sorting through his thoughts. No way could he concentrate on the tedious tank status reports now. He was too wired. No, he had a better idea, a much better idea.

Going back to his desk, he pressed the intercom. "Captain Lin, would you come in a minute?"

"Yes, General,"

The young woman came in his office and he waved her to one of the visitor's chairs. She was wearing her usual military uniform – a green jacket and green skirt with a white shirt. She perched on the chair and he went back to his desk and sat down.

"Lin, I know things have been difficult over the last several weeks."

She nodded, but said nothing.

"Since this problem started with the Americans, I have been, shall I say, difficult to be around."

"It is understandable, sir. You have been under a lot of pressure."

He took off his thick glasses, laid them on the desk. "I have. However, that is no excuse for the way I have treated you recently."

She waved that away. "Not a problem, sir."

"Good. As you may have overheard, the U.S. president has changed his tune. The Chinese-American 'agreement' is back in place. We help them and they help us."

"Yes, sir, I did listen in on the conversation. It is wonderful news."

"I agree." He smiled. "Now that things are back on track, I was hoping you would be agreeable to resuming our special arrangement."

Her face broke into a wide grin. "That would please me very much, General."

"Excellent, Lin. If possible, I'd like to start today."

Standing up, she went to the door and locked it. Then took off her military jacket and laid it on the chair. Her crisply starched shirt strained against her curves.

As he watched intently, she slowly unbuttoned her shirt and sensuously took it off. Then she unzipped her skirt and let it drop to the floor. Unhooking her bra, she shrugged out of it, and leisurely pulled down her panties. Completely nude, she sashayed around the desk and leaned over and gave him a quick kiss on the lips.

Chang was breathing hard now and his groin was straining against his pants. He tried to pull her down for a longer kiss.

She laughed and pushed his hands away. "Not now. We'll do that later."

Lin dropped to her knees in front of him and pushed his legs apart. She began unbuttoning his uniform jacket.

"Lay on the floor, Lin," he said, his voice hoarse. "I'll get on top."

She chuckled. "No. We do it my way first."

Still sitting, he leaned his head back against the chair, knowing the woman could be headstrong. But he also knew she was an expert when it came to this.

She unbuckled his belt and unzipped his trousers. With both hands she reached in and began to stroke him lightly. She was firm but gentle, as if knowing that he was already close.

He grunted from the pleasure, reached out with his hands and caressed her full breasts.

"You like that, General?" she asked coyly.

Groaning in response, he tried kissing her again. Her head moved to one side and she gently pushed his hands away from her.

"Just lay back and relax, sir. I'll do all the work."

He sighed, knowing she was right, and let his hands drop to his sides.

Lin stopped stroking him, lowered her head and began to lightly kiss the sides of his shaft. The feeling was electric and he almost exploded.

Stopping the kisses, she gave him time to catch his breath.

After a moment, she began kissing his shaft again, then took it in her mouth. The feeling was pure ecstasy. He took deep breaths in order to hold himself back.

Gripping the armrests tightly, he watched her head bob up and down as she picked up the tempo. The pleasure and pain combined into one and he could feel himself almost coming.

Lin slowed her movements, obviously trying to extend his pleasure a while longer.

She pulled away from him and sat back on her haunches and smiled. "Enjoying yourself, General?" she whispered.

His breath ragged, he nodded vigorously. Then she began to rub her hands slowly over her own luscious body, which was now covered with a light sheen of perspiration. The teasing excited him even more and he groaned with anticipation. It was clear from the expression on her face that she was enjoying this as much as he was.

"The best is yet to come," she said, as she moved towards him.

Kneeling in front of him once again, she lowered her head and took him in her mouth, very slowly, until his whole shaft disappeared. After holding him tight there for almost a minute, she glanced up at him, her stunning eyes bright with lust. The beautiful moment lasted for another minute until his loins screamed for release and he exploded in her mouth, the sexual sensation more powerful than any he'd had before.

***

Atlanta, Georgia

The first thing Erica Blake noticed when she walked into the motel room was the moldy smell. The stench hung in the air of the small, scruffy place. Going to the A/C, an antiquated wall unit, she pressed the on-button but nothing happened. Shaking her head slowly, she went to the window and cranked it open. The incoming breeze was hot but fresh, and she knew it was the only way to air out the place. She had paid cash for the room, so the last thing she wanted to do was complain. Most of the guests at this dump, she guessed, rented rooms by the hour. Complaints would be a red-flag to the day-manager, who probably had 911 on speed-dial. He was used to loud hookers and heroin addicts, not patrons who cared about cleanliness and air-conditioned comfort.

After a quick look out the window, all she saw was outside was a littered, almost empty parking lot. A few clunkers showing lots of rust were parked haphazardly. But seeing nothing else, she pulled the blinds closed.

Going into the grungy bathroom, she washed her face and hands with the tepid water. Then, still fully clothed, she went to the bed and lay down on the lumpy mattress. The springs were loud as she tossed on the bed, trying to find a comfortable spot. She was dead tired from her long bus ride and was asleep in minutes.

She woke with a start three hours later, staring at the cracks in the ceiling. Her muscles were stiff so she stretched out on the bed, trying to get the kinks out. As she lay there, her thoughts raced through her options. On the plus side, she was no longer in D.C. She had successfully evaded the NSA goons. She had cash in her pocket, a gun, and a burner phone. On the debit side, the goons were still after her. She was no longer an FBI agent and the only people she trusted were Lewis and Steve.

The image of Steve's face crossed her mind and lingered. Maybe she'd made a mistake years ago when she'd asked for a divorce. She missed him and wished they were still together. A feeling of dread overcame her as she thought about the danger he was facing now. Then a car honked outside and she heard two men arguing in the parking lot. The harsh sounds brought her back to reality.

Looking down at her clothes she realized she was still wearing the jeans and polo shirt from yesterday. Priority number one was to shower and buy fresh clothes.

Her stomach rumbled. Besides three Snickers Bars and a Sprite, she'd had nothing to eat for over a day. That was her second priority.

Climbing off the bed, she headed for the shower.

An hour later Erica was sitting at the counter of a Denny's off of Peachtree Street. The restaurant was half-full with mostly blue-collar workers and construction types.

Wearing the cargo pants and a man's short-sleeve shirt she had bought at a nearby Wal-Mart, she sipped coffee and glanced at the menu. She tugged at the bill of her baseball cap, pulling it lower to cover more of her face.

Her waitress came over and refilled her cup. The black woman appeared to be in her mid-forties. She was short and pudgy, with sad, brown eyes. Her name tag read *Sarah*.

"Ready to order?" the waitress asked with a heavy Southern accent.

Erica looked up. "What's good here, Sarah?"

The woman chuckled. "It's all good."

Erica rolled her eyes. "I bet. I'll have the Grand Slam Special, with extra bacon. And put butter on the toast."

"Sure thing, hon." Sarah wrote it down, moved away.

Erica sipped coffee and idly scanned the newspaper she'd bought on the way in. The headlines were all about the crappy economy and the soaring unemployment in Atlanta. Below the fold was a story about an anti-Chinese demonstration that had taken place yesterday in downtown.

Sarah brought over a large, steaming plate and set it down in front of her.

Erica attacked the food, wolfing it down in minutes. She even ate the bland grits.

"Somebody was hungry," Sarah said as she refilled the coffee cup.

Erica pushed aside the empty plate. "Hadn't eaten in a while."

"You in from out-of-town?" the waitress asked.

Erica tensed. "What makes you say that?"

"Just making conversation, hon. I just know you're not a regular here."

"That's true." She stared at the waitress. She seemed safe enough, and she decided to trust her instincts. "My name's Erica. I'm staying at a dumpy motel now but I'm looking for a better place. Know of anything?"

The woman grinned. "I own a duplex not far from here. It's small, but clean. My son and I live in one side, and I rent out the other. But the redneck asshole who was renting it just split. I'm looking for a new tenant."

"How much?"

Sarah told her.

"I'll take it for a week. Maybe longer."

Sarah gave her a perplexed look. "But you haven't even seen it yet."

Erica smiled. "Your uniform is clean, your shoes are shined and your hair is neatly combed. Somebody that takes care of the way they look is bound to have a place better than the dump I'm at now."

"You're pretty smart," Sarah said, chuckling, "for a white girl." She held out her hand and the women shook. "I get off here at two this afternoon. I'll give you the address and we can meet there then."

***

Erica turned up the A/C of the one-room apartment and cool air came out of the vent. It felt good. Then she checked out the bed, noticed the clean sheets. Lastly she ran the tap in the worn but spotless bathroom and flushed the toilet. It all worked and she walked back to the room.

"Looks good, Sarah," she told the other woman.

Sarah cocked her head. "I'm sorry, but I'll need cash, up-front. The last guy stiffed me for a week's rent. I won't make that mistake again."

"I understand." She dug the money out of the front pocket of the cargo pants and gave it to her.

"Thank you kindly," Sarah said. "And like I said before, my son Dwayne sometimes runs the TV too loud. Just bang on the wall and I'll see he turns it down."

"Sure."

"By the way, Erica, where's your stuff? Don't you have any luggage?"

"Nope. I'm traveling light."

"I guess so. Well, if you need anything, just holler."

The woman left and Erica locked the door and turned on the small TV, set the volume on low. Then she pulled out her cell phone and punched in a number. Senator Lewis's recorded voice came on the line and Erica hung up. She wasn't about to trust voice-mail.

***

NSA Rendition Center
Aberdeen, Maryland

Steve McCord sat on the cold floor of the jail cell, with his back against the wall. The 8' x 8' cell was a concrete bunker. Besides the solid steel door at one end and a dim light bulb hanging from the ceiling, there was nothing else.

The excruciating pain in his mouth was blinding and he rubbed his temples, trying to push away the throbbing. They had torn out all of his teeth, yanking them out one-by-one, until finally, after blacking out and being revived several times, he had broken down and told them what they wanted to know.

He coughed and more bright red blood seeped out of his mouth. The prison jumpsuit he wore was already covered with it. He wiped his mouth with one hand and rubbed off the sticky red substance on his pants leg.

But what hurt more than his ragged, bleeding gums was the fact he had given her up. He would never forgive himself for betraying Erica.

Coughing again, more blood spewed down his chest.

Just then he heard clanging and glanced up to see the door creak open. Two men in black uniforms holding stubby rifles came into the room, followed by a third man he recognized immediately. It was NSA agent Logan. Steve cringed, pressed his body against the wall.

"You don't look so good, my friend," Logan stated with a sneer. He squatted down and looked at Steve at eye-level. "You've lost a lot of blood – you may not make it."

"Damn you!" Steve yelled, as more blood seeped from his mouth.

"Still feisty, huh? We'll see how you feel by tomorrow. We're taking you on a little trip."

Logan stood up and turned to one of the guards. "Load him into the jet. Be careful with the blood. You don't want to mess up your uniforms." Then he left the cell.

***

Hart Senate Office Building
Adjacent to the U.S. Capitol
Washington, D.C.

Senator Megan Lewis was scared. She paced her office, her thoughts racing. Her close friend, Secretary of State Audrey Cruz, had gone missing. It had been over a day and no one knew where she was. The FBI and D.C. police had been called in, but so far there were no clues to her whereabouts. Megan knew the woman well. Intimately well. She knew Cruz would never leave without telling her staff her plans. Cruz wasn't wired that way.

Megan had a sick feeling about the whole thing. She had spoken personally to the lead FBI agent on the case and felt they were doing everything to find her. The senator had also tapped all of own her sources in Washington. But the disappearance was an enigma.

Luckily, the press hadn't gotten hold of the story yet, otherwise D.C. would turn into a circus. Better that the FBI keep looking for her, at least for another couple of days. But if that didn't work, she'd go to the press herself. Maybe some citizen, somewhere, would spot her.

Lewis stopped pacing and sat behind her desk. She took a sip of her now cold coffee as she processed all that had happened. Senator Carpenter's death. The President's assassination. Admiral Stanton. McCord being arrested. Now this. *Was Cruz's disappearance part of it too?* A chill went down her spine. *Jesus. What the hell's happening?* None of it made sense. Then a new thought flashed in her mind. She had made a lot of inquiries about these events. True, she had only asked her trusted sources. But what if somebody was tracking her? What if she herself was in danger? She knew she was a powerful senator, a key powerbroker in Washington circles. But someone had killed the president. *I could be next.*

Just then the intercom on her desk buzzed and she heard Lisa's voice. "Senator, the Colonel is here to see you."

"Show him in, Lisa."

Megan stood up and buttoned the jacket of her Versace black suit. Then she went around the desk, just as her door opened and the tall, slender man came in the office. Unlike his past visits, the colonel was wearing civilian clothes – a white, button-down shirt and gray slacks. Before, he had always worn his blue Air Force uniform. Lisa left the room and closed the door behind her.

"Jack, it's good to see you again," Megan said, offering her hand. Colonel Jack Norton was one her most trusted sources of information.

The man gave her a brief smile and they shook. "Good to see you also, Senator."

"Have a seat," Megan said as she motioned to one of the deeply upholstered wingback chairs in front of her desk. She sat on the other one.

"Thank you, Senator."

She chuckled. "What's with the civvies? Can't say I remember seeing you in that before."

"In light of what's going on," Norton replied. "I thought it best to have a lower profile."

She nodded, turned serious. "That sounds ominous. You told Lisa you had something important to talk about?"

The man fidgeted in his seat, as if he were uncomfortable in the civilian clothes. "Yes, ma'am. I thought it was too sensitive to discuss over the phone."

Megan crossed her legs and leaned forward in her seat. "Now you're scaring me. What the hell's going on? Pardon my French."

His eyes nervously scanned the room. "Ma'am, I need to do something before we talk."

"What do you mean by that?"

The colonel reached into his pants pocket and pulled out a silver colored device, the size and shape of a large pen. "Senator, I need to scan this room for electronic surveillance."

"Are you crazy, Jack? You think somebody's bugging my office? I'm a U.S. senator, for Christ sakes."

"I'm sorry, ma'am. But after you hear what I have to say, you'll understand."

She sighed and waved a hand in the air. "Go ahead, then."

Norton stood, turned on the device and slowly walked around the room, holding the pen-like instrument in front of him. After that, he picked up the phone on her desk and inspected it closely, even unscrewing the receiver caps to look inside. He put the device back in his pocket and sat back down. "It's okay, ma'am. It's safe to talk."

Megan nodded. "Okay, Jack. Enough bullshit. Let's hear it."

The man lowered his voice. "What I'm about to tell you is absolutely confidential. I only learned of it by accident. And I still have to verify it with a couple of other sources, before we take any action. But I felt I had to come to you right away. My life and your life are at risk, if we don't handle this right."

She sensed the urgency and gravity by the tone of his voice. The colonel was a veteran of two wars and a highly decorated fighter pilot. If he said it was a grave situation, she knew it was deadly serious.

"Senator, have you ever heard of something called Operation BlackSnow?"

She thought a moment, shook her head. "No. What the hell is it?"

"As you know, one of my duties is supervising a team that handles the Air Force surveillance satellites. Recently, one of my NCOs picked up a coded transmission. It was encrypted, but my guy is sharp. Anyway, he spent time deciphering it then he passed the info on to me. It appears there is a pending military operation. An operation called BlackSnow."

"Who sent the transmission, Jack?"

"It came from the Pentagon, somebody very high-up, from what I can tell."

"So, what is this operation?"

"The Pentagon is planning a nuclear first strike."

Her jaw dropped. "A nuke attack? On who?"

"I don't know, Senator. The transmission wasn't clear on that."

Megan leaned back in her seat. "I'm skeptical, Jack. This could all be some contingency plan. I'm sure the Pentagon runs simulations all the time. This could be some type of war game scenario."

The colonel shook his head. "That's true. But this was too detailed. It mentioned specific submarines. It also referred to some type of countdown."

"What do you mean?"

"It implied there was a countdown to when the attack would take place."

She leaned forward in the seat. "When?"

"Ten days from now."

"Damn," she muttered. She folded her arms in front of her, her thoughts racing. "I don't know, Jack. I'm still thinking it could be a war game."

"I have more, Senator."

"Go ahead."

"When I found out about this, I started working my sources at the Pentagon. I've been there five years and I know a lot of people."

"You do. You've given me very useful intel in the past."

"Thank you, Senator. Anyway, after checking my sources, I found one who had overheard a conversation recently. Two senior officers, a four-star general and an admiral were heard talking about an operation called BlackSnow. And it didn't sound like a war game. It sounded real."

"If it is true, and the military is planning something like this, the Joint Chiefs of Staff would be involved. And President Taylor would have to approve it."

The man nodded. "That's why we have to be careful how we handle this information. We have to be absolutely certain it's true."

"I agree. You said you were double-checking other sources?"

"Yes, ma'am. I have my team scouring the transmission logs for any other references to BlackSnow. If there's more, we'll find it."

"How long will that take?"

"A day, maybe two."

"Good. When you have that I'll go to the Senate Majority Leader and the President. Confront them with this. A nuclear war is unthinkable, no matter what the motivation."

"Yes, ma'am. One other thing. Watch your back. A lot has happened in Washington recently. It may all be connected."

She nodded, stood up and extended her hand. "Thank you for bringing this to me, Jack. You won't regret it."

He stood and they shook. "I'll call you as soon as I have more, Senator."

The colonel left the office and closed the door behind him.

Megan went back to her desk and sat down. She mulled the situation for a few minutes, then made a quick decision. Pressing on the intercom, she said, "Lisa, please come in."

The young aide entered and Lewis waved her to one of the chairs.

"Lisa," she began, picking her words carefully. "As you know, some very disturbing things have taken place in this town lately. The colonel has just shared additional information that is even more alarming. I won't tell you what we discussed until he gets further confirmation, but let's just say it's frightening. And in light of Audrey Cruz's disappearance, I've decided to hire a security detail for my own protection."

Lisa's eyes went wide. "You think you need bodyguards?"

"I do. I want you to retain a private security force to protect me. Two bodyguards at all times should be enough."

The aide nodded. "When do you want them to start?"

"Immediately."

9 Days to Zero Hour

Camp David
Thurmont, Maryland

President Taylor jogged up the hill, his lungs aching from the effort. He followed the winding dirt trail, his legs almost ready to give out.

This part of the Presidential retreat was a pristine forest, with tall spruce towering over him. Dense, verdant green vegetation sprouted everywhere.

In spite of the dreaded exercise, he loved Camp David. He liked the solitude and the utter silence of the place. The only sound was his ragged breath and the occasional call of a bird.

His wife, in much better shape and a faster runner, was somewhere up ahead on the trail. Behind him were two Secret Service agents, running at an easy pace.

Taylor slowed his jog, then stopped altogether to catch his breath. He sucked in the fresh scent of the woods, planted his hands on his hips. He had sworn to himself that he would lose weight and had even started using the treadmill in his White House bedroom. The election wasn't that far away. But he hadn't realized how out of shape he was until he began to run this morning. Now his heart pounded, his mouth was bone dry, and his legs felt rubbery. His jogging clothes, drenched in sweat, clung to his body.

"Are you okay, sir?" one of the agents asked from behind him.

"No problem…Tom," Taylor replied haltingly, gulping in more air. Then he took a swig from the bottle of Perrier he was carrying.

After a moment, he began running again and crested the hill a few minutes later. From that vantage point he could make out the clearing below and just beyond that the cluster of rustic wooden buildings of Camp David. He spotted his wife, followed by her own Secret Service agents. She was still sprinting and was almost at the buildings.

Knowing he'd never make it down there at a fast pace, he took another sip of water and slowed to a walk.

When he reached the clearing, the agents spread around him and he continued his walk.

Taylor saw a man in a business suit striding towards them. The president blocked the bright sun with his hand and recognized the man instantly. It was General Corvan.

"Mr. President," Corvan said, "we need to talk. In private, sir."

"Sure, General." Taylor turned to the lead agent. "Tom, give us some space."

The agents moved away and Taylor turned back Corvan. "Let's go sit by that tree. I need to get out of this sun."

The two men walked over to the large maple and the president sank to the ground, leaning his back against the tree trunk.

Corvan squatted down, facing him.

"I didn't think getting in shape would be this tough, General."

"Yes, sir."

"But I keep telling myself it's worth it."

"Yes, sir."

Taylor tipped the bottle to his lips, took a long swallow. Then he said, "What have you got?"

"I didn't want to disturb you here, sir, but some new info has surfaced."

"On BlackSnow?"

"Yes, sir."

Taylor leaned forward. "Well?"

"As you know, we've been trying to keep the status of Audrey Cruz quiet for as long as possible."

The president nodded his head.

"Sir, we think a local news outlet has picked up the story. A TV station."

"How did it leak out?"

"I don't know, sir. Could have been the local cops."

"Crap. I wanted to keep her disappearance out of the media a while longer."

"Yes, sir. It looks like they'll go on-the-air with it today."

Taylor leaned back against the tree. "Okay. I guess it was inevitable. Write up a press release. Say the White House will assist the FBI with the investigation into her disappearance."

"Yes, Mr. President."

"What else, Corvan?"

A frown crossed the general's face and the man hesitated, as if he didn't want to go on.

"What is it, damn it?" the president hissed.

"Sir, it appears that a technical specialist not part of BlackSnow may have cracked an encrypted message about the operation."

Taylor scowled. "What the hell?"

"He's part of an intelligence unit at the Pentagon. An Air Force NCO."

"Air Force? Damn it. Those guys can't be trusted."

"I know sir."

Taylor tried to control his rage, took a deep breath. "Go on."

"As you ordered, we've had NSA taps on personnel at the Pentagon who weren't part of the operation. To make sure we could contain situations like this."

The president waved a hand in the air. "Get on with it, Corvan."

"One of the taps picked up a phone conversation of an NCO, an Air Force Master Sergeant. The sergeant mentioned BlackSnow several times and quoted specific, detailed information about the plan."

"Christ, all mighty. Okay, let's not waste time, Corvan. Here's what I want you to do. Get a hold of Garcia. Explain the situation. Let's eliminate this problem."

"With extreme prejudice?"

"Is there any other way, General?"

"No, sir."

***

Atlanta, Georgia

Erica Blake pulled the brim of her baseball cap lower as she leaned against the side wall of the duplex. She was waiting for the cab to arrive, staring intently at the car traffic on the street and the pedestrians on the sidewalk. But no one seemed to notice her and she relaxed. Shoving one hand in the side pocket of her cargo pants, she felt the reassuring shape of the .38 revolver.

A yellow taxi cab slowed in front of the duplex and stopped. Glancing both ways first, she crossed the sidewalk and got in the cab.

The driver, a swarthy man with longish hair, turned to face her. "You want to go to electronics store?" he asked in a heavy Pakistani accent.

"Yeah," she replied. "The closest one."

"There's Best Buy on 14th street."

"Good. Let's go."

Five minutes later he pulled into the parking lot of the big-box store.

She paid the driver in cash, got out, and walked into the large building, scanning the aisles for computers. Seeing the sign, she strode over, began to peruse the wide variety of laptops.

A young, blond kid wearing a blue polo shirt walked over to her. Flashing a smile, he asked, "Looking for a computer?"

"No," she shot back. "I need a new toaster."

He looked confused at first, then chuckled. "Yeah. We've got this Toshiba on sale." He pointed to a sleek laptop with a big screen. "It's a beauty. It has everything you'll ever need. Multimedia capacity and —"

She looked at the price tag. "Too much. I just need to browse the web and do e-mail."

Erica hadn't realized how much she depended on the internet until she no longer had computer access.

His eyes lit up. "Hah. In that case, I have the perfect machine for you." He pointed to another, smaller laptop. "This Dell netbook. Ten inch screen. Super light-weight."

Glancing at the price, she picked up the computer. It was small and light and would fit in her backpack with no problem. "I'll take it."

"Don't you want to turn it on, try the keyboard first?"

She glared at him. "I said I'll take it! Is that so hard to understand?"

The guy took a step back, said, "Sure. No problem." Taking out a key from his pocket, he unlocked the case below the display and took out a box. "If you follow me, I'll ring it up for you."

Giving him a sweet smile, she said, "That wasn't so hard, was it?"

Ten minutes later she was outside the store, calling the cab company for a ride back. She had decided a few days ago not to get a car, but instead rely on the city's public transport and cabs. She knew the NSA would probably be monitoring car registrations and tags, and hadn't wanted to tip them off.

As soon as she hung up she realized something odd was happening on the street in front of the Best Buy. Traffic was stalled and cars were honking loudly. A large, unruly demonstration was streaming past on the sidewalk. The protesters were yelling and carrying hand-made signs with anti-Chinese slogans. The crowd was so large that it had spilled onto the street and the store's parking lot. The marchers were heading east, toward downtown, but there were so many of them she couldn't see where the line of people began. The group of demonstrators must have been blocks long.

Glancing up, she saw a helicopter circling overhead. It had the local ABC News logo on the side. A chill went down her spine.

Then a large van with the same logo pulled into the parking lot. A camera crew climbed out, followed by a redhead carrying a microphone. The woman pointed at the crowd, then at the façade of the store, obviously telling them to film the protest and the general location.

As one of the cameras followed the crowd, a second one began scanning the building.

Clutching the computer box under one arm, Erica decided to ditch the cab and get away on foot. Sprinting away from the front doors, she went into the alleyway.

But she had the sick feeling the camera caught her, just before she ducked out of sight.

***

Special Operations
Marine Corps Detachment
Training Facility, Building 14
Fort Bragg, North Carolina

Bobbie Garcia was in his office watching a ballgame on ESPN when his cell phone buzzed. The Yankees were at bat in the bottom of the 7th inning and he didn't pick up for a moment. A lifelong fan, he tried to watch the team as much as possible. The batter struck out and he unclipped the phone from his belt and took the call.

"Bobbie," he heard his wife Maria say, "it's me." Her voice sounded excited but worried also.

"What's wrong?" he asked.

"Sorry to bother you at work, but we need to talk."

He muted the TV. "Okay. Shoot."

"Bobbie, I'm pregnant."

Stunned, he uttered, "But you're on the pill."

"It's not perfect, you know that."

Shocked, sad, and elated all at the same time, he was speechless.

"Bobbie, I know the timing's not right. But I want this baby." Then she whispered, "I hope you do too."

The image of holding a newborn infant in his hands, his own flesh and blood, flashed in his mind and suddenly his future looked brighter. A wave of excitement flooded him. "I love you, Maria. I want this baby too."

He heard her yelp, then she began to cry.

"What's wrong?" he asked.

"Nothing's wrong. I'm just happy. Happy for both of us."

Garcia glanced at his watch. "Listen, I don't have a current assignment. I'll leave now and come back home for a bit."

"I love you, Bobbie."

"I love you too."

He hung up and was about to turn off the TV when his cell buzzed again.

Taking the call, he held the phone to his ear.

"Garcia," he heard the general say, "we have a new problem. We need your team to take care of it. Immediately."

"Yes, General."

"I just sent you an encrypted e-mail. It has all the details."

"Yes, sir."

The line went dead and Garcia took his laptop off sleep-mode and opened the e-mail. He read it twice, printed it out, and deleted it.

Getting up, he left the office and went into the cavernous training room. Seeing Sergeant Thomas hunched over a partially disassembled M-60 machine gun, he called him over. Wiping his hands, the sergeant walked up to him.

"What's up, Captain?"

"I've got something for you. Let's talk in my office." The two men went back to the room and Garcia closed the door behind him.

He handed Thomas the printed e-mail. "Sergeant, there's a situation I want you to handle. An Air Force NCO who works at the Pentagon. The details are all there."

Thomas quickly read the note and looked up. "I'll take care of it."

"Do it when the man's off-duty. Take as many of the team as you think you'll need."

"Yes, sir. You're not coming with us?"

"No, I need to head home today. I'll be back tomorrow. Call me on my cell, if you need anything."

Thomas nodded. "No problem." The man turned to go.

"And Sergeant, as usual, memorize the note and burn it."

"Yes, sir."

***

Board of Directors Conference room
ZQM Euro Bank
Zurich, Switzerland

Sitting at the head of the sleek conference table, Director Henry Mueller listened to the tall, thin man seated at the other end of the table, trying to restrain himself from interrupting. Felix Hoffman had always been a thorn in his side, but the man was a fellow board member and a very influential German banker, so Mueller tried to be diplomatic.

Hoffman droned on for another five minutes, covering in detail the results of the bank's quarterly earnings. This topic had already been reviewed by a bank staffer earlier in the meeting, so the repetition was unnecessary.

The other eight board members were fidgeting in their seats and glancing at their watches when Mueller held up a hand. "Thank you, Herr Hoffman, for that excellent analysis of our earnings. You should be commended for your attention to detail. However, I'd like to conclude that part of the meeting and move on to another matter."

Hoffman frowned, obviously not pleased, but the other members quickly nodded their assent.

Mueller spread his hands flat on the table. "As you all know, not long ago, we were presented with a very lucrative proposal from our American friends. Seeing the great value of this plan to our bank, as the director of this board I quickly accepted. Pending your approval and the approval of our respective governments of course."

Hoffman frowned again. He was the only board member who had objected to the proposal and it took every ounce of persuasion that Mueller could muster to convince him.

"And, as you know," Mueller continued, "we all *finally* agreed that we should pursue it."

Hoffman held up a hand. "I still think it is a bad deal, Director. The Americans cannot be trusted. As recent events have proven."

Mueller pursed his lips. "I wanted to review the deal, exactly because of those recent events. Many of you have been badgering me about the status of the arrangement, and this is the perfect opportunity to inform you of the progress."

The German tapped his Mont Blanc pen loudly on the table. "Please go on, Herr Mueller. This should be entertaining."

The director took a deep breath and let it out slowly, trying to control his anger. "My primary contact with the Americans is Megan Lewis, one of the most powerful senators in the United States."

Hoffman leaned forward in his seat. "A stunning-looking woman, something I'm sure you've noticed." He raised an eyebrow. "Let's hope your relationship with her is strictly business, Herr Mueller."

The director's face flushed red. "Please do not interrupt me again. I'd like to bring the board up-to-date."

The German held up his palms. "Of course."

"Soon after I informed Lewis that we had approved the proposal, President Wilson was assassinated. He, along with Lewis, were the chief architects of the plan. Since his death, the new president has been noncommittal. However, I have some excellent news to report on that front."

The board members leaned forward in their seats and several smiled.

"Senator Lewis recently met with President Taylor and he was receptive. He is obviously new in his position, and I'm sure wants time to evaluate it, especially in light of the upcoming election in the U.S." He paused for effect. "But I got the impression from the senator that it appeared he would support it."

The members of the board broke out into loud applause, all except for Hoffman. When the clapping died down, the German banker said, "Are you sure it's not just wishful thinking on your part? We have a board election coming up soon and your position as Director will be voted on by all of us. As you know, I will be running against you. I may not be the most liked member, but I'm one of the most important. My own bank owns a significant number of shares in this firm, something I'm sure you haven't forgotten."

"How could we forget, Herr Hoffman? You remind us constantly. Just remember, I have the support of everyone else here."

"Almost everyone," the German retorted. "We'll see when the election is held."

Glancing around the room, Mueller noticed a few of the men lower their eyes, as if trying to avoid his gaze. *Not a good sign*, he thought.

He turned back to Hoffman. "It is not wishful thinking on my part. I believe the deal will go through. Each of us will be enriched in ways we could never dream about before."

"When will we know for sure?" the German asked.

Mueller shrugged. "I would say it's a matter of days." He paused and smiled. "The Americans are fairly desperate for us to buy their Treasury bonds."

"Will you know by our next meeting?"

The director nodded. "That's ten days from now. Yes, I'm certain we will know by then."

8 Days to Zero Hour

Atlanta, Georgia

Erica Blake woke up with a start and for a moment was confused where she was. Sitting up on the narrow bed, she glanced around the cramped bedroom of the duplex apartment. It all came back.

On the nightstand sat six empty bottles of Budweiser. She vaguely remembered watching TV while sipping beer, then nothing. Looking down, she realized she was still wearing the same shirt and pants from yesterday.

Rubbing her eyes, she sluggishly rose off the bed, stripped off her clothes, and jumped in the shower. Ten minutes later she was clean and wearing fresh clothes – a gray polo shirt and baggy jeans. Pulling her damp hair into a ponytail, she stuck her omnipresent baseball cap on her head. Stuffing her gun, cash and phone in her pockets, she finally felt ready to go out. It was ten in the morning and her stomach was growling for food.

There was a knock on the door and she peered through the peephole. Sarah stood there, dressed in her Denny's uniform.

Erica opened the door, yawned. "Hi, Sarah. What's up?"

"Looks like somebody had a long night," Sarah said, chuckling. "You must have worn out the poor man."

"I wish. No, just a hangover."

"Been there, hon." Then the waitress's face turned serious. "I'm heading off to work, but wanted you to know something. I had a couple of hang-up calls last night and I saw a black car stop in front of the duplex early this morning." The woman lowered her voice. "May be nothing, but I'm guessing a girl like you, without luggage, and paying cash for everything, may have a past."

Erica tensed, and her thoughts flashed to the news camera yesterday. "Thanks, Sarah. I appreciate it."

The woman gave her a sad smile. "If you need anything, call me at the restaurant or go over and see Dwayne. It's still summer vacation and all that lazy son of mine does is watch television." She waved and walked away.

Erica closed the door, the hunger gone. Pacing the room, she realized she had to leave Atlanta. Now.

It would take too long to walk to the Greyhound station, so she pulled out her phone and began to punch in the cab company's number.

Just then she heard a car pull into the duplex's driveway. Peering around the edge of the closed blinds, she saw it immediately. A black Ford sedan with cheap hubcaps and heavily tinted windows. It had government car written all over it.

Two men in dark suits and aviator sunglasses climbed out of the car, looked around. One of them walked to Sarah's front door and the second came her way.

There was a loud knock on her door. "I'm with the Census Bureau," she heard. "We're doing the survey."

Pulling the .38 out of her pocket, her eyes darted around the room. There was no back door, and the only window besides the front one was in the bathroom. And that one was very small — she'd have trouble squeezing through.

"I don't do surveys," she replied, moving to the left of the closed door.

"I'm sorry, ma'am. But it's a legal requirement. Every citizen has to be counted in the census."

Her heart pounded in her chest. "I'm sick. Come back later."

Then everything happened in an instant. Through the thin wall of the apartment she heard a scream for help, followed by a muffled shot. Then she heard her own door being kicked in.

The cheap wood splintered and the lock gave way. The man in the suit crouched into the room, holding a Glock in front of him.

Erica leveled the .38 and fired two shots, the loud noise echoing in the small room. The man flinched back, but didn't drop. *Damn,* she thought, *he must be wearing a Kevlar vest.*

He whirled around to face her just as she fired two more rounds. Screaming, the man clutched his leg and crumpled to the floor.

The smell of gunpowder hung in the air as she sprinted out of the apartment. Reaching the sidewalk, she heard a man's voice from behind. "Stop, Blake! Or I'll shoot!"

Quickly spinning around and dropping to one knee, she fired the revolver's last two rounds. He tumbled backward, but not before firing his own gun.

Erica saw his muzzle flash and immediately felt a blinding pain in her shoulder.

She staggered to the ground, clutching her bleeding upper left arm. Gritting her teeth to stave off the intense throb, she almost passed out but recovered a moment later.

Sitting up, she glanced at the wounded man who lay moaning a few feet from her.

Police sirens wailed in the distance, coming closer.

Struggling to her feet, she strode over to the fallen man. Bleeding but conscious, the man reached for his Glock, which lay on the ground next to him.

Using her revolver, she struck him in the temple and he slumped, unconscious. Reaching into his pants pocket, she grabbed his car keys, then picked up his pistol and slipped it in the waistband of her jeans. But she knew she needed one more thing from him.

Ignoring the pain in her arm, she awkwardly pulled off his suit jacket and put it on. It was way too big for her, but would hide the bleeding.

Realizing she only had seconds before the cops arrived, she ran to the Ford sedan and fired it up. Backing out of the driveway, she turned around on the street and stomped on the gas, the car lurching forward. She sped west, desperately looking for signs to the interstate.

Twenty minutes later she was speeding south on I-75, with Atlanta's tall skyline in the rear-view mirror. Erica felt a sharp jab of pain and she glanced under the coat at her wound. She knew the bullet hadn't hit an artery, or she'd be dead already. It looked like the shot was a through-and-through, but it was still bleeding and she had to stop the flow.

But she pushed that thought aside. The cops at the scene would have talked to the NSA agents by now. An APB for her and the car had probably already been issued. She had to ditch the car's license plates.

A large sign loomed ahead. The next exit was for Atlanta's Hartsfield Airport.

Jerking the wheel right, she crossed two lanes and got on the off-ramp, ignoring the blasts of horns from other cars. Driving past the secondary turn-offs for the terminals and car rental returns, she spotted the Long Term Parking sign and took that exit.

Minutes later she was inside the massive, multi-story concrete structure, which was almost completely full of cars. On the 3rd level she found an empty slot and backed into it.

Resting a moment to alleviate the pain, she then rummaged through the glove compartment, looking for anything to use as a tourniquet. She found a man's handkerchief and she painfully shrugged off the jacket. Wrapping the cloth around her bleeding upper arm, she tied it tightly, gasping from a fresh stab of pain.

That done, she dug a quarter out of her pocket and got out of the car.

Looking around first to make sure no one was nearby, she walked to the rear of a nearby Impala and crouched by the license plate. She unscrewed the plate and went back to the Ford. Taking off its plate she replaced it with the new one. Since she was in a long-term lot, she hoped the owner of the Impala wouldn't be back for days, maybe longer.

Climbing back in the Ford, she pulled out of the slot and sped toward the exit, her tires squealing all the way.

An hour later she was near Macon, still heading south on I-75. Glancing at the gas gauge, she knew she'd have to stop soon. Spotting an Exxon sign for the next exit, she swung into the right lane and slowed down. Exiting the interstate, she pulled in front of one of the pumps of the large gas station. It was all self-service and the machines only took credit cards. She'd have to go inside to prepay in cash.

Getting out of the car, she awkwardly shrugged on the jacket and walked inside the building, which included a Subway restaurant and a large convenience store.

With her arm still throbbing, she walked the aisles of the store, picked up a bottle of Bayer and a box of large bandages. Realizing she'd need more items, she grabbed a small shopping basket and dumped in the aspirin and bandages. Then she walked around the store, grabbed a map of the U.S., a six-pack of Coke, and a bottle of No-Doz. Finally, she found the food aisle and clutched a dozen candy bars.

Walking back to the cash register at the front of the store, she stood in line to pay. When it was her turn, she said, "This stuff and thirty dollars of gas on pump six."

The attendant behind the register was an Asian man, short and wiry. His name tag said Mike, but she doubted that was his original name. Wordlessly, the man rang up her stuff and told her the total in broken English.

She handed him the cash and he gave her the filled plastic bag. "You…want…receipt?" he asked.

"No, thanks. Don't think I'll need it."

Walking back to her car, she put the bag in the passenger seat and then pumped the gas.

Getting in the vehicle, she turned on the engine and pulled out of the station. A minute later she was back on the highway.

She knew she had to get out of Georgia fast. Probably out of the country.

***

U.S. Senate Chamber
Washington, D.C.

Megan Lewis was sitting in the large chamber, talking with another senator. They were discussing the upcoming vote on the defense budget when her cell phone rang.

Plucking the phone out of her Dior shoulder purse, she looked at the caller ID. She held up a hand and said, "Excuse me Senator, I need to take this."

She stood and walked to a quiet area of the room, away from the other lawmakers.

"Hello," she said, holding the phone to her ear.

"It's me," she heard – it was Colonel Norton's voice, but it sounded tinny as if he were far away. "I'm on a secure line, Senator."

"Good. What's up?"

"Remember the conversation we had the other day?"

"Yes, Jack. I know exactly what you're talking about."

"Perfect. Although this is a secure line, I'd rather not get too specific. Things are getting dicey."

"I understand."

"Senator, I've just received confirmation from several sources. The operation is real. Very real."

Stunned by the news, she was speechless a moment.

"Senator, are you still there?"

"Yes, Jack. I'm still on. You said things are dicey. What do you mean?"

"One of my sergeants, the one that cracked the encrypted message, he's gone missing."

She broke into a cold sweat. Audrey Cruz missing and now this. Damn. She glanced at the corner of the chamber, spotted her two bodyguards standing by the wall. No question she'd made the right decision on that.

"Okay, Jack. I understand what's happening."

"Good, Senator. But watch your back. Some heavy shit is coming down."

"I hear you."

The line went dead and she put the phone back in her purse. She was about to walk back when it rang again.

Grabbing it quickly, she took the call. "What is it, Jack?"

But instead of the colonel's voice she heard Erica Blake's.

"Hi, Senator," the young woman said.

"Erica, I'm glad you called. I've been worried about you."

"Things have been hectic, to say the least."

"I can imagine, Erica. Don't tell me where you are, it's better that way."

"I agree."

"Do you need anything, Erica? I can wire you money."

"I'm okay, for now. But maybe soon. I'm on the move right now. I just wanted you to know I was still alive."

"It's good to hear your voice. By the way, what we talked about before, the connection between the various…incidents…I just got confirmation. They're all connected. It's big. Bigger and much worse than I imagined."

"Damn."

"My thought exactly. Whatever you do, don't come back to D.C. Things are getting scary, even for me. I've hired bodyguards."

"Jesus Christ."

"Amen to that. Listen, Erica, I've got to go. But keep in touch. And if you need anything, call me."

"Thank you, Senator."

***

The Oval Office
The White House
Washington, D.C.

Matt Taylor stood by the three tall windows and stared out at the Rose Garden. He was in a sour mood and even the peaceful garden scene wasn't helping.

"Mr. President, General Corvan is here to see you," he heard Alice say over the intercom.

"Show him in, Alice," he replied, as he sat down behind his desk.

The general came in, nodded, and sat down on one of the wingback visitors chairs.

"I'm in a foul mood, General. Please don't make it worse."

"Yes, sir."

"What do you have?"

"Sir, all of the preparations are going smoothly on BlackSnow. I was just at the Pentagon and met with the key generals and admirals. The technical aspects of the operation are all in place."

"That's good to hear. What about the Air Force sergeant we talked about the other day? Have you dealt with that?"

"Yes, Mr. President. He won't be a problem anymore."

"Excellent."

"We do have one other issue, on a related matter."

Taylor shook his head slowly. "I guess it's unavoidable, in a complex operation like this. What is it?"

"Do you remember that FBI agent? Erica Blake?"

The president nodded.

"The National Security Agency guys found her in Atlanta. Unfortunately there was a shootout and she got away."

"Damn it, Corvan. She's one woman. How could she get away from them a second time? Are those idiots incompetent?"

"I can't answer that, sir. I do know she's on the loose and they're trying to locate her. She wounded two NSA agents and now there's a nationwide manhunt for her."

Taylor gritted his teeth. "I'm tired of this. Forget the NSA. Send Garcia after her."

"Yes, Mr. President. Do you want her terminated?"

Taylor shook his head forcefully. "No. Bring her in alive, if possible. We need to question her to find out who else she's been talking to."

"Yes, sir."

The president leaned back in his chair, was quiet a minute. Then he said, "Corvan, looking at the bigger picture, I think BlackSnow is going as well as can be expected. We've had some minor setbacks, like this FBI woman, but other than that, I'm pleased with our progress."

"I agree, Mr. President. Do you think you can stall the Chinese until Zero hour?"

Taylor barked out a laugh. "Yeah. I think I've got those jerks snowed."

"That's good. What about Megan Lewis and the Swiss proposal? How do you plan to handle that?"

"She's a very influential senator. I could use her support in the election. I'll stall her too."

"Good thinking, sir."

Taylor closed his eyes and swallowed hard. He hadn't had a drop of liquor in three days and he felt the pain of withdrawal. But BlackSnow was only a week away and he had sworn to himself he'd stay off the booze until after the operation was over. He knew he had to keep a clear head. Too many things could still backfire.

"Are you okay, sir?" he heard Corvan ask. The president opened his eyes, let out a deep breath.

"I'm fine, General."

A worried look crossed Corvan's face. "You look a bit pale," the general said. "Maybe I should get your doctor in here?"

Taylor waved a hand in the air. "No. It's nothing. I stopped drinking a few days ago, that's all. I want my mind sharp."

Corvan nodded.

"Got anything else for me, General?"

"No, sir." The man stood up. "I'll call Garcia now. And give you an update this afternoon."

The president nodded absently, having already forgotten about the FBI woman. His thoughts had drifted back to the logistics of Operation BlackSnow.

"We'll talk later, Corvan." He swiveled his chair and stared out the windows, the peaceful view of the Rose Garden momentarily calming him. But a moment later his disposition turned dark as the lurking dangers of the next week flooded his mind.

7 Days to Zero Hour

Special Operations
Marine Corps Detachment
Training Facility, Building 14
Fort Bragg, North Carolina

Bobbie Garcia paced his office as he considered his new assignment. The general had been explicit in his instructions. Find Blake. Interrogate her. Then send her to the special place.

The problem was she could be anywhere right now. The NSA guys had screwed up big time. They had her cornered and let her get away. He shook his head. Those clowns were good at gathering intel but not very proficient at field work. Now it was up to him to clean up their mess.

There was a knock at the door and he said, "Come in."

Sergeant Thomas opened it and peered around it. "Anything on her whereabouts, Captain?"

"Not yet. But get the jet ready. We'll go as soon as something breaks."

"Yes, sir." The man nodded and closed the door.

Garcia continued pacing and a few minutes later his cell phone rang. Unclipping it from his belt, he held the phone to his ear.

He heard an unfamiliar voice. "This is James Moseley."

"Who are you?"

"I'm with the National Security Agency. Assistant Director of the Atlanta office."

"How'd you get my number, Moseley?"

"General Corvan."

Garcia didn't like getting calls from people he hadn't personally worked with, but hearing the general's name made him feel less suspicious.

"What's the code word for today, Moseley?"

"Red spinach."

"Okay," Garcia said, relaxing. "You're good."

"I just got off the phone with the general and he told me to contact you directly. I've got info on Erica Blake."

Garcia's interest shot up. "What do you have?"

"She was spotted in El Paso, Texas, close to the border with Mexico. She ditched the car she took from us and was last seen on foot. We think she'll cross the border. I should have a more exact fix on her location later today."

"Good. I'll head down there right now. But don't have your guys try to pick her up. You've done enough damage already. I'll take care of this with my crew."

There was a pause on the other end. "Listen, two of our men were wounded. We're not happy about this either."

"Yeah, I hear you, Moseley. Call me as soon as you have more." He hung up and left his office to find Thomas.

***

Hart Senate Office Building
Adjacent to the U.S. Capitol
Washington, D.C.

Megan Lewis stepped out of her office and approached her assistant's desk. "Have you reached Colonel Norton, Lisa? I told you I needed to speak with him immediately."

The young woman looked up, a frown on her face. "I just got off the phone with his office. They...can't locate him...haven't seen him all day."

"Christ. What the hell is going on? Call his private cell number."

"I did, ma'am. It just rings and rings. The voice mail message that he had is gone."

Megan clenched her fists, trying to control her anger. She had wanted to talk to Norton to tell him what she planned to do, but that looked unlikely. The man could be dead.

Making a snap judgment, she decided to go ahead with her plan. Time was running out. "Lisa, call the White House. Now. Tell them I have to meet with the president today. Tell them it's urgent."

"Yes, ma'am," her assistant said as she picked up the phone.

***

El Paso, Texas

Erica Blake walked on the crowded sidewalk of downtown, feeling like hell. Her arm throbbed and she was exhausted from the long drive. And she was starved – she'd only had the candy bars and Coke to keep her going.

She pushed those thoughts aside, thankful she was still a free woman. A police car had followed her for a few minutes as soon as she pulled into town, so she decided to ditch the Ford sedan. Driving into a parking garage, she lost the tail and parked the car in an empty slot, then quickly walked away.

It was a brutally hot day, the sun beating down from a cloudless sky. Her polo shirt clung to her from sweat and dried blood. But she was thankful for the jacket she wore. It was too big, but it concealed her wrapped arm.

The city smelled of asphalt, smog, and exhaust from the cars that packed the streets. She pulled her cap lower over her eyes and tried to blend in with the other pedestrians. Many of the people were Hispanic and she caught snatches of conversations in Spanish.

Desperately wanting to stop and rest, instead she pushed on, knowing she had to keep going. She had to get out of town and across the border. She hoped she could lose herself there, in some remote corner of Mexico, until she could figure a way out of this mess.

As she strode on the sidewalk, sidestepping the other pedestrians, she kept an eye out for a parked car she could steal. But the area was too open, with too many people around.

Finally she spotted a three-story parking garage at the end of the street and headed there. She needed wheels and that was her best bet.

***

The Oval Office
The White House
Washington, D.C.

President Taylor sat behind his desk, feeling a lot better today. The yearning for booze wasn't as strong and the massive headaches he'd been having had receded to a mild throb. *Maybe I'll stop drinking completely*, he thought. He barked out a harsh laugh, knowing that would never happen. He liked the stuff way too much.

As he sat alone in his office idly reading budget reports, the upcoming election crossed his mind. Once BlackSnow was complete, he'd start campaigning hard. Now that he had tasted the power of the presidency, his overriding goal was be to get elected next year. Glancing around the famous office, he smiled to himself. The place was addictive, just like the booze.

"Mr. President," he heard Alice's voice over the intercom, "Senator Lewis is here to see you."

He straightened his tie and buttoned his suit jacket. Then he stood and walked around his desk. He hated the woman, but would need her help in the upcoming election.

The senator walked in, wearing a fashionable, probably very expensive, navy pant suit.

"Megan, it's good to see you again." He held out his hand and they shook.

"Mr. President, thank you for seeing me on such short notice."

"No problem. Now that I'm president, I realize the value of your counsel. Your work on the Swiss proposal was first rate." He pointed to the couches in the front part of the office. "Why don't we sit there – it'll be more comfortable."

She looked surprised at first, then smiled. "Of course, Mr. President."

They sat across from each other and he said, "Would you like some coffee or tea? I can have Alice bring us some."

The woman leaned forward in her seat. "No, thank you, sir. I'm fine."

Taylor unbuttoned his snug suit jacket. "You told Alice you had something urgent to discuss?"

"Yes, sir. As you're acutely aware, many tragic events have taken place in our country recently."

He shook his head slowly for effect. "Yes, tragic. Very tragic."

"The president's assassination, the death of Senator Carpenter, Secretary Cruz's disappearance, the death of the Admiral Stanton...."

Taylor flinched when he heard the admiral's name. He thought he had kept that quiet, but somehow Lewis had picked up on it. He forced himself to calm down and see where the conversation was heading. But a feeling of dread settled in the pit of his stomach. "Yes, I agree, it's been a strange sequence of events."

She frowned. "I believe they're all connected, Mr. President."

"What do you mean?"

"Sir, I've recently learned of a secret operation, an operation that I think links all of these events."

His jaw dropped in what he hoped was a look of astonishment. "What? What are you saying? That there's a conspiracy?"

"Yes, Mr. President. As soon as I confirmed the facts, I decided to come to you. This secret operation is so immense it would change the course of history for our country and probably the world."

Taylor swallowed hard, his mind racing. Then he said, "I'm glad you came to me. As president, I'll make sure I get to the bottom of any conspiracy."

The frown stayed on her face. "That's what I was hoping," she said, but not with much conviction.

"Tell me more about this operation, Megan. Who and what's involved?"

"I found out about it from a friend of mine, an Air Force colonel named Norton."

Taylor shrugged. "I don't know the name."

"He works at the Pentagon, runs an intel group there. Anyway, he confirmed there's a group of top generals who are planning a nuclear first strike. They even have a timetable for implementation."

"A rogue group of military officers? A nuclear attack? Are you sure of your facts, Megan? It sounds preposterous."

"I thought so too, sir. At first. But I believe it's the truth. The people who uncovered the plot are all disappearing. Norton's missing, as is the NCO who cracked the secret transmission."

Beads of sweat formed on his forehead and he took out a handkerchief and dabbed them away. "I see. The whole thing sounds ominous. Is there a name for this operation?"

"Yes, Mr. President. It's called BlackSnow. Operation BlackSnow."

Taylor shook his head forcefully. "I've never heard of it."

A skeptical look crossed her face. "Are you sure, sir? There are some very high level people involved."

He grimaced and bolted out of his seat. "Are you questioning my veracity? We've had differences in the past, but when our country's future is at stake, we're all in this together!"

She seemed taken aback by his outburst. "I'm sorry, sir. I apologize. It's just been so crazy lately."

He sat back down. "I understand. Now, tell me more about this, what did you call it? BlackSnow?"

"I hadn't heard of this operation until a few days ago. But I believe what Norton told me is true. And now that so many people have disappeared or died, it reinforces the case that it exists. There are too many coincidences."

Taylor nodded, plastering an earnest look on his face. "You may be right, Senator. Maybe all the tragic events are connected. And from what you're telling me, there seems to be a major effort to keep this operation a secret." He paused for affect. "You said these generals were planning a nuclear first strike. On who?"

"Norton didn't know."

"I see. You also said there was some type of timetable?"

"Yes, Mr. President – it appears it will take place about a week from now."

"Oh, my God! That soon? I've got to get to the bottom of this, and fast. There's no way I will authorize a nuclear first strike." Taylor shook his head slowly and let out a long breath. "God damn it, I can't believe this could be happening under my watch. I'll find these people, whoever they are, and have them arrested. You can bet your ass I will!"

Relief flooded her expression. "Thank you, Mr. President. I'm glad I came to you with this."

"As am I, Megan. Give me a couple of days to ferret out the truth. I'll have the Attorney General and the Joint Chiefs begin an immediate investigation. Using the Patriot Act, I'll have these conspirators charged with insurrection and placed in military confinement. In the meantime, I'd appreciate if you kept this to yourself. I wouldn't want to spook these bastards. They might flee the country."

Lewis smiled. "I agree, sir. I'll keep this quiet. I want to make sure this group is put behind bars before something unspeakable happens." She leaned back on the couch, and her body seemed to relax. "You don't know how relieved I am right now."

He stood, walked over to her and extended his hand. She stood also and they shook.

"Thank you, Senator. You've done our country a great service by exposing this conspiracy." He gave her a wide smile. "I'm going to award you the Presidential Medal of Freedom."

She blushed. "That would be an honor, sir."

Lewis left the office, closing the door behind her.

Taylor, his heart pounding and his thoughts racing, began pacing the large office.   After a few minutes, he took off his jacket, loosened his tie and rolled up his sleeves. Then he pressed the intercom on his desk. "Alice," he bellowed, "get Corvan in here. Now!"

Three minutes later Corvan came in the office.

Taylor stopped pacing, said, "Close the door, General. We've got a massive problem." He pointed to one of the wingback chairs. "Grab a chair."

"What is it?" Corvan asked, alarm in his voice.

Taylor went around his desk, slumped in his seat. "Just met with Senator Lewis. Incredibly, she's found out about BlackSnow."

"What? How's that possible? We've had a super-tight lid on this operation."

Taylor shook his head. "The Air force colonel, Norton, told her."

"Shit…I'm sorry, Mr. President. Pardon my language."

The president waved a hand in the air. "Forget it."

"Sir, Colonel Norton has been terminated."

Taylor shot him a dark look. "But not soon enough."

"No, sir."

"Okay, Corvan. Let's focus here. What the hell do I do about Lewis? I need her for the election. But if she spreads the word about BlackSnow, you, me, we're all screwed."

"I understand. I'm assuming she's keeping it quiet for the moment?"

"Yeah. I gave her a song and dance, told her I'd investigate immediately and arrest anyone connected to it." He let out a cold, harsh laugh. "Jesus, I'm becoming too good a liar. I guess that's what makes a great politician."

"What do you want to do, sir?"

"Let me think, damn it!" Taylor folded his arms across his chest and closed his eyes.

After a moment, he opened them, said, "I've got to cut the Senator loose. Damn the election. BlackSnow is too important. I'll figure out a way to win without her help."

"Garcia's tied up. Do you want me to send an NSA team to take Lewis out?"

Taylor grunted. "After they screwed-up the last assignment? Hell no." He rubbed his jaw. "Where's Garcia now?"

"He's going after Blake. They've got a pretty good fix on her location."

"Put that on the back-burner, Corvan. Redeploy him to take care of Lewis. She's the priority now."

"Yes, sir."

"And. I don't want the senator taken alive."

"Terminate her with extreme prejudice?"

A wicked smile spread over the president's face. "Yeah. I always hated that bitch."

6 Days to Zero Hour

Command & Control Center
Chinese Military
Beijing, China

General Wu Chang stood in the Center and stared at the ten massive video screens that covered the far wall of the huge room. The bombproof bunker was located five floors below street level, in a highly-secure military installation just outside the city.

The screens showed live feeds from ten different Chinese satellites. From this room, Chang and his staff monitored foreign military activity around the world.

"Give me a close-up on Screen 6," Chang said to Lieutenant Wong. A wiry man in his twenties, Wong was one of five military officers who manned the consoles arrayed in the middle of the room.

"Yes, General," Wong replied.

Screen 6 was showing an overhead view of a large group of American warships, heading through the Straits of Hormuz in the Middle East. The ships appeared as dots on a blue background of the ocean, but as the satellite zoomed in, the details of the craft came into focus. Individual jets parked on an aircraft carrier were clearly visible.

Chang observed as the fleet churned north. Satisfied, the general said, "Now give me a close-up on the American Pacific Fleet."

Wong toggled a switch and Screen 3 zoomed in. The dots were replaced by an armada of military warships, navigating on choppy, dark-blue water. The ships, Chang knew from the coordinates superimposed on the screen, were approximately one-hundred miles west of Los Angeles, California. The Demarcation Line was also superimposed on the screen and Chang watched intently as the ships cruised west, then slowed, and began to turn around, well shy of the Line.

"This is excellent," Chang muttered to himself. It was clear the new U.S. president was following his predecessors' agreement with the Chinese government. "We own the Americans."

"What's that, sir?" Wong asked.

"Nothing. Carry on, Lieutenant."

Just then the general's cell phone rang and he unclipped the phone and held it to his ear.

"It's me," he heard Captain Lin's sultry voice on the other end. "Ready for more, General?"

Chang was immediately aroused. The woman is insatiable, he mused.

"I'm busy right now, Captain," he replied.

"General, get your ass back here. I want to do nasty things to you."

Chang's mind flashed back to their last encounter and his willpower melted. Glancing at his watch, he said, "Give me twenty minutes."

"Hurry," he heard her say breathlessly. "I'm wet for you now."

***

Hart Senate Office Building
Adjacent to the U.S. Capitol
Washington, D.C.

Megan Lewis was confused. As she sat behind her desk in her office, she thought about her options. Her meeting with Taylor had turned out much better than she had expected. She had figured the bastard would deny everything and tell her she was crazy. But instead, he'd promised an immediate investigation. *Maybe he isn't involved. Maybe it is a rogue group of generals acting on their own.* He had seemed incredibly sincere. And Taylor's offer of a Presidential Medal of Freedom! That was truly unexpected. The medal, she knew, was the highest award a U.S. president can bestow on a civilian. She smiled, savoring the thought of the medal. *It would definitely enhance my presidential ambitions.*

A dark thought clouded her mind. *What if Taylor is lying? What if he's trying to stall me?*

Still confused, she pressed her intercom. "Lisa," she barked. "Get in here."

The assistant came in her office seconds later. "Yes, ma'am?"

"I need to speak with General Owen Tarkington at the Pentagon. Get a hold of him."

"But I'm working on the budget analysis. The vote is in two hours."

"Screw that, Lisa. Find the general."

"Yes, ma'am."

The assistant left and Lewis tapped her gold Cross pen on her desk for a full minute. Then Lisa's voice came over the intercom. "I have the general on the line, Senator."

Megan picked up the receiver and in a syrupy sweet voice said, "Owen, thank you for returning my call."

"No problem, Senator. Haven't heard from you in a while."

"I've been *so* busy lately." She let out a girlish laugh. "We'll get together soon, I promise. We had fun last time, didn't we?"

There was a throaty laugh from the other end. "Senator, you can rock my world anytime. What do you need?"

"Just a small favor, Owen. I'm in the middle of something. Something big. It's called Operation BlackSnow. Top-secret, national security stuff. I just need to find out something. Am I in the know or in the cross-hairs? You're high-up in the Pentagon. I need you to find out for me."

"I haven't heard of the operation. But promise me a good time soon, Senator, and I'll find out."

She laughed. "You got it, Owen."

"Okay. I'll call you back."

Megan hung up. She pressed the intercom again. "Lisa, bring me coffee. A whole pot."

"Yes, ma'am."

The senator leaned back in her chair and waited for the return call.

An hour later, Megan stared at the empty coffee cup and empty pot on her desk and rubbed her sour-feeling stomach. Regretting drinking the whole thing, she knew she'd had no choice. She always drank a lot of coffee when she was nervous and she had been on edge all morning.

The intercom buzzed and she heard Lisa's voice. "Senator, I have General Tarkington on the line."

"Put him on."

She picked up the receiver.

"Megan," she heard him say, "I've got info for you." His voice sounded edgy – all the playfulness was gone.

"Okay. Go ahead."

"You're in deep shit, Senator. I only found out a vague outline of the operation." He paused for a moment, then said. "I don't want to know more about it. In fact, this is the last call you'll get from me. This is too big, way too big. I've got a career to protect."

"Okay, Owen. What did you find out about me?"

"If I were you, I'd get the hell out of town."

"What do you mean?"

"There's a contract out on you. You're persona-non-grata."

"A contract? You mean I've been targeted?"

"Get the hell out of D.C., Megan. Better yet, get out of the country."

"Who's behind it?"

The line went dead and she replaced the receiver. A feeling of cold dread settled in the pit of her stomach.

***

Juarez, Mexico

Erica Blake glanced at the cracked mirror in the shabby, cramped bathroom. She was in a cheap motel just outside downtown, a cash-only place populated with hookers, johns and crack-heads. A perfect place to hide.

Erica touched the ugly wound on her left arm, flinching from the pain. She was standing, naked and clean, having just taken a tepid shower. The dried blood and grime was gone from her weary body. But she was also very pale. She leaned her face toward the mirror to inspect her snow-white appearance. She'd lost a lot of blood over the last several days, something her lightheadedness and wobbly legs confirmed. Desperately needing medical care, she also knew she had to stay hidden. The NSA had spooks everywhere, even here in Mexico.

Going back to bedroom, she collapsed on the thin mattress. Glancing at her cell phone on the cheap nightstand, she weighed her options. Running low on cash, she wanted to call Lewis. But what if the NSA was monitoring the senator's calls?

Deciding not to call, her thoughts drifted to Steve. *Where is he? I need to find him and help him.*

As she lay on the bed, she glanced around the dingy room and accepted the fact she wouldn't be helping anybody. She'd be lucky to keep herself alive. Her .38 rested on the nightstand, its black, stubby shape familiar and comforting. Fortunately, she'd been able to buy a box of ammo in Juarez earlier in the day.

She traced a finger on her wound, lightly touching the raw skin. She felt a trickle of sticky substance and realized she was still bleeding. *A doctor. That's what I need. A doctor that takes cash and asks no questions.* Her thoughts drifted, her vision blurred and she passed out.

***

Bethesda, Maryland

Bobbie Garcia was angry. He'd tracked Blake to the Mexican city of Juarez, right across the border from El Paso. Juarez was a big place, but he was certain he would have found her exact location quickly. The NSA had confirmed the woman was wounded during the shoot-out in Atlanta. She'd be looking for medical help, and he and his team would swoop in.

As he sat in the black SUV, he forced himself to calm down by taking long gulps of the air-conditioned air. He couldn't blame Corvan for changing the mission. Things happened. Priorities changed. But he wanted to prove, once again, how good he was. That he was the best. The NSA had lost Blake twice. He and his team would handle it the first time. Shelving those thoughts aside, he stared out the window of the vehicle.

The SUV was parked across the street from Senator Lewis's stately home. Lewis had already left her office in D.C., and was being tailed by Sergeant Thomas. Garcia's plan was to wait for her to get home and let her get settled in for the night. He and his team would move in, then terminate the two bodyguards and kill her. Then they would transport the bodies to the safe house in Virginia and incinerate them. The house had an industrial oven that had come in handy several times before.

Just then Garcia's cell buzzed. He unclipped it and held it to his ear.

"We've got a problem," he heard Thomas say.

"What?"

"We lost her."

Garcia's hand gripped the phone tightly. "How the hell did you let that happen?"

"One of the bodyguards was driving. He must have noticed us following.…"

The captain gritted his teeth. "Jesus, Thomas! Keep looking for her! Call me back in five. With good news, this time!"

"Yes, sir."

Garcia disconnected the call and began to drum his fingers on the steering wheel. He had a really bad feeling about this. He ground his teeth as he mulled over everything that could go wrong.

5 Days to Zero Hour

On Interstate 95
Ten miles north of Philadelphia, PA

Megan Lewis was in the backseat of the stretch Cadillac as it raced north on the interstate. Sitting across from her was one of her bodyguards, while the other one drove the spacious limo. The bodyguards were rugged, stony-faced men. Men of few words. But they were good. She was certain they had already saved her life. One of them had spotted a tail when she left her office, and making a split-decision, she'd decided to run. The conversation with Owen had spooked her.

Since then they had driven quickly but aimlessly around Washington D.C. and then north through Maryland and now into Pennsylvania. Making only a few stops for gas, they had continued driving as she urgently tried to come up with a plan.

Dawn was breaking and the first rays of pinkish-gray daylight streamed in the windows. As she sipped coffee from a to-go cup, her mind churned. *It's clear I'm in the cross-hairs. Taylor lied. Anyone capable of assassinating an American president wouldn't hesitate to take me out. That's for damn sure.*

Shaking her head slowly, she finally came to a decision. Pulling her cell phone from her shoulder purse, she punched in numbers. Glancing at her watch, she guessed Henry Mueller would be having lunch about now. Zurich was six hours ahead of her local time.

The line rang for a long time, then went to voice mail so she hung up. *Damn. I need to speak with him live.*

Beads of sweat formed on her forehead and she punched in the numbers again. This time the call was answered.

"Megan," she heard him say in a cheerful voice, "good to hear from you. I just noticed your number on my phone display and hoped it was you, not one of your assistants."

"Henry," she replied, her voice strained. "I need your help."

There was a pause on the other end. "You don't sound yourself. Are you okay?"

"I'm in a bind. More than that, really. I'm in deep trouble and I need help."

"Of course. Anything. You know that."

"Henry, this line may not be secure. This call has to be quick and cryptic. Don't mention specific names or places."

"Yes, I understand."

"I need to get out of the country. Fast. I can't fly commercial – people are after me."

"You're an important American senator. Are you saying you're not safe there?"

"That's right."

"Sounds ominous. Listen, Megan, I have several Lear jets that I use for business travel. I have one on stand-by in the city where we first met. In fact we had a quick meeting at that airport five years ago. Do you remember it?"

Megan racked her brain, came up empty for a moment. Then it dawned on her. JFK airport in New York City.

"I got it, Henry."

"Good. I'll make a call now and have the pilot wait for you. By the way, where do you want to go?"

Her mind raced. "I want to fly to Australia," she lied. "I'll be safe there."

"Okay. I'll make the arrangements. I'll call you back later with more specific information. And be careful."

She breathed a sigh of relief. "Thank you, Henry."

Megan disconnected the call and put her phone away. She leaned forward and said, "Head to Kennedy Airport. Fast."

***

The Oval Office
The White House
Washington, D.C.

President Taylor, Treasury Secretary Longstreet and the Budget Director were standing by the president's desk, conferring on the national debt when the intercom buzzed. "Mr. President," Taylor heard Alice say, "General Corvan is here to see you. Says it's urgent."

The president turned to the two men. "I'm sorry, gentlemen, but we'll have to continue this discussion later."

"But, sir," Longstreet replied, "the debt problem is urgent too."

Taylor held up a hand. "Sorry. National security trumps that. We'll talk later today."

"Yes, Mr. President."

The two men left the room, and the general walked in and nodded. "Hello, sir."

Taylor went behind his desk and slumped in his chair. "Thank you for saving me from another tedious Power Point presentation. The treasury secretary may be an economic genius but he always puts me to sleep." He leaned forward in his seat. "Alice said you had something urgent?"

A frown crossed the general's face. "Yes. I spoke with Garcia several times late yesterday and again early this morning. I didn't want to bother you until I was sure. Garcia's crew lost Senator Lewis."

Taylor's hands formed into fists. "Lost her?"

"Yes, sir. They were following her but she gave them the slip. Looks like her bodyguards are highly skilled and picked up the tail."

"Shit! I can't believe this is happening."

"I'm sorry, sir."

"This is bad, Corvan. Really bad. We have to eliminate her. She knows way too much."

"I understand."

The president rubbed his temple with one hand. A massive headache was brewing. "I know you understand. You have just as much to lose as I do."

"Sir, unfortunately I have more bad news."

Taylor grunted. "What? What else?"

"The NSA has been monitoring Lewis's calls for the last few days. They picked up a call today. They didn't get all of it, but enough to know that the senator is flying out of the country." The general glanced at his watch. "In fact, she may already be gone."

Taylor clenched his jaw and desperately longed for a scotch whiskey. "God damn it, where did she go?"

"Australia."

The president shook his head slowly. "That's a big place. We'll have trouble finding her."

"I've already alerted our contacts there and the NSA is monitoring flights into Australia."

"Find her and kill her."

"Yes, sir. Do you want me to send Garcia after her?"

Taylor was quiet for a moment, then said, "We're only days away from BlackSnow. I'd rather not have him that far away. Contact one of our friends at the CIA – send one of their black ops teams after Lewis. God knows we don't want to send an NSA field unit after her."

"Yes, sir. What about Blake? Maybe Garcia should go back to finding her."

The president waved a hand in the air. "Sure. Fine. Anything else, Corvan?"

"No, sir."

"Okay. Now leave me alone. We can talk later."

The general stood. "Yes, Mr. President." He turned and left the room, closing the door behind him.

The president pressed the intercom. "Alice, I don't want to be disturbed for half-an-hour."

"Yes, sir," she replied.

Taylor stood and walked over to the ornate wooden cabinet at the far side of the room. Reaching in his pocket, he pulled out a key and unlocked one of the drawers of the cabinet. Then he pulled out a glass and a large bottle of 30-year old scotch and took them back to his desk.

4 Days to Zero Hour

Juarez, Mexico

"*Ustedes aceptan dolares Americano?* Do you take cash? American dollars?" Erica Blake asked the short, plump woman in the stained nurse's outfit.

The nurse gave her a crooked smile, her discolored teeth showing. "*Si.* That is all we take." She let out a throaty laugh. "No American Express cards here."

Erica was in the waiting room of a clinic that the night clerk of her motel had recommended. No questions asked kind of place, the clerk had said.

The dingy room was filled with shabbily-dressed men of all ages, wearing makeshift bandages and walking with crutches and canes. From the furtive looks they gave her, Erica was pretty sure most of them had something to hide. Juarez had a rep for being a lawless town and the clientele here seemed to prove it.

There was no A/C in the place and Erica brushed at the sweat rolling off her forehead. "How long a wait to see the doctor?" she asked.

"*Eso depende,*" the nurse replied. "That depends. A hundred bucks gets you to the front of the line."

Erica thought about that for a moment. She was running low on cash, but she desperately needed to get treated. "Okay." She pulled some bills from her pocket and handed it to the woman, who grabbed them quickly. "*Sigame, senorita.* Right this way."

Erica followed the nurse into the back area, a large room that had been partitioned into small cubicles. The cubicles were dimly-lit and grimy and were full of patients, many groaning or crying. It looked like two doctors and a handful of nurses were shuttling between the rooms. They reached the end of the narrow corridor and the nurse pointed to an empty cubicle. "Doctor Flores will be with you in a minute." Then she laughed. "And be careful with that *puto*. He likes to grab *tetas*." The nurse left and Erica sat on the elevated table in the center of the room, its tufted plastic covering torn and faded.

A minute later a middle-aged man with a wide mustache and black, slicked-back hair came in the cubicle. He pulled the screen closed behind him. He wore a doctor's white lab coat and a stethoscope hung from his neck.

"*Yo soy Doctor Flores*," he said theatrically. "I can see from your looks you are an American? *Eres mui bonita, senorita.*"

Erica crossed her arms in front of her. "Actually I'm Canadian."

"My mistake. *Perdoname.* What is your name, pretty lady?"

"Susan. Susan McMillan."

"A pretty name for a pretty lady."

"Doc," she said brusquely. "I'd like to chat, but I need medical treatment."

"Of course. Of course. What is the problem?"

She pointed to her shoulder. "I've got a deep…cut on my upper arm."

"I see. Please take off your jacket so I can take a look at it."

Erica slowly shrugged off the too-big jacket, careful not to re-open the wound. Then she rolled up the short sleeve of her polo shirt.

Flores took off the makeshift gauze and bandages and inspected the ugly wound. "How did this happen? It's more than a cut, *senorita*. This is a gunshot wound. Luckily for you, the bullet went all the way through your arm."

"Doesn't really matter how it happened. I just need you to sew it up. But I got to know how much first."

He stood back from her and gave her a wide smile. "How will you be paying?"

"Cash."

His eyes lit up. "We could work out a different payment plan, if you prefer."

"Like what?"

"A pretty woman like you, I am sure you have something to trade."

The lecherous man was giving her the creeps. Shaking her head slowly, she said, "I'll pay cash. How much?"

He looked crestfallen. "Pity. Cash is five-hundred dollars, U.S. And that includes a shot for the pain and a prescription for Percodan. The pills will help with the pain. I will need half before I start, the balance when I am done."

She shrugged. "Okay. Let's do it right now." She pulled the dwindling wad of cash out of her pocket, counted it out and handed it to him.

"Please take off your shirt and lay on the table," he said.

She gave him a hard look. "I'll keep the shirt on – just cut off the sleeve."

He sighed. "As you wish, *senorita.*"

Erica lay on the torn plastic cushion and stared at the bare, dim light bulb that dangled from the ceiling.

He cut off her sleeve and rolled a cart next to the table. As he picked up a hypodermic needle, she said, "Aren't you going to wash your hands first?"

He seemed surprised at her question. "Of course, I must have forgotten." He left the cubicle and returned a minute later. Then he methodically put on rubber gloves and picked up the hypodermic. "The shot will dull the pain. First I will clean the wound and then cut away the dead skin. After that I will suture the wound. *No te procupes.* Do not worry. I have done this many, many times."

He gave her the shot and after a minute Erica felt her arm go numb. "Go ahead, doc."

The man began to work on her and to her surprise, he seemed very proficient. He was done ten minutes later.

Snapping off his gloves, he said. "By your pale complexion, I can tell you have lost a lot of blood. I recommend you take it easy for a while, eat lots of protein and drink lots of fluids."

Sitting up on the table, she inspected her neatly bandaged arm. "Good job, doc." She pulled out the balance of the cash and handed it to him.

"If you ever need any other medical attention, *yo estoy a tu servicio.*" Florez gave her a theatrical bow. "I am at your service." He gave her another bright smile. "Have dinner with me, Susan McMillan. I could show you the better parts of our…lovely city."

She stood, awkwardly put on the jacket. "Got to run, doc. Got a long day ahead of me."

He ran a hand over his slicked-back hair. "Pity."

An hour later she was back at the motel. On her walk back she had stopped at a cantina and wolfed down a heaping plate of enchiladas and washed it down with Dos Equis beer. It was the first real food she'd had in days and she savored the rich taste as it was going down. But now, as she sat on the lumpy mattress, she began to regret it. Her stomach grumbled and she rubbed it. But she took comfort that her arm had been patched up – she wouldn't have to worry about bleeding out.

Getting up, she went to the bathroom to clean up and change into a new shirt. After that, she'd pack the few meager possessions she'd bought and stuff them in her backpack. It was time to leave town.

***

Bobbie Garcia disconnected the call and re-clipped the cell phone to his belt.

"That was Moseley, the NSA guy," he said to Sergeant Thomas, who was sitting next to him on the front seat of the rented, dark gray Yukon. The vehicle was parked on a side street, not far from downtown Juarez. "They've tracked her location."

Thomas nodded. "Good. How'd they get it?"

"Moseley's worked with the *Federales* here in Juarez a couple of times before. Drug-enforcement stuff. Anyway the Mexican feds just got a tip from a local doctor, a real sleaze-bag from what Moseley said. Anyway, this doctor treated a woman fitting our description to a tee. And she had a GSW in the arm. The NSA guy is certain it's Erica Blake."

"What's the doctor and the *Federales* get out of all this? Why would they help us?"

"This is Mexico, Sergeant. It's all about the money. I guess the NSA isn't shy about spreading it around."

Thomas shrugged. "Our tax dollars at work."

"I guess so." Garcia put the clinic's address into the Yukon's navigation system on the dash. A moment later he said, "The clinic is not far from here."

Garcia cranked up the vehicle and eased his way into traffic.

Ten minutes later the Yukon was cruising slowly past the decrepit façade of the clinic. "This is it," the captain said. "My guess is she's holed up at some cheap hotel nearby."

"I agree," Thomas responded.

"We'll scout the immediate five block area, then expand the circuit if we have to."

"Yes, sir. How do you want to play this?"

"Get your stun gun ready. We'll take her as soon as we see her."

Thomas frowned. "In broad daylight?"

"This is Juarez. Kidnappings are a part of life here. Anyway, I'm not taking a chance on losing her. We see her, we grab her."

"Yes, Captain." The sergeant pulled a large, black handgun from a bag by his feet and rested it on his lap.

They drove around the area in an ever expanding circle, and fifteen minutes later rolled past a shabby-looking motel with faded paint. "That's a possible," Thomas said.

Garcia nodded, as he looked in the rear-view mirror. "We'll check it out." Driving to the end of the street, he did an illegal U-turn, went back to the motel and parked in the parking area that fronted the place.

Just then Garcia spotted an attractive woman wearing a baseball cap come out of one of the first floor rooms. He'd studied Blake's picture on the flight down, knew her facial features and body shape well.

"We just caught a lucky break, Sergeant," he said excitedly. "That's her! Let's go!"

Garcia pulled his Glock from his waistband and jumped out of the car, while Thomas gripped the stunner and also climbed out.

As they rushed toward Blake, she must have heard something because she whirled around and faced them. Her eyes went wide and she reached in her pocket. Pulling a revolver, she aimed their way, but not before Thomas fired three rounds. The gun made muffled sounds and her body flinched back. She staggered and crumpled to the ground.

Garcia reached her a second later. "Help me carry her back," he said to Thomas. He grabbed the woman's shoulders, while the sergeant lifted her by the legs. They carried her back quickly to the SUV and put her in the cargo compartment.

By this time, other motel guests had come out of their rooms to see what had caused the commotion. Seeing them, Garcia waved the Glock in the air and they hastily jumped back in their rooms.

The two men climbed back in the Yukon and drove away.

"What now?" Thomas asked, as the SUV sped along the busy street, weaving in-and-out of traffic.

"We go back to the airfield, take the jet on a little trip."

An hour later they pulled into the parking lot of the private airfield outside of Juarez. There was no tower here, just a long asphalt runway. A row of single and twin-engine prop planes were parked off to one side of the landing strip. Their Gulfstream jet, also parked there, stood out, its sleek black shape and swept-back wings gleaming in the mid-day sun.

Private rent-a-cops armed with semi-automatic rifles and shotguns patrolled the area. Crime was a constant problem in Mexico and armed security was necessary as a deterrent. The planes were an inviting target for theft. General Corvan had paved the way before their flight here, paying the airfield's owner generously for usage of his runway. No questions asked.

Garcia climbed out of the Yukon and waved to the guards, who nodded back. Thomas also got out and they went around to the back of the vehicle and opened the tailgate door. There they zipped open a black body bag and placed Blake's unconscious body inside. Then they carried the bag to the Gulfstream, and with the pilot's help, loaded it into the plane.

***

Bobbie Garcia leaned back in the jet's leather seat and stared out the small round window. They were flying at an altitude of 35,000 feet and the vast expanse of water below looked like a tranquil blue lake. They cruised over puffy cumulous clouds, their white shapes blending beautifully with the blue much further below. *It's a peaceful scene*, he thought. *It's a shame I can't share it with Maria.* She would have liked it. Maybe soon, though. When all this was over.

He heard a groan and he glanced back in the plane. Sitting in the seat across from him was Blake, her hands tied to the armrests. She groaned again and he realized the woman was regaining consciousness. Her eyelids fluttered and a moment later she was fully awake. She said nothing, just craned her neck around, taking it all in.

Thomas, who was sitting across the aisle in the otherwise empty plane, got up and walked up to him. "You want me to stun her again, boss?"

Garcia shook his head. "No. No need. She's not going anywhere."

The sergeant nodded and went back to his seat.

"Where am I?" Blake asked.

Garcia didn't answer at first, but rather studied the woman. Although she looked pale, she was a striking-looking woman. The pictures hadn't done her justice. If she hadn't been an FBI agent, she could have had a future in modeling.

"You're in a plane," he finally replied.

She glared. "I figured that. Where we going?"

"You'll find out soon enough."

"Why did you kidnap me? Is this a ransom? For money?"

He laughed. "No."

"Who are you?"

"My name's not important. The only thing that matters is that you're in our custody."

She frowned. "Are you law-enforcement?"

He laughed again. "In a matter of speaking."

"My name is Susan McMillan," she said. "I'm a Canadian citizen. I demand you take me to a Canadian consulate."

"Your name is Erica Blake and you're an ex-FBI agent. There's a nationwide hunt for you. You shot and wounded two NSA agents in Atlanta. I know all about you, Miss Blake. So, you can drop the act."

A flash of fear crossed her face and she went quiet.

"What no more questions, Erica?"

She shrugged. "What the hell. At least tell me your name."

"I guess it can't hurt now. My name's Bobbie."

"Okay. Who do you work for, Bobbie? The NSA? CIA? DoD? You have a military look. My bet is Department of Defense. Special Ops?"

He grinned, said nothing.

Blake's face brightened as if she'd just figured something out. "You're part of the conspiracy."

"What conspiracy?"

"This big plan that links all the events," she said. "Carpenter's death, the President's assassination, all the rest of it. You're involved in some way."

Garcia shrugged. "You've been watching too many Hollywood movies, Erica. There is no conspiracy. I'm just a guy following orders."

"If you are connected to this insane plan, whatever it is, you may know what's happened to my ex-husband. He went missing a while back. I need to find him. Please, Bobbie," she pleaded. "Even if you can't tell me anything else, tell me about him."

"What's his name?"

"Steve McCord."

Garcia recognized the name immediately. He was the CIA agent the NSA guys had taken and interrogated. A frown crossed his face.

"What is it? What's happened to Steve?"

The captain was determined not to tell the woman anything, but her beseeching expression melted his resolve. "Okay, I guess it can't hurt. McCord was arrested and questioned. He's still alive."

Her face flooded with relief. "Thank God! Where is he?"

He waved a hand a hand in the air. "We're going there now."

"We are?"

"Yes. But don't get your hopes up too much. He's in bad shape, from what I heard. He may not make it."

3 Days to Zero Hour

Gimmlewald, Switzerland

Megan Lewis strolled on the sidewalk of the picturesque village, admiring the boutique shops and bistros that lined the main street. But, at the same time, she kept a wary eye for anyone who could be tailing her.

After a refueling stop in Sydney, Australia, Mueller's plane had flown her to Bern, Switzerland. Waiting for her at an airport locker, there was a phony Swiss passport and two new credit cards reflecting her new identity. Henry had thought of everything – she would have to repay the man, as soon as she got the chance.

At the Bern airport she rented a car and drove to this small town. Henry had told her the place was a perfect hideout. It was in a remote part of the country, far away from the hectic banking centers of Zurich and Geneva.

After checking into the small but exclusive inn under her new name, Megan altered her appearance as much as possible. Dying her hair black and putting on black frame eyeglasses, she also shed her expensive designer suit and replaced it with a pair of baggy Levi's, a cheap blouse and white Adidas sneakers. She bought a disposable camera and dangled it from her neck. Standing in front of her room's mirror yesterday, she looked nothing like the stylishly-dressed senator, but rather, a carefree tourist on holiday.

Spotting a quaint café at the corner, she decided to have lunch.

Minutes later she was seated at small wooden table next to the sidewalk. A tall waiter handed her a menu. "Would you like something to drink?" he asked in German.

"A white wine," she replied in the same language. "How is the Zürcher Geschnetzeltes here?" she asked, referring to the veal and mushroom delicacy popular in the country.

"Excellent, Madame."

"Good. I'll have that."

The man nodded and moved away.

After drinking the first glass of wine and ordering another, her food order came and she began to eat. Savoring the rich veal and warm loaf of bread, her thoughts turned to her somber new reality. In spite of the fact she was in a picturesque village with breathtaking mountain views and quaint shops, she was still a woman on the run. *Killers are after me. Trained assassins whose job it is to find me, no matter where I am.*

Gulping down her second wine, she signaled the waiter for another.

On the plus side, she was in a country far away from the United States. Switzerland was a neutral country, and it would be difficult to extradite her back to the U.S., since she had committed no crimes. She also had plenty of money available. Years ago she had set up secret Swiss and Cayman bank accounts. And she had a good friend she could trust. Henry Mueller. Her thoughts drifted to the Swiss banker, to their last tryst. It had been exciting and fun, which puzzled her. She had sex with men only when it benefited her in some strategic way. But being with Henry had been different. Better, for some reason she couldn't pinpoint. But she had to be careful. Mueller was married and she had heard his spouse was a very jealous trophy wife.

As she sipped her third wine, she pushed all those thoughts aside.

Leaning back in the wooden chair, she gazed at the nearby lake, where small sailboats with bright-colored sails glided over the azure waters. The air smelled clean and fresh, unlike the smog back in Washington. She tried to focus on the scenery and enjoy the bright sunshine and cool breeze of the day.

Because she knew that once night fell, she would unsuccessfully try to sleep. The terror of being captured and killed lurked every night.

***

Prison Complex
Guantanamo Bay Naval Base
Guantanamo, Cuba

Erica Blake clutched the thick jail bars that fronted her 6' x 6' cell and eyed the old clock on the corridor wall. It read 2:00 p.m. Yesterday she'd been brought to the antiquated prison, stripped, hosed-down, and given an orange jumpsuit to wear. Then locked up in this cell and fed twice. She'd been told nothing.

She'd demanded an attorney, but the two armed U.S. Marines who guarded this wing stayed silent. It was clear that listening to inmate complaints wasn't high on their priority list.

The clock clicked to 2:01 p.m. and the metal door at the end of the corridor opened. A man in a U.S. Navy uniform with officer's insignia came in and the Marines came to attention.

The three of them strode to the front of her cell and one of the jarheads said to her, "Step back, please."

Erica backed away from the cell door and the Marine guard unlocked it. The officer stepped in the cell and the guard relocked it behind him.

"I'm Ensign Tulley," the naval officer said. "I'm a JAG attorney, assigned to your case." The ensign was in his early twenties, athletically built with a boyish face. His blond hair was closely cropped in a high-and-tight crew-cut.

"What am I doing here, Tulley?"

"Miss Blake, you've been charged under the Patriot Act for terroristic acts against the government of the United States. You're being held as an enemy combatant."

Her jaw dropped. "What the hell? How can that be?"

His boyish face reddened and Erica guessed that this was probably his first case.

"I'm sorry, ma'am. But it's all right here." He was holding a manila envelope which he handed to her.

Opening it, she read through the document quickly. It appeared very official and was signed by the Attorney General of the U.S. Her heart sank and she handed it back. Then she sat down on the threadbare metal cot.

Tulley turned to the two Marines, who were still standing at parade rest outside the cell. "Gentlemen," he said, "I need to have a private conversation with my client."

The Marines saluted and went back to their post by the corridor door.

"May I sit down?" the officer asked Erica. "We need to prepare for the next steps."

She shrugged and he sat on the far side of the cot.

"How old are you, Ensign? You don't look old enough to drive."

He blushed again. "I graduated from the Naval Academy six months ago. With honors."

"I'm sure. Is this your first case?"

He nodded, said nothing.

"Great," she added.

"Miss Blake, you're in a lot of trouble. I'm here to help you."

Sighing, she said, "Okay, Tulley, looks like we're stuck with each other. Is this a privileged conversation? I'm your client, so you can't repeat what I say, right?"

"That's right, ma'am."

"Let me tell you what happened. Two NSA agents, posing as Census takers and without identifying themselves as law-enforcement officers, drew guns on me and tried to kill me. I had to defend myself. After I fled, I was tracked down by a secret, black-ops team and brought here."

A dubious look crossed his face. "I'm sorry, ma'am, but your story sounds far-fetched. Why would the NSA want to arrest you in the first place? I've read your file. You have a history of insubordination, and in fact, you were fired by the FBI. Your record also indicates you may have a drinking problem. Is it possible you were drunk or on drugs and that's why you shot the NSA agents?"

Erica's hands formed into fists and her heart raced. "Listen, Ensign, let's get one thing straight. Everything I'm telling you is true." She stabbed a finger on his chest to make her point.

Tulley held up his palms. "Okay. I'm on your side. Let's say I believe you. Why would the National Security Agency want to arrest you? And why were you charged under the Patriot Act?"

She breathed a sigh or relief. At least he was listening to her. Her voice dropped to a whisper and he leaned in, straining to hear. "Let me tell you everything, Tulley. It's going to be hard to believe, but all of it is true. I first started working on this about a month ago, when I was assigned to Senator Carpenter's death in Washington, D.C." Then she proceeded to tell him, in detail, the web of conspiracy she had discovered. Ten minutes later she was done.

The young officer, his mouth open, was speechless. Eventually he said, "Jesus Christ."

"You believe me, Tulley?"

"Ma'am, there's been so many strange events happening in the U.S. lately. Things that don't make any sense. This conspiracy, or whatever it is, does seem to tie it all together."

Erica nodded. "Yes, it does. Now, can you get me out of here?"

He looked doubtful. "That's going to be difficult. Since you're charged as an enemy combatant, your rights to due process are forfeited. You'll be tried here, at Gitmo in a military court. I'll request an immediate hearing, but…it may be years before your case is heard."

Her anger boiled over. "So that's it? That's all you can say? What good are you?"

The ensign recoiled as if he'd been slapped in the face.

"Sorry," she added. "You didn't deserve that. But you've *got* to help me."

"I'll do all I can, ma'am. Is there anyone who can corroborate your story?"

She decided she had to trust him completely – he was her only chance of getting out of this prison. "U.S. Senator Megan Lewis," she replied. "She's a friend of mine. She's been able to confirm the names of some of the conspirators."

"Good. I'll contact her today. The senator may have connections high-up at the Justice Department. Maybe she can pull some strings so you can be tried in a civilian court back in the States."

Erica felt a ray of hope.

"Miss Blake, is there anyone else that can corroborate your story? The more the better."

"There's a police detective in Fairfax County, Virginia. Detective Gray. I worked with him on the Carpenter case."

"Okay, I'll call him too. Having two people who confirm your story, especially a senator and someone in law-enforcement will help me get an expedited hearing with a military judge."

"Thank you, Ensign. There's something else I need your help with. The guy that kidnapped me in Juarez – he said my ex-husband was being held here, in Guantanamo. I need you to find him."

"What's his name?"

"McCord. Steve McCord."

A frown crossed his face.

"What is it, Tulley?"

"I haven't seen him, but I've heard his name. He is here, in another wing of the prison. From what I've heard, he's in bad shape, ma'am."

That was the second time she'd heard this and a chill went down her spine. "Please, Tulley, find him. Do everything you can to help him."

The man nodded but the frown didn't leave his face.

2 Days to Zero Hour

The President's private study
The White House
Washington, D.C.

President Taylor stood in the middle of the small office, intently watching the Fox News broadcast. The TV screen showed images of anti-Chinese demonstrations in various cities. Kansas City, Dallas, Portland – it was the same everywhere. The protests hadn't abated, but rather seemed to be heating up. Americans were fuming about the Wilson assassination, and anger was boiling over. A second Chinese consulate had been burned down, this time in Dallas. The president grinned, savoring the timing of it all.

There was knock on the door and he muted the sound on the TV.

Alice stuck her head around the door. "Mr. President, the general needs to see you."

"Sure, Alice, send him in."

General Corvan stepped in the room and said. "Sorry to bother you, sir, but I have some news."

"No problem, Corvan," Taylor replied, smiling. Watching the demonstrations had put him a good mood. "Have a seat."

"Thought I'd find you in the Oval Office, sir." The general glanced around the cramped, utilitarian office.

Taylor sat behind the modest desk. "This is less formal, Corvan. Gives me a chance to relax a bit." He didn't add that the study had no windows, making it easier to sip scotch without being interrupted.

"Of course, sir."

"What do you have?"

"Some good news and some not so good news."

The president smiled. "Give me the good first."

"Yes, sir. Erica Blake, the former FBI agent, is now in custody. She's been incarcerated in our special place."

"Excellent. The bitch deserves it."

Corvan nodded. "Per your orders, she was charged under the Patriot Act. She won't be going anywhere for a very long, long time."

"Good. Now give me the other news."

"Sir, as you know, we've been in the process of tracking down Senator Lewis."

Taylor's mood turned dark at the mention of the woman's name. "Well?"

"We believe she took a flight to Australia. Sydney, to be exact. The NSA believes she's in that city now, or in the general vicinity."

"And? What are you doing about it? I want her found!"

"Yes, sir. I've commissioned a CIA wet-work team. They're on the ground in Sydney now. I'm sure they'll find her."

"Good." He leaned back in his chair, ran a hand over his bald head. "Everything else on track for BlackSnow?"

"Yes, Mr. President. I had another meeting this morning with the other generals and admirals. All the logistics are in place."

"Excellent. Has Admiral Peters been prepped for Zero Hour? Remember, the Chairman of the Joint Chiefs is an important cog in this operation."

"Yes, sir. I've rehearsed it with him several times."

"Good."

Just then there was a knock on the door and Alice once again stuck her head around the door. "Sorry to bother you," she said, "but General Wu Chang is calling from Beijing."

Taylor shook his head slowly and muttered, "What does he want?" Raising his voice he said, "Okay, Alice, put him through."

Alice nodded and closed the door.

The president shrugged and rolled his eyes. "I'm looking forward to when I don't have to babysit that guy."

The general grinned and the red phone on the desk began to ring.

Taylor picked up the receiver and held it to his ear. "General Chang, how good of you to call. How's the weather in Beijing? It's hot here in D.C."

"Mr. President," Taylor heard Chang say, "this isn't a social call." The man's heavily accented English sounded stressed.

"What's the problem, General?"

"The Premier just called me. He's been watching the American news. This latest consulate burning has us on edge, Mr. President. You *must* announce the findings on the assassination. Now."

"Of course, General. I've also been watching the burning of your consulate in Dallas. It's tragic. Very tragic. I'm going to order National Guard units to begin guarding your U.S. Embassy and all of your consulates, effective immediately. Be assured that I won't tolerate any more violence against your people or your property."

"That is good news, Mr. President. I appreciate that. But when are going to give your national address on the assassination?"

"Very soon, General. You can tell the Premier that I will be speaking to the nation in a matter of days."

"That is good to hear."

"Don't worry, Wu, I don't want to further damage the partnership between our two nations. I have just as much at stake as you do."

"That is correct, Mr. President. Just yesterday I authorized another purchase of your Treasury bonds."

"And we appreciate it, Wu. I appreciate it, personally. Maybe over the next couple of months, you and the Premier will consider paying us a visit. The weather at Camp David will be excellent then. I can assure you the fall foliage is beautiful there."

"I would welcome that, Mr. President. I have never been there before."

"Excellent. I'll alert my staff so they can begin making preparations. We'll have a State Dinner in your honor, right here at the White House."

"A State Dinner – that would be very special." By Chang's tone of voice, Taylor could tell the general regarded the dinner as a great honor.

"Good. In that case, I'll let you get back to work. I know you're a busy man. We'll talk soon. And don't worry about security for your consulates. I'll start protecting them with the U.S. military."

"Thank you, Mr. President."

The line disconnected and Taylor replaced the receiver.

"That went well," the president said. "Another crisis averted."

"Yes, sir," Corvan replied. "I'm assuming you want me to start coordinating with the Defense Department for deployment of National Guard units to their consulates?"

The president glanced at the calendar that hung on the wall of the office, then looked back at the general. He barked a harsh laugh. "No! The hell with the Chinese."

1 Day to Zero Hour

Prison Complex
Guantanamo Bay Naval Base
Guantanamo, Cuba

Erica Blake jogged-in-place in the prison cell, the perspiration dripping from her forehead. She wasn't used to the sweltering Cuban heat and her baggy orange jumpsuit clung to her body, drenched with sweat. With nothing to do but wait, the hours and days had seemed endless. Exercise had been her only solace. The clock on the corridor wall said 9:50 a.m., only two minutes after she'd looked last.

Dropping to the grimy floor, she began doing sit-ups. Her arm was healing, but it would be months before she could do push-ups. Still, between the jogging and the sit-ups, she had been able to stay somewhat sane. She did fifty, then sat up on the concrete floor. Winded, she gulped in air and regretted it immediately. The pungent smell of the prison filled her lungs – feces, urine, vomit and other foul odors she couldn't identify.

The Marine guards at the end of the corridor stood ramrod straight, holding their rifles across their chests. Besides bringing her tasteless mush to eat three times a day, they had no interaction with her. Except for a few brief words, the guards were silent.

From her cell, Erica had been able to observe the other prisoners being held in this corridor. Most of them appeared to be Middle Eastern men, with long, shabby beards. They spoke what sounded like Arabic. From the sluggish, listless way they moved in their cells, it seemed they had been at the prison a long time.

The door at the end of the corridor opened and Ensign Tulley walked in. He spoke briefly to the guards and the three men approached her cell. One of the Marines unlocked the door and the young officer entered. The guards relocked it and moved back to their post.

"I have some information," Tulley said, a frown on his face.

Erica stood up and faced the man. "It's not good, is it?"

"No ma'am, it isn't. Why don't you sit down?"

"I'll stand, Ensign."

"As you wish. After we met the other day, I called Senator Lewis's office in Washington. The senator has been missing for several days. Nobody on her staff knows where she is."

Erica shook her head slowly. "Jesus."

"I also checked with the D.C. police and the Bethesda, Maryland police, where she lives. No one's seen her or heard from her. Her housekeeper reported her missing. I talked to her also."

"They got to Lewis," Erica said. "And she'd even hired bodyguards."

The ensign nodded. "Her bodyguards are missing too."

"I told you, this is big."

"Yes, ma'am. The other name you gave me, Detective Gray."

"Yeah?"

"He took early retirement from the Fairfax County police force. And now he's out of the country, on vacation."

"Convenient."

"I agree, Miss Blake, this has a real bad smell to it. Unfortunately, without those two people to confirm your story, your charges are going to be difficult to defend. I requested an expedited hearing on your case, but was turned down."

Any flicker of hope disappeared. "What else could go wrong?"

"Actually, ma'am, there is one other thing I need to tell you about. But I'd like you to sit down first."

Erica shrugged, plopped down on the cot.

"It has to do with your ex-husband, ma'am."

She looked up at the ensign's eyes and saw the hesitation there.

"You found Steve?"

"Yes, I did," he said, his voice heavy with sadness. "I'm sorry to tell you, but Steve McCord died this morning."

She didn't comprehend the words at first, then the finality of it hit her like a ton of bricks. Her heart pounded and her stomach churned. "Steve? Steve's dead? Are you sure?"

"I'm afraid so. The doctors at the military hospital here in Guantanamo did what they could, but…."

Erica put her head in her hands and began to weep. She cried uncontrollably, her pain-wracked thoughts filled with images of Steve. The only man she'd ever loved.

***

Special Operations
Marine Corps Detachment
Training Facility, Building 14
Fort Bragg, North Carolina

Bobbie Garcia looked at his computer screen and grinned. The latest wire transfer had gone into his secret bank account, increasing his previous balance. Once again, the general had kept his word. And in just days, this whole operation would be over.

He and Maria would be able to start their new life together. Smiling to himself, he decided he would buy her a new car. She'd always had to settle for used, high-mileage Chevys or Fords. This time it would be different. He'd surprise her with a brand-new Lexus or Mercedes-Benz, in metallic blue, her favorite color. He closed his eyes as he visualized the sleek car, even smelling the aroma of the rich, leather interior.

Just then his cell phone rang. He grabbed the phone and held it to his ear.

***

The President's private study
The White House
Washington, D.C.

President Taylor leaned back in his chair, closely studying Admiral Peters, the Chairman of the Joint Chiefs of Staff. The admiral was a small man, thin and wiry, with piercing, icy-blue eyes. The navy man was sitting on one of the visitors chairs. General Corvan was sitting next to him, and the two men waited patiently for the president to speak.

Peters had not been part of the original group that had created BlackSnow, but rather a later addition. But Corvan had vouched for him and the general had rarely let him down.

"Admiral," Taylor began, "I understand from Corvan that you've been fully briefed on your…role…at Zero Hour."

"Yes, Mr. President," Peters replied confidently.

"Good. I don't want any slip-ups. In that room will be people who aren't in on our operation. The Secretaries of Defense, Treasury, and Commerce, along with a few others. I want them convinced."

Peters nodded. "Don't worry, Mr. President. It will go smoothly."

"Okay, gentlemen. Are all the other preparations in place?"

"Yes," Peters said. "The submarines are in position. All they need is the go-ahead sequence codes."

Taylor rubbed his jaw. "Excellent. Corvan, is everything set up for the trip?"

"Yes, sir. We'll leave for San Diego tomorrow morning. The dedication ceremony for the new aircraft carrier is set for the afternoon. Since it's a big event, I've confirmed that all of your key Cabinet members will be going."

"Very good," Taylor said. "Okay, gentlemen, if that's all, I've got some other work to do." He waved a hand in the air. "Budget stuff, you know how it is."

"Of course, sir," Corvan replied. The general and the admiral stood and left the room, closing the door behind them.

Reaching into a desk drawer, Taylor pulled out a glass and a bottle of scotch, placed them on his desk. He poured himself a double, picked up the glass and downed it one long swallow. The harsh liquor burned his throat as it went down, but a moment later the lightheaded buzz kicked in and calmed his nerves. Tomorrow was a big day. The biggest of his life. A lot was riding on it.

Then he put the glass and bottle back in the drawer. He knew he would need a clear head tomorrow and one drink was all he would permit himself. There would be plenty of time for more after it was all over.

***

Gimmlewald, Switzerland

Megan Lewis took a sip of the chardonnay, savored the taste. It was a rare French vintage, but she didn't expect anything less from the handsome banker. Henry Mueller, who was sitting across from her, smiled. "How do like the wine?" he asked. The two were having dinner in a small, but elegant restaurant not far from her inn.

She returned the smile. "Exceptional, Henry. Thank you for this dinner and for everything you've done for me. I truly appreciate it."

His face turned serious. "You're welcome, Megan. As I told you before, you'll be safe in this town. Not many people visit it. And it's not on any tourist maps."

She nodded, then took a bite of her veal.

"I can't believe what's happened to you, Senator. And the things that are going on in your country…it is beyond belief."

"Believe it. Everything I told you, it's all true."

He leaned in closer. "I'm assuming the deal we had…." His voice trailed off.

"I'm afraid that's gone, Henry. President Taylor is hip-deep in this insane BlackSnow operation."

A sad look crossed his face. "A pity. I had my heart set on that land in Wyoming."

"We're all disappointed. I'm convinced my life will never be the same. I have a new reality to deal with. I may never be able to return to the U.S. By the way, have you told your bank anything about any of this?"

"No. I told them the deal was still in the works that we would find out something soon."

"Good. If I were you, I'd stall them as long as possible."

"I will, Megan."

"The less people who know I'm here, the better."

"Don't worry. I won't tell anyone you're here." He raised his wine glass. "I propose a toast. To better times."

She halfheartedly picked up her glass, clinked it with his. "To better times," she muttered. Deep down she knew better times were not ahead. Quite the contrary.

He must have sensed her darkening mood because he placed one of his hands over hers and gave her a brilliant grin. "Cheer up. Living in Switzerland is quite nice. It is a beautiful country. And you are well off financially. After a time, you'll see. Your life here will be better than you imagined. Think positive."

His positive attitude was infectious and she gave him a small smile.

Mueller squeezed her hand. "And, of course, Zurich is not too far away. I can visit you whenever you like, or need…."

She understood his implication right away. Mueller would never replace Audrey, but he would be a welcome distraction from all the negative events in her life right now. "You know, Henry, the inn where I'm staying is close. Why don't we have a nightcap there, after dinner?" She gave him a sly grin. "I *do* need to repay you for all you've done for me."

He glanced at her nearly empty plate. "If you are done with your dinner, we could go there right now."

Megan chuckled. "Hot to trot?"

"I am not familiar with that American expression."

"It means you're in the mood to make love."

The man nodded, took out his wallet, pulled out a thick sheaf of Swiss francs and put them on the table.

Megan stood and said, "I'm ready."

Zero Hour

Aboard Air Force One
Flying at 42,000 feet over Missouri

President Taylor listened idly while Treasury Secretary Longstreet droned on, his Power Point presentation seemingly endless. Taylor, Corvan and the secretary were in the plane's conference room, seated around the oval conference table. Through the windows to his left, Taylor saw a perfect blue sky. From this altitude the weather appeared serene, much different than the rain and storm clouds they'd left back in D.C. this morning.

The red phone on the credenza rang and General Corvan stood and picked up the receiver. Taylor glanced nervously at his watch – BlackSnow was beginning.

Corvan listened for a moment, then hung up the phone. "Mr. President," he said, "that was Admiral Peters. He needs to brief you on an urgent national security problem."

"I see," Taylor responded. "In that case, get the rest of the Cabinet in here. We may need their input."

"Yes, sir."

Corvan left the room and came back a minute later, trailed by the Cabinet members who were on the plane. They were followed by Admiral Peters, the Chairman of the Joint Chiefs of Staff.

Taylor motioned with a hand. "Have a seat, ladies and gentlemen."

After the group had settled around the table, the president said, "I've just been informed that we have a grave national security threat. The Chairman needs to brief us on this urgent matter. Go ahead, Admiral."

Everyone turned to face Peters, whose hands were placed flat on the table in front of him. His white naval uniform was crisply starched and the commendation ribbons on his chest were perfectly aligned. Taylor noticed that Peters was wearing his Navy Cross medal today, the highest honor awarded to a member of the U.S. Navy, a subtle reminder that the admiral was a war hero.

"Ladies and gentlemen," Peters began, "as the President has just stated, we have a crisis on our hands." His voice was steely and he enunciated every word carefully to underscore the gravity of the situation. "Ten minutes ago, our satellites picked up an unusually high rate of activity at all of mainland China's ICBM complexes. Trucks and personnel were shuttled to all of their intercontinental ballistic missile silos."

A hushed silence fell over the group and the admiral paused for effect.

"Five minutes ago," Peters continued, "our satellites detected the opening of one-hundred and sixty-three missile silos. That's their entire land-based ICBM capability. The destructive force of that many nuclear missiles is massive. It would obliterate most of the United States of America."

As the words sank in, the room erupted into boisterous shouting, as the various Cabinet members tried to talk over each other.

Taylor stood. "Please, everyone! Settle down. We need to focus here and yelling isn't going to help." He sat down as the ruckus quieted.

"Admiral," the president asked, "How sure are you about these satellite transmissions? Could they be wrong?"

"Mr. President," Peters replied, "We have multiple satellites covering the same areas. There's a triple redundancy of the images and they all show the same thing. The silo doors are open."

"I see," Taylor said, his voice grave. "Could they be doing some kind of test?"

"Sir, we've been monitoring the Chinese for decades, just like we monitor the Russians, Iranians and North Koreans. The Chinese have never before opened all the silo doors at all of their complexes. If it were a test, or a repair issue, they would open a few at a time, just like we would." He paused a moment, then added. "And there's another ominous sign, sir. In the last few minutes, we've been able to decipher several of their coded transmissions – their military forces around the world have been placed on the highest alert. One transmission even included a list of American cities. I would say that is a smoking gun, Mr. President."

Taylor leaned forward in his seat. "Is it your judgment, Admiral, that the missiles are targeting the United States?"

"Yes, sir. I believe the Chinese are poised to launch a massive nuclear first strike against our country."

"My God!" the president exclaimed, his face scrunched in a deep frown. He turned to Corvan. "What do you think, General?"

"Mr. President," Corvan replied, "the Chinese assassinated President Wilson. I believe that was just the beginning. This pending nuclear attack is a continuation of their plan. I think they intend to wipe us off the face of the planet."

Taylor nodded, then turned to the Defense Secretary, who was seated to his left. "What do you think, Stan?"

The Secretary of Defense was an affable but meek man. He'd only gotten the job because he had been a popular congressman from Florida, an important swing state in elections. "I'm not sure what to think," the secretary said. "I'll support whatever you decide."

The president looked around at the others in the room. "Does anyone else have something they want to add?"

The Commerce Secretary raised a hand and Taylor said, "Go ahead."

"Sir," the secretary said, "perhaps we should call the Chinese and ask for an explanation."

"So the bastards can lie to us?" Taylor shot back, his voice dripping with venom. "Hell, no! They killed Wilson, an American icon, for God's sake. And now they're getting ready to nuke us back to the Stone Age."

The Commerce Secretary flinched back and quickly said, "You're right, Mr. President."

Taylor turned back to the admiral. "How much time do we have, Peters?"

The admiral looked at his watch. "Five minutes. Maybe less."

The president shook his head slowly. "Jesus. What are my options, Admiral?"

"You have no choice, sir. We have to nuke them first."

Taylor steepled his hands on the table in front of him. "You're recommending we launch a pre-emptive first strike on the Chinese?"

"Yes, sir. It's the only way to prevent them from wiping us out."

Corvan raised a hand. "I concur, Mr. President. You have no choice. Our country's future is at stake."

"What are the logistics, Admiral?" Taylor asked.

"Our Pacific Ocean Trident submarine fleet is stationed underwater, in the Yellow Sea," Peters replied. "That's east of the Chinese mainland. They're fairly close to Beijing and Shanghai. The fleet is composed of sixty Trident D5 SLBM subs. They have the latest in advanced 'Whisper' technology, which make them almost undetectable. Each of the subs carries a payload of twenty-four, multi-warhead nuclear missiles. That's a total of 1,440 missiles. The missiles are SLBMs – submarine launched ballistic missiles, which are smaller than land-based ICBMs, but still pack a hell of a punch. I recommend we use the Trident fleet. They're the closest to China and their missiles would reach them the fastest. They would deliver a massive strike on the Chinese. Even if only half of our missiles reach their destination, they would still take out all of their ICBM complexes and many of their major cities."

The Labor Secretary spoke up. "I thought the Line of Demarcation, the treaty that President Wilson agreed to, kept our naval vessels close to the U.S.?"

Taylor nodded. "I secretly rescinded that for our subs. After the assassination, I didn't think the Chinese could be trusted."

"Good thinking, sir," the secretary replied.

The president rubbed his jaw. "So, we hit them with the Tridents. Corvan, do you agree?"

"Absolutely, sir."

"Stan, what about you?"

The Defense Secretary nodded. "Yes, Mr. President. I agree."

Taylor glanced around the room one last time. "I have no choice, ladies and gentlemen. I have a sworn duty to protect the lives of over 320 million Americans. And I intend to do just that." There was a chorus of agreement from the group and the president added solemnly, "God help us all."

Taylor turned to Peters. "It's a go, Admiral."

"Yes, Mr. President." The naval officer stood and stepped out of the room for a moment. He came back, followed by an Army major who was carrying a large, black briefcase. Taylor recalled the nickname for the briefcase – it was referred to as the nuclear 'football'. Using the case, the president of the United States, along with the senior military officer, keyed in the sequence codes that authorized a nuclear attack.

The Army major laid the case on the table in front of the president and opened it. Taylor, when he had assumed the presidency, had been briefed on the procedure. But he had never seen the case open before. The inside contained a computer screen and a keyboard. But it appeared much more durable than a typical computer – it was constructed with heavy-gauge black metal.

The gravity of the situation suddenly hit Taylor and beads of sweat formed on his forehead. He had prepared for and visualized this very moment for a long time, but he never thought he would be nervous when it actually took place. A cold chill went down his spine as Admiral Peters tapped in his own sequence numbers on the keypad.

"It's your turn, Mr. President," the man said when he was done.

His hands slightly shaking, Taylor tapped in his numbers.

When he was done, Peters said, "Thank you, Mr. President."

The major closed the case and the admiral said, "I'm going to the Com room, sir. I need to transmit the final instructions to the subs and put all of our military forces on DEFCON 1." He looked at his watch. "Our attack will begin in approximately three minutes."

Taylor nodded and the admiral and major left the room.

The president turned to Corvan. "Get the Chaplain in here. I'd like him to lead us in a prayer."

***

Command & Control Center
Chinese Military
Beijing, China

General Wu Chang stood by the bank of small monitors at the left of the room, watching silently as the latest satellite feed from Germany streamed on one of the monitors. NATO was conducting a military exercise outside of Berlin and the general was studying the NATO tank formations. He liked the approach they were using and had decided to copy it for his own tank battalions on the Chinese-Russian border.

Just then Colonel Zhu walked up to him, a worried look on his face.

"General," Zhu said, "one of our naval vessels patrolling the Yellow Sea, the destroyer *Nanchang*, has picked up an undersea sonar signature. From the shape of the undersea vessel, it appears to be a submarine. The *Nanchang's* commander believes it is an American sub."

Chang grimaced. "That's impossible, Colonel. That area is off-limits to all American warships. Have the commander check again. He must have made a mistake."

"I personally talked with him, sir. He's double checked the readings. And another of our warships, the cruiser *Qingdao* has verified it with their sonar. There is a U.S. submarine there."

Chang's heart began to pound. *What the hell is going on?* he thought. *Why would the Americans station a sub so close to China? Are they spying on us? Or maybe it's having navigation problems and went off-course?* Whatever the reason, he had to find out.

The general picked up the phone on the desk in front of him and quickly punched in a number.

"Captain Lin," he said when she answered. "Call the American President. Now. I have to speak with him immediately. Tell his assistant it is urgent."

He hung up and waited by the phone.

It rang a minute later and he picked up the receiver. "Mr. President?" he asked, but it was Lin who answered.

"Sir," she said, "I spoke with Alice Moore, President Taylor's assistant. She says the president is traveling right now on Air Force One. He has received your message and will call you back in a few minutes. They have to set up the satellite connection. He apologizes for the delay."

Chang felt a bit better after hearing the apology. "Okay, Lin. Put the call through to here. I'll stay at the Control Center until he calls."

He hung up the phone and sat down on the empty chair by the desk. Then he picked up the phone again and punched in another number – a moment later he was put through to the Chinese Premier.

"Premier," Chang said, "one of our ships picked up a sonar signal which appears to be an American submarine in the Yellow Sea."

"I see. What do you make of this, General? The Americans have been so cooperative of late."

"I agree, sir. Especially with the president's invitation for us to visit Washington in the Fall. I believe this sub, if it is American, must be having technical problems and is off-course. I have called President Taylor and he is due to call me back in a few minutes. I don't believe this is a serious situation, but nevertheless I wanted to inform you."

"Thank you, General. Do you think we should put our naval fleet on standby alert?"

"I will talk to Taylor first and see what he has to say. If I am not satisfied, I will issue the alert. I will keep you informed, Premier."

The premier disconnected and the general hung up the phone.

Just then the phone rang and Chang picked it up. "Yes?"

"Sir," Lin said, "I have the President on the line."

"Thank you, Lin." There was a click on the line and Chang heard Taylor's voice.

"General," the president said, his voice syrupy sweet. "Sorry for the delay in getting back to you. Your assistant said you had something urgent to discuss?"

"Mr. President, our naval warships have detected what we believe is one of your submarines stationed underwater in the Yellow Sea." Chang's voice took on a hard edge. "That is a clear violation of the Demarcation Line."

There was a long pause on the other end. Then Taylor said, "I apologize, General. You are correct. One of our submarines is having computer problems and is way off course. This is terribly embarrassing. I apologize profusely for the error on our part. My Navy people are at this very moment working to fix the glitch. I can assure you that sub will be heading back to San Diego as soon as it is fixed. And do not worry, it is one of our training subs, which have no offensive weapons on-board. Please forgive us, General."

Chang was comforted by the president's pleading, almost pathetic response. "No harm done, Mr. President. Remove the vessel and we will be satisfied."

"Do not worry, General. Rest assured – I personally guarantee its prompt removal. By the way, I hope you're looking forward to your visit to the U.S. In addition to the State dinner, I have an extra surprise for you."

His interest peaked, Chang asked, "And what is that?"

"I know that you are a married man, General, but I'm also guessing you appreciate female beauty of many forms. I have a friend I'd like you to meet. This beautiful young woman is curvaceous and alluring. A blue-eyed blonde, she is a personal favorite of mine. I have enjoyed her intimate company for years. I've already discussed it with her, and she would be honored to meet you and…satisfy your desires. And it would be strictly confidential. No one would find out. How does that sound, General?"

Chang had always been an admirer from afar of exotic blondes, which were so rare in China. As he visualized the woman in his mind, he became aroused.

"General? Are you still there?"

"Yes, Mr. President." Chang's voice dropped, so that the others in the Center wouldn't hear him. "Yes, during my visit, I would like to spend time with this person. I would not want to insult your generosity."

"Excellent. I'll set it up. I've experienced her charms many times and I can assure you, you will not be disappointed."

"I'm looking forward to it, Mr. President."

"Very good, General. Is there anything else? If not, I'll let you go. I know you're a busy man."

"No, nothing else. You have been...very informative. Thank you."

***

Aboard Air Force One
Flying at 41,000 feet over Missouri

President Matt Taylor hung up the phone, feeling sick to his stomach. He hated groveling to the Chinese bastard, but knew it wouldn't be for much longer. He was sitting by himself in the plane's conference room – the Cabinet had cleared out minutes before.

After taking a gulp from his cup of black coffee, he picked up the phone. "Get Corvan and Peters in here," he barked.

A moment later the two men came in the room and closed the door behind them.

"Is the attack under way?" Taylor asked Peters.

"Yes, Mr. President," the admiral replied. "The Trident submarines fired their missiles a minute ago. They're on their way. Our satellites are tracking the trajectories – the first strikes will land shortly."

Taylor rubbed his jaw. "Good. Corvan, are the camera people ready?"

Corvan nodded. "Yes, sir. As soon as you like, you can address the American people. I've contacted all of the networks – NBC, ABC, CBS, Fox and ZNN. They will pick up the feed and carry your address live."

"Excellent. Get the makeup girl and wardrobe person in here. I need to look dignified and commanding."

"Yes, sir," Corvan replied.

A few minutes later, Taylor sat behind his desk in his Air Force One office, staring at the TV camera which stood ten feet in front of him. The camera director counted down to zero with his fingers and the camera lens ready light changed from red to green.

Corvan, who was standing to one side of the cameraman and director, nodded and Taylor began speaking.

"My fellow Americans," the president said, "I come to you with grave news. Earlier today I learned that the Chinese government was on the verge of a massive nuclear first strike against the United States." He paused for effect. "This harkens back to two previous, heinous attacks in our country's history – Pearl Harbor and September 11th. After much deliberation, and with the advice of my Cabinet and National Security team, I made a difficult decision. I made this decision in order to protect our country and you, my fellow citizens. To forestall this treacherous Chinese attack, I ordered a nuclear missile strike on China."

Taylor paused, then continued. "As you know, the Chinese government was responsible for the assassination of a great American, my predecessor President Wilson. So this latest deceitful act should not come as a complete surprise. Please be assured that I did not take this decision lightly. But I have a sworn duty to the Constitution and to the American people to preserve and protect this great land of ours."

Taylor leaned forward in his seat. "There will be difficult days ahead. But we will get through them. I strongly believe that we, as a nation, will come together and speak in one voice, much like we did after the attacks of September 11th. And rest assured that everything I do will be guided by the principle of ensuring the safety and security of every American. Good day and God bless our country."

The camera light went from green to red and Taylor breathed a sigh of relief. He leaned back in his seat and saw Corvan walk up to him.

"That was excellent, Mr. President."

"Thank you, General."

Taylor glanced out the plane's windows. The sky had turned dark and threatening, the bright blue giving way to almost black. It looked like a powerful storm was brewing, even at this altitude.

***

Command & Control Center
Chinese Military
Beijing, China

General Chang had gone back to watching the NATO tank drills on the small monitors when Colonel Zhu came up to him.

"General, we're picking up something ominous on satellite 365."

Chang looked up from the small screen. "Okay, Colonel, put the image on Screen 2."

The colonel went to a console, punched in numbers and the image on one of the massive video screens on the far wall shifted quickly. It now showed a blurred overhead picture of a blue ocean with black dots streaking over it.

"What am I looking at, Colonel?" Chang asked, confused by the image.

"Sir, the satellite has picked up a large group of missiles. They broke the surface of the Yellow Sea. The missiles are heading for our mainland!"

"Are you saying we are under attack, Colonel?" the astonished general asked.

"Yes, sir! There is no doubt about it. Missiles are headed our way."

"Where are they in the Yellow Sea?"

"Sir, they originated in the approximate area where we spotted the American submarine."

"There's no way one sub could fire that many missiles."

"I agree, General. There must be a fleet of submarines there."

"My God," Chang exclaimed, his heart pounding in his chest. "I can't believe the bastard Americans are attacking us!" His mind racing, he said, "How much time before they hit us, Colonel?"

"Minutes, General."

"There's no time to consult with the Premier. Alert our ICBM bases. I'm authorizing an immediate attack against the United States. I have no choice. How long before our missiles can lift off, Colonel?"

Zhu glanced at the wall clock. "Approximately fifteen minutes, sir. The silos need that much time to prepare."

"Do it, Colonel! Do it now!"

Zhu picked up a phone and yelled orders into the receiver. Then he sprinted to a computer console and began to furiously tap in instructions.

A shrill alarm began to howl in the Center and there was a flurry of activity as technicians rushed to all of the work stations in the room.

A moment later the colonel ran back to where Chang was standing. "It is done, General."

"Good. How long before our missiles lift off?"

"Very soon, sir."

"Heaven help us, Zhu."

"Yes, sir."

Just then one of the large screens on the wall flashed brilliant white. Then the image flickered and turned dark.

"What was that screen showing, Colonel?"

"That image was a satellite feed of the city of Shanghai."

"Oh, my God."

A moment later Chang heard an ear-splitting explosion, felt the floor vibrate under his feet, and saw a blinding white light engulf him. In a split-second he felt an excruciating burning pain sear through every part of him.

Then everything went black as he and the room were vaporized.

1 Day after Zero Hour

Cheyenne Mountain Complex
North American Aerospace Defense Command
(NORAD)
Colorado Springs, Colorado

President Matt Taylor stood in the empty conference room looking through the glass wall at the frenzy of activity below. In the massive amphitheater, NORAD personnel worked feverishly at hundreds of computer consoles. At the far end of the cavernous room, giant video screens displayed satellite images from all parts of the world.

The NORAD complex was located deep inside the granite mountain range. Taylor knew the hardened site had been constructed to withstand a direct strike from an enemy nuclear missile, something that gave him comfort. From this site, military personnel controlled the U.S. arsenal of land-based ICBMs, the Strategic Air Command with its fleet of long-range bombers, and the U.S Navy's Trident submarine fleet.

As he stared at the screens on the wall, his thoughts drifted to the horrific events that occurred yesterday. Although the attack had gone as planned and had been successful, several Chinese missiles had been launched.

He was jittery from stress, no sleep, too much coffee, and too much aspirin. A blinding migraine had settled in his head and nothing seemed to clear it. But at least he hadn't resorted to his old friend, booze. And knowing his wife and two sons were safe here, in the complex, eased his anxiety. Bringing them along on Air Force One had been smart on his part.

Turning away from the scene below, he glanced at the TV monitors to his right. The TVs were tuned to ZNN and Fox News, but he had muted the sound earlier. The horrific images were more than enough – he didn't need to hear the talking heads.

The news coverage had been non-stop since yesterday, the streaming images of a devastated Washington D.C. and Los Angeles competing for attention. Two Chinese ICBM missiles had evaded the U.S.'s anti-ballistic missile defense, and effectively obliterated the centers of both of those American cities.

A new stab of pain formed in his temples and he rubbed his forehead, trying to push it away. The ache, he was sure, was a reminder of the casualties the U.S. had suffered. Early estimates were in the range of 600,000 dead in LA and 200,000 in the D.C. area.

The phone on the conference table rang and Taylor picked it up. He listened a moment, said okay, and hung up.

Moments later General Corvan and Admiral Peters stepped in the room and closed the door behind them.

The president slumped onto a chair and motioned for the two to do the same.

Corvan grinned and said, "Mr. President, the satellite images have now confirmed it. Operation BlackSnow was a success. We've destroyed all of the Chinese ICBM complexes, their military bases, and at least thirty of their major cities. Beijing, Shanghai, Guangzhou, Tianjin, Wuhan, Shantou, and Shenzhen have all been wiped out. We won, Mr. President."

Taylor glanced at the TV screens, picked up the remote and turned off the sets. "Yes. But at a damn high cost. I didn't expect so many Americans would die."

Peters, his expression grim, said, "This is war, sir. There are always casualties. The important thing is the United States has won."

The president nodded and pushed aside his negative thoughts. "You're right, Admiral." He turned to Corvan. "What's next?"

"Sir," the general replied, "I recommend two things. First, we should launch a second nuclear strike. Hit China with our land-based ICBMs and bomber fleet. This would effectively destroy every city, every town and the entire infrastructure in China. The American people have suffered losses. They need revenge. After a second, massive strike, China will cease to exist."

Taylor rubbed his forehead. "What's the second thing you recommend?"

"Sir, I believe we should declare Martial Law in the U.S. It would allow Army and Marine units to be deployed to the affected areas. They can give assistance to local police and other emergency responders."

The president turned to Peters. "What do you think, Admiral?"

"I agree, sir."

Taylor nodded. "Okay, gentlemen. Let's go ahead with both. Corvan, write up an Executive Order declaring Martial Law. I'll sign it immediately."

"How long of a period do you want the Law to last, sir?" the general asked.

"Indefinitely."

"Yes, Mr. President."

Taylor leaned forward and faced the admiral. "Peters, go get the nuclear 'football'. I want to blow those Chinese bastards off the face of the map."

"Yes, sir."

2 Days after Zero Hour

Prison Complex
Guantanamo Bay Naval Base
Guantanamo, Cuba

Erica Blake knew something was wrong, she just didn't know what. The routine at the prison had changed dramatically.

After hearing loud sirens going off yesterday, she saw the two Marine guards leave the corridor. They hadn't returned. Meals had stopped coming, in spite of the shouting from the other prisoners on this wing.

Erica gripped the bars of her cell and stared at the clock on the corridor wall. The minutes crawled forward, time seeming to stand still. Her empty stomach growled, but she was more worried about the lack of drinking water. Her parched throat felt like sandpaper.

The Muslim prisoners who filled the other cells began a wailing, Arabic sounding chant and she picked up scraps of paper from the floor, wadded them up and stuck them in her ears. Then she went to her cot and sat down, trying to will away the empty time.

An hour later she heard a door clanging open and she sprang up, hoping to see the Marines in the corridor passing out water bottles.

But instead she saw Ensign Tulley striding toward her cell. Using a bulky metal key, the young officer opened her door and came in. She noticed that his usually crisply starched naval uniform looked wrinkled and slept-in today. His eyes were weary-looking, with dark circles under them.

"It's good to see you, Ensign," she said. "What the hell is going on?"

A frown creased his face and he shook his head slowly. "Things are bad, Miss Blake. You won't believe what's happened."

She shrugged. "I'm stuck in this shit-hole. Could they get worse?"

Tulley sat down on the end of the cot. "Yeah. They could, and they have."

Erica plopped down on the other side of the bunk. "Okay. Enough with the bullshit. Just tell me what's happened."

He nodded, but the grim expression stayed on his face. "Miss Blake…screw it – it's time I called you by your first name. Erica, there's been a nuclear war. China has been wiped out. And we've suffered terrible losses. Los Angeles and Washington, D.C. are partially gone."

"Gone? What do you mean gone?"

"Chinese missiles destroyed large parts of the downtown areas. The city centers were vaporized. Fires are rampant in the surrounding areas. The news reports estimate human casualties at close to a million."

"Oh, my God." The shock hit her like a punch in the gut and she was speechless a moment. "What happened, Tulley? Who started it?"

"President Taylor was on TV, said the Chinese were going to hit us first, so he ordered an attack."

She nodded, as a dawning realization hit her. "Maybe this was all part of the plan. Operation BlackSnow. The conspiracy."

Tulley rubbed the back of his neck. "That's what I think, too. It all fits together."

"Jesus Christ."

"There's more, Erica."

"More?"

"Martial law has been declared in the United States," he continued. "The Army and other military units are being deployed in the LA and D.C. areas to help restore order. Civil liberties are being suspended until the crisis is over." He paused, took a deep breath. "The stock market is in shambles – it was closed today, after a 4,000 point drop yesterday. It's going to take a long time for the country to come back."

"You said downtown D.C. is gone? What about Congress? The Senate and the House?"

"All of those buildings were destroyed. Congress was in session. The newscasts say most of the legislators are presumed dead. The president was traveling when the attack happened and now he's at an undisclosed location, along with most of the Cabinet."

She shook her head slowly. "God all mighty."

"There's more. All U.S. Navy units from Guantanamo are being re-deployed back to the States. I'll be leaving on a Navy cargo ship tomorrow. I've been re-assigned to Norfolk."

"What about me?"

He grimaced. "I'm working on that. I've talked to the military judge a couple of times already. I'm trying to get you out of here. After all that's happened, I believe your story. You're not guilty of anything."

She motioned with her hand. "What about the other prisoners here?"

He shook his head. "Don't know. From what I've heard, the Marine guards are leaving too. My guess is, the prisoners will stay locked up."

"With no food or water?"

"I'm afraid so. But I can't save them. You're my client. I'm going to do everything I can to legally get you out of here."

"Thank you, Tulley."

The grim expression was still on his face. "Don't thank me yet. It's going to be difficult. Damn difficult."

He turned around and left the cell, locking the door behind him.

A sinking feeling settled in the pit of her stomach.

***

Special Operations
Marine Corps Detachment
Training Facility, Building 14
Fort Bragg, North Carolina

Bobbie Garcia sat behind his desk in his office, staring down at the empty tumbler in front of him. Picking up the bottle of Jack Daniels, he poured himself his fourth drink and downed it one swallow. The harsh liquor burned his throat, but the light-headed buzz was beginning to dull the pain.

The image of Maria's face flashed in his mind and the pain came back with a vengeance. While he had been here at Ft. Bragg, she had been home in D.C. Minutes before the blast hit, he had been on the phone with her, talking happily about their future plans. Their apartment, along with thousands of others, had been obliterated.

General Corvan had called him later that day to give his condolences. The satellite images, the general said, confirmed that the area of D.C. where the apartment was located was now no more than a pile of burning rubble. Garcia requested a leave-of-absence to search for her body, but the general had denied it, saying the radiation levels were extremely high and would remain that way for a long time. And, Corvan added, Garcia was needed here at Ft. Bragg in case his services were required again.

Pouring himself another drink, Garcia sipped it, the depression and bitterness over Maria's death settling over him like a suffocating blanket, literally sucking the air out of his lungs.

His eyes misted over and he closed them, all while sipping the Jack Daniels.

Sometime later he heard a knock at his door. Putting the bottle and glass in a drawer, he said, "Come in."

Sergeant Thomas walked in. "Captain, I'm giving the team a refresher course on sniper techniques. Would you like to listen in, sir?"

Garcia shrugged, mumbled, "Naw. You go ahead, Sergeant."

"You okay, sir? You don't look well."

A bolt of anger shot through Garcia. "Get the hell out of my office!"

Thomas backed away, did a quick salute, turned and left the room.

Garcia put his head in his hands and wept uncontrollably.

3 Days after Zero Hour

Gimmlewald, Switzerland

Megan Lewis was in her suite at the inn, watching the international newscast on the large flat screen TV. The chaotic images of the two devastated American cities were being replayed, along with new commentary updating human casualties. The dead were now estimated to be over a million Americans. Estimates of the number of wounded varied wildly, depending on which source was quoted. But the number was large and growing every day, according to several news outlets. As more wounded survivors were found, they were being transported to hospitals in nearby states. The regional hospitals had been flooded with patients and could not take more.

The Army Corps of Engineers, FEMA, and Homeland Security personnel had been deployed quickly around the affected areas and were providing assistance to the local police and fire units. Massive fires were still burning, but authorities expected they would be contained in a few weeks' time.

Some things would take longer to solve. Radiation from the nuclear fallout, the newscaster said, would contaminate the devastated areas for years, much like Hiroshima and Nagasaki experienced after their bombing in World War II.

The newscast changed and a different anchor's face filled the screen. The new reporter was an exotic-looking Nordic woman, and Megan turned up the volume.

"…and although," the anchor said, "the downtown areas of Washington and Los Angeles were destroyed, the rest of the U.S. does not appear to be affected. There were no other missile strikes on any other American cities. We also have some further, good news to report. Our correspondents, who cover a wide variety of locations from around the world, are now confirming that Europe, Canada, Latin and South America were spared during the nuclear exchange. They are reporting no infrastructure damage, nor loss of life. There was also no damage to Africa, India, Australia, Russia and some parts of Asia. China, however, is another matter altogether." The anchor paused a moment, then continued. "Because of the colossal devastation to that country, no reporters have been able to go near it. But satellite images from at least ten different governments confirm that China has been completely destroyed. All their cities and towns, and even a large part of their countryside, have been reduced to piles of burning rubble. Nuclear radiation levels there are extremely high and the fallout has drifted over parts of Japan and South Korea. Those countries are advising their citizens to remain indoors as much as possible."

Megan turned off the set and began to pace the room. She had been watching the news for days, transfixed by the horrific images in the United States. The initial shock had given way to a deep sadness. Her friends, family, and colleagues, most of who lived in D.C., were most likely dead. And if not dead, then badly wounded or sick from the radiation.

As she paced, her own situation crossed her thoughts. She felt fairly safe here, hiding in this remote corner of Switzerland. If she kept a low profile in the small town, the odds were Taylor's men wouldn't find her. And since she had plenty of money, she could live here indefinitely. Mueller wasn't too far away, and his visits would be a welcome distraction.

Now that Martial law had been imposed, she mused, there was no way she could return to the U.S. Taylor would have her arrested with impunity. Better she remain here, biding her time.

Megan's thoughts raced, as she put aside the sickening images of the dead and wounded, and turned to the politics of it all. She tried to visualize what America would look like in a year or two. Although she was distressed about the senators and congressmen who had perished, the calculating side of her mind saw a bright side. She realized that most of her competitors for top government jobs were gone. *Maybe, just maybe*, she thought, *my presidential ambitions aren't dead.*

A small smile spread on her lips.

***

Cheyenne Mountain Complex
North American Aerospace Defense Command (NORAD)
Colorado Springs, Colorado

President Matt Taylor was sitting at the head of the long table, in the conference room overlooking the NORAD amphitheater. Also sitting around the table were the members of the Cabinet, several high-ranking military officers, and the acting heads of FEMA and the FBI. The former chiefs of those agencies had died during the attack.

Having just concluded a lengthy meeting discussing the federal government's response to the devastation in LA and D.C., Taylor said, "Thank you, ladies and gentlemen. I commend you on all your efforts during this time of national crisis. That will be all for today. We'll reconvene at the same time tomorrow." He paused and noticed General Corvan raising a hand. "Yes, General?"

"I need a word with you, sir, after the meeting."

"Of course."

The group in the room stood and filed out, leaving the two men alone in the conference room.

Taylor rubbed his jaw. "Considering everything that's happened, things are going as well as can be expected. Don't you agree, General?"

"Yes, sir, I do."

"The American people are pulling together. It reminds me of the days after September 11th, once the initial shock wore off."

"Yes, Mr. President."

"We've got a long road to recovery, but I believe that in time, we as a country will be better off." Taylor paused, went quiet a moment as he mulled over the events of the last week. "General, did I ever tell you why I named the operation BlackSnow?"

"No, sir, you never did. Although I did wonder about it."

The president smiled. "Because I knew that after we blew up the Chinese, the black and gray nuclear ash over that country would mix with falling snow – hence black snow."

Corvan nodded. "Very true."

Taylor leaned forward in his seat. "You said you needed to talk to me about something?"

"Yes, sir. Early this morning I got a call from Master Sergeant Thomas."

"Refresh my memory. Who is that?"

"Sir, that's Captain Garcia's 2nd in command."

"Of course, I remember now."

"Mr. President, Thomas is very concerned. Garcia's wife was killed in D.C. and since then, the captain has been acting...irrationally. He's been drinking heavily on the job, and has stopped communicating with the team. Thomas told me Garcia is distraught and very bitter."

"That doesn't sound good. Not good at all. Garcia knows a lot about BlackSnow. If he cracks from the stress, no telling what would happen."

"I agree, sir. The captain is an excellent operative. But, frankly, I'm worried."

"What do you recommend?"

"Sir, we need to cut him loose."

Taylor mulled this over a moment. "I agree." He stood up, faced the glass wall and watched the activity in the amphitheater below. "Take care of it. I don't want to know the details."

***

Prison Complex
Guantanamo Bay Naval Base
Guantanamo, Cuba

Erica Blake heard the corridor door creak open and she sprang to her feet. She had been lying on her cot for hours, trying to will away her thirst and hunger.

Seeing Ensign Tulley approach her cell, she watched as he unlocked the door and came in. The ensign was wearing camouflage fatigues today, the white naval uniform gone. She also noticed he was wearing a sidearm and was carrying a duffel bag.

But the frown he had on his face yesterday was still there.

"Sorry I couldn't come sooner," Tulley said. "But things are getting crazy out there."

"What's happening?"

"We're pulling out today. The base is a madhouse, trying to get everything ready to go."

"What about me, Tulley?"

"I'm sorry, Erica. I couldn't get the judge to change his mind. Since they've decided to leave the other prisoners here, he didn't want to make an exception."

"So I'm screwed."

He shook his head. "Maybe, maybe not. I can't get you out of here legally. But there is another way, if you want to take the chance."

"What are you talking about?"

"There's a freighter leaving Guantanamo tomorrow. They're taking some of the supplies and fuel from the base to the Panama Canal Zone. The cargo ship is a private vessel, but I've talked to the captain. He owes me a favor, and he's willing to take you on board. He would drop you off before they reach the Zone. After that, you'd be on your own."

A glimmer of hope filled her. "That sounds a hell of a lot better than dying in here."

"Yeah. That's what I thought too. There are a few logistical problems, but I think we can overcome them."

"Like what?"

"I've got to get you off this base and to the docks, without getting shot."

She chuckled. "No problem."

"I wish I had your confidence. Lucky for us, with so many people leaving today, the place is going insane. I think I can sneak you out."

She nodded. "First things first. Do you have any water? I'm dying of thirst."

He put the duffel bag on the floor and unzipped it. He rummaged around, pulled out two water bottles, offered them to her.

Grabbing one, she unscrewed the top and gulped the contents. She coughed, then took the second bottle and drained it in seconds.

"That's better," she said, wiping her mouth with her hand.

"I've got a few more things for you." He pulled out a green fatigue uniform and handed it to her. "The size is too big," he said, "but it'll have to do." He also grabbed a green cap from the bag. "Pull your hair up and put this on too."

Erica unzipped her baggy orange jumpsuit and let it fall to the floor. The young officer blushed at seeing her in her underwear, but she ignored his reaction and began to put on the uniform and cap.

The fatigues were at least three sizes too big and he took off his belt and handed it to her. "Take this. Cinch the belt tight and you should be okay."

"Thanks, Tulley."

He reached inside the bag again, pulled out two more items. One was a small, chrome plated revolver, probably a .32 caliber. The other item was a wad of cash.

"Here," he said, "you'll need this."

She took them and put them in her pockets. Giving him a quizzical look, she asked, "Why are you doing all this? You're taking a hell of chance."

He shook his head slowly. "I believe your story. I don't think you're guilty. I can't let you die here." He paused, gave her a small grin. "Maybe, after you get settled, wherever that is, you can pay back the money. I don't make a hell of a lot as an Ensign."

She grinned back, stuck out her hand. "Don't worry, if I make it out alive, I'll pay you back. With interest." They shook hands.

"Okay," he said, "let's go. Follow behind me and don't say a word. I've got a Humvee parked outside."

She nodded, and he turned and walked out to the corridor, with Erica right behind. The other prisoners in the wing, seeing her leave, began to yell loudly in Arabic.

There were no guards in the hallway and Tulley and Erica passed through a maze of poorly-lit, grimy corridors until they finally reached the main hallway of the prison. This area was also deserted of Marine guards.

Using a set of metal keys, Tulley unlocked a series of barred doors. A few minutes later they were outside the antiquated prison building.

The sunlight was blindingly bright outside, making Erica squint.

Glancing around the parking area in front of the prison building, Erica saw rows of Humvees and trucks being loaded feverishly. There were Navy seamen and Marines everywhere, but they all seemed absorbed with the hectic work.

The ensign locked the heavy prison door behind him and pointed to a Humvee parked next to the building. "I'll open the storage panel in the cargo area of the jeep," he said. "It'll be a tight fit for you, but we have no choice. And whatever you do, stay quiet. We still have to drive through the main security checkpoint at the front gate of the prison complex. Hopefully, since I'm an officer, they won't inspect the Humvee too closely." He paused and frowned. "But if they do, we're both screwed."

Tulley walked to the rear of the Humvee, with Erica right behind. The area was under an overhead canopy that extended from the building and was fairly secluded from the rest of the parking lot. The ensign opened the vehicle's cargo door, then opened the lid to the storage bin. She crawled inside the small space, fitting her body around tools in the bin. He closed the lid shut and everything went dark.

Panicking for a second from a feeling of being trapped, she slowed her breathing and forced herself to relax.

The Humvee's engine growled to life and she felt the vehicle pull away.

A minute later it slowed down, then stopped. Hearing voices, she tried to make out what they were saying, but they were too muffled.

Hearing the opening and slamming of the vehicle's multiple doors, she squeezed her hand into her pocket and pried out the revolver. If they opened the storage bin lid, she was toast. But she wasn't going to go down without a fight.

Instead of seeing the lid open, she heard the Humvee start up again and move away.

The vehicle picked up speed, swinging around curves of a bumpy, poorly-maintained road.

Sometime later the Humvee slowed and came to a stop. She heard loud voices in what sounded like Spanish so she tightened her grip on the revolver.

4 Days after Zero Hour

Special Operations
Marine Corps Detachment
Training Facility, Building 14
Fort Bragg, North Carolina

Bobbie Garcia was in his office, watching the latest news on his computer. He had been monitoring the news clips for hours, looking for any hopeful signs. But there were none. The images of D.C. were depressingly the same – burning rubble, towering plumes of black smoke and collapsed twisted metal. Deep down, he knew Maria was dead.

But he kept at it, feeling that if he kept watching, she would by some miracle come back to him.

Just then there was a knock on his door. He looked up briefly, ignored it.

There was a second, louder knock and the door opened. Sergeant Thomas came in the room and closed the door behind him.

"I told you, Sergeant. I don't want to be interrupted. Now, get out of here."

Thomas locked the door and said, "I'm sorry, Captain. I have orders."

Garcia grimaced. "I'm giving you a direct order. Get the hell out of here!"

"Sorry, sir." Thomas drew a Walther P99 semi-automatic from the back of his waistband. The captain noticed the pistol had a suppressor attached to the barrel.

Pointing the gun at Garcia's chest, Thomas said, "The general called me. Gave me a direct order. I'm really sorry about this, Captain. We've known each other a long time and I admire you. But I follow orders."

Garcia's jaw dropped. "What's going on here? What in God's name are you saying?"

"No more talking. It's over for you, sir."

Garcia's mind raced, the depression that had enveloped him for days suddenly lifting. "Wait a second. Since you're going to kill me, don't I least get a final request?"

A frown crossed Thomas's face, but a moment later he nodded. "Okay. That's fair. What is it?"

Garcia pointed to his laptop. "I've got encrypted files in there, with passwords for my off-shore bank accounts. I'll show them to you. You can have all the money. It's not like I'll need it. I just have one favor to ask. I want you to have a church service performed for Maria. She was Roman Catholic and I know she would have wanted that."

"You'd give me the passwords for such a simple thing?" Thomas said, eagerness in his voice. "You can count on me. I'll take care of it."

"Thank you, Sergeant. That means a lot to me. Let me pull up the files now."

Thomas lowered the gun and Garcia began to tap on the laptop's keyboard.

A second later the captain grabbed the computer with both hands and threw it full-force at the other man. The laptop hit Thomas in the face and the sergeant flinched back and yelled in pain. As the pistol clattered to the floor, Garcia lunged out of his chair and flew into the other man, knocking him off his feet.

The two grappled, punching wildly at each other while trying to reach for the gun.

Garcia kicked Thomas in the groin and the man howled in pain. Seizing the opportunity, the captain grabbed the gun, pointed and fired three shots in rapid succession. The pistol made a muted clapping sound and the sergeant crumpled and went quiet.

Garcia checked Thomas for a pulse, found none and picked up the laptop from the floor. Stuffing the computer into his go-bag, he quickly glanced around the small office. Realizing everything he would need was in the bag, he stuck the pistol in his waistband.

Racing out of the office, he knew he had to get out of there fast.

Instead of being the hunter, he had now become the hunted.

***

Aboard the ocean freighter Vizcaya
Heading west on the Caribbean Sea

Erica Blake, still wearing the fatigue uniform, stood on the top deck of the huge freighter. She leaned on the railing and stared at the choppy seas. The cargo ship had left the port in Guantanamo early that morning, after the crew had finished loading the vessel. On the massive, lower deck of the ship, hundreds of 40 foot long cargo containers were stacked six and seven high.

The ship's captain, a swarthy man, had shown her to a tiny berth yesterday, pointed out the ship's mess hall, and then left her alone. It was clear from his courteous demeanor that she was a welcome guest. No doubt he owed Tulley a big favor.

As she watched the ship cut through the angry, blue water, her thoughts turned to the future. Besides the gun and the wad of cash, she had nothing. But, she mused, she was still better off than the rest of the prisoners back at Gitmo.

Two Years Later

The President's Office
Federal Building
Denver, Colorado
(Provisional Capital of the United States)

President Matt Taylor was proud of himself. Looking at his reflection in the mirror, he admired the fit and trim man he had become. Thanks to a strict exercise regime and a low-fat diet, he had shed sixty pounds. It also helped that he hadn't had liquor in a year.

He closed the center button of his Armani blue suit, and adjusted his red tie. The Presidential election was being held in six months, and he was ready. Practicing a sincere smile, he held it a moment. *Perfect*, he thought.

Glancing around his modest office, which was Spartan compared to the Oval Office in D.C., he knew the situation was temporary. After the election, he would commission the construction of a new White House, here in Denver. A new congressional Capitol building would come next.

The clock on the wall showed 9:00 a.m. and he turned and left the room. Followed by the two Secret Service agents who were posted in the corridor, he made his way to the Situation Room, which was located at the end of the long hallway.

Taylor stepped in the large conference room and the assembled Cabinet members rose to their feet.

Smiling, he said, "Have a seat, ladies and gentlemen." He took the chair at the head of the table and looked at the assembled group as they sat down.

His Chief of Staff, General Corvan was to his right, while Admiral Peters, Chairman of the Joint Chiefs, was to his left. The other Cabinet members had been with him since he assumed the presidency, except for the replacements made necessary by the attack on Washington. The new people he had chosen were loyal friends and participants in the still-secret Operation BlackSnow.

Taylor leaned forward in his chair. "As I mentioned during our meeting yesterday, I have asked Treasury Secretary Longstreet to speak with us today, and give us an update on the country's economic status. He has coordinated with various government agencies to give us this report." He turned to the secretary. "Mike, why don't you begin?"

"Of course, Mr. President," Mike Longstreet replied, as he turned on the Power Point projector that sat on the table. The projector flickered to life and a map of the United States was projected on the far wall.

"As you know," Longstreet began, "after the nuclear missile strike on Los Angeles and Washington D.C., the federal and state governments of the United States focused a massive relief effort to the devastated areas. FEMA, along with the military, evacuated the hundreds of thousands of wounded. They also resettled the nearby populations, those areas affected by nuclear fallout, to other states. Decontamination of the fallout areas continues to this day. But I'm pleased to report that the radiation levels have dropped to such a degree, that debris removal and reconstruction is taking place at a much faster pace than we anticipated. This activity has been sped up by the rescinding of Martial law, which as you know, took place six months ago."

The images on the wall shifted to scenes of bulldozers and cranes clearing concrete debris and twisted metal. Those scenes were replaced by images of concrete trucks pouring foundations and workers laying utility pipes.

Taylor held up a hand. "And just to add, I have conferred with the appropriate agencies, and they expect that within five years, parts of LA and D.C. will be resettled."

The assembled group began to clap and Longstreet waited for that to subside.

"Now," the secretary continued, "I'd like to turn to financial issues. As I'm sure you're aware, before the heinous Chinese attack on our two cities, that country held a majority of the U.S. national debt. Over the previous ten years, China had been buying a majority of our Treasury bonds."

Longstreet paused a moment, then continued. "One very beneficial result of the war is that since the country of China no longer exists, that massive debt has also ceased to exist. For all practical purposes, the United States is debt free."

The members of the Cabinet clapped again, this time more loudly.

"Now that we are debt-free," Longstreet added, "we no longer have to pay interest on the debt. This has freed up a massive amount of capital and helped our economy grow significantly."

The images changed to a graph of the U.S.'s Gross Domestic Product.

"As you can see on this graph, our GDP has tripled since two years ago." The secretary paused and smiled. "Also, we have seen tremendous growth in the American manufacturing sector. Up until the war, China was the world's largest manufacturer. Since then, our industrial production has quadrupled – all of our industries have benefited and grown – automobiles, electronics, aviation, furniture, clothing, you name it. That has contributed to achieving our current national employment level, which, for all intents and purposes, is full employment. It is my estimate, and that of many economists, that the U.S., in a few short years, will once again be the world's sole superpower."

There was more clapping, this time louder, and Taylor waited until it died down. "Thank you, Mike, for that excellent analysis." The president paused, looked around the room. "I think you will agree that the United States is definitely headed in the right direction."

The Cabinet clapped again and the president smiled widely. "Just make sure you vote for me in the upcoming election," he added, chuckling.

There was a roar of approval from the group, and Taylor said, "That will be all for today, ladies and gentlemen. We'll reconvene tomorrow, at the same time."

The president stood and the Cabinet members got up also. As they filed out of the room, Taylor shook hands with each of them.

The president and General Corvan stayed behind, and when they were alone, Taylor asked, "How do you think it went?"

"Excellent, Mr. President."

"I thought so, too. All the economic numbers are good. The country is doing well. By the way, I think I'll keep Secretary Longstreet after the election – he doesn't seem so boring now."

"Yes, sir."

Taylor turned and gazed out the broad windows of the room, which overlooked downtown Denver. It was a bright, sunny day, with almost no clouds. "Did you get the Gallup poll numbers, Corvan?"

"Yes, sir. The latest polls show you're leading in the presidential race by a wide margin. You're twenty points ahead of the closest candidate, the businessman from Atlanta."

Taylor turned back to the general. "Good news. Very good news."

Corvan smiled. "I always knew BlackSnow would work. The country is better off, and so are you."

The president nodded. "I love it when a plan comes together."

***

Monterrey, Mexico

Bobbie Garcia walked through the kitchen and into the garage of his house, a home he had rented under an assumed name. The garage, much like the rest of the house, was cramped. The room was just big enough to fit his Jeep, leaving a small area in front of the vehicle for a storage cabinet.

It was brutally hot in the closed garage and Garcia wiped the sweat from his forehead. The garage smelled of oil and mildew, but he had spent so much time in the place that he was used to it.

Unlocking the storage cabinet, he opened its doors and turned on the bare light bulb that hung overhead. Inside the narrow closet was a wooden table covered with an olive-green tarp. He pulled off the tarp and let it drop to the floor.

A high-powered snipers rifle sat on the table, a bi-pod supporting the barrel. He caressed the precision scope and the trigger mechanism. Then he ran a hand over the barrel, feeling the latent power of the lethal weapon.

Ever since Martial Law had been lifted in the United States, he had been planning for this very moment. The time when he would slip back into America and seek revenge. A fugitive for two years, Garcia had hid out in this northern Mexican city, waiting for the right time. It had taken him months to assemble the customized rifle and now it was ready.

He would get his revenge. For Maria's death and for the attempt on his own life. Of that he was certain. Not caring if he lived or died, he only cared about one thing. To make sure General Corvan and President Taylor paid. Paid with their lives.

***

Gimmlewald, Switzerland

Megan Lewis jogged on the park's trail, as it wound around the edge of the lake. The air felt fresh and cool – Switzerland's short summer was giving way to sunny, brisk days and cold nights.

It was midday, but only a few people were in the park. Mostly college-age youths and a few middle-aged people like herself, all wearing jogging clothes.

Megan stopped to catch her breath, spotted a nearby bench and walked over. Sitting down, her thoughts turned to her plan for today. She had been contemplating it for months and realized the time had come. She couldn't wait any longer.

Pulling her cell phone from a pocket, she dialed a familiar number. It rang a minute, then Mueller's voice came on the line.

"Henry, I'm glad I caught you."

"Great to hear from you," he replied, his voice warm. "I was just leaving for a meeting with the bank's other board members. But I always have time for you."

"That's sweet, Henry. Listen, I've given a lot of thought to the plan I've been discussing with you."

"I see," he said. "What did you decide?"

"I'm going ahead with it."

"Are you sure, Megan? It would be dangerous for you."

"My mind is made up. I'm going to run for the Presidency of the United States."

"I had a feeling you would. You're a beautiful, but stubborn woman. I knew I wouldn't be able to talk you out of it."

"I have to do it, Henry. My country needs me."

"I understand. As I told you before, I and my bank will financially support your candidacy. I will set up a special bank account, with extensive funds. We'll match and surpass whatever amount of money Taylor raises."

"That's good to hear. I really appreciate it."

"I'm still worried about your safety. How will you deal with that?"

"I've thought it all through, Henry. I'll hold a press conference in Switzerland, announcing my candidacy for president. Once I do that, it'll be difficult for Taylor to send his goons after me. Plus, I plan to hire a large group of bodyguards."

"I agree with your thinking."

"Henry, can you set up the press conference in Zurich? And invite the press from around the world?"

"Of course. I'll start working on that today. I have a lot of contacts. I'll put that to good use."

"Excellent. Thank you."

"How soon before you leave for the States, Megan?"

"After the press conference and after I retain the bodyguards."

"I can help you with that too."

"Good. I estimate I'll leave for the U.S. in a matter of days. The election is in six months. I need to start campaigning immediately."

"I will miss you."

"I'll miss you too, Henry. Our…relationship…has been very special. But don't worry, I'll come back and visit."

"That is good to hear. I'll call you later with information on the press conference."

"Thank you, Henry."

She turned off the phone and put it back in her pocket. Then she gazed out over the lake and watched as a noisy flock of birds flew over the water.

Megan felt good, now that she'd made the decision.

There were risks ahead, but also the potential for the ultimate reward. Visualizing winning the election, she saw herself being sworn in as president. *President Lewis. It sounds great. Damn great.*

A broad smile crossed her face.

Feeling invigorated, she continued her jog.

***

Recoleta Park
Buenos Aires, Argentina

Erica Blake walked through the large, crowd-filled park, occasionally stopping to browse the numerous vendor carts that dotted the area. Some of the vendors sold food and the aroma of spicy meats and strong coffee filled the air.

It was Saturday and many families were out, strolling along the park's paths or picnicking on the lush green lawns. Music was everywhere – coming from street musicians, from an amateur band on the stage, and from radios people carried.

But the party-like atmosphere did nothing to brighten Erica's mood. She had been depressed for months, the mental wear of being a fugitive had taken its toll.

She had assumed a new identity and altered her appearance, dying her hair blonde and cutting it short, and donning wire-frame eyeglasses. But she never felt safe, always felt like they were just one step behind her. Nightmares of U.S. government goons breaking down her apartment door while she slept haunted her.

Passing a newsstand, she browsed the selection of newspapers. Picking up a copy of *La Nacion*, Buenos Aires largest daily, she spotted a small café at the corner and headed in that direction.

Sitting at one of the outside tables, she ordered coffee and spread the newspaper in front of her. Most of the news was about Argentina's sour economy, but one article below the fold peaked her interest.

Economia de los Estados Unidos creciendo rapidamente, the headline read. U.S. Economy Booming. After two years in her adopted country, she had become fluent in Spanish.

Sipping coffee, she read through the article, which described the robust economic recovery the U.S. had experienced since the Chinese-American war. The article also mentioned the upcoming American presidential election. President Taylor was a candidate, and based on current polls, his chances for re-election were very good.

As she read Taylor's name, a surge of anger filled her. The despicable man had been responsible for Steve's death. Even after all this time, the visceral hatred she had for the president had not diminished. And now it appeared he would be president for the next four years.

She grimaced, then shook her head slowly, knowing she had to do something, anything, to prevent that from happening.

Pushing aside the newspaper, Erica made a snap decision. She would go back to the U.S., regardless of the risk. Steve's death would be avenged. She didn't know how she would do it, or even if she had a chance of success. But she would do everything in her power to stop Taylor from being elected. She owed Steve that much.

A feeling of relief and hope filled her. Now she had a goal.

Taking a last sip of the coffee, she paid her bill and began strolling through the park again.

The day looked brighter as she took in the local colors, the sounds and the smells, knowing it would be her last visit to the park.

END

***

About the author

Lee Gimenez is the award-winning author of 15 novels, including his highly-acclaimed J.T. Ryan series. His novel FIREBALL, a J.T. Ryan Thriller, was a Finalist for the 2019 Author Academy Award. Many of his books were Featured Novels of the International Thriller Writers Association, among them CROSSFIRE, FIREBALL, The MEDIA MURDERS, FBI CODE RED, SKYFLASH, KILLING WEST, and The WASHINGTON ULTIMATUM. Lee is a multi-year nominee for the Georgia Author of the Year Award, and was a Finalist in the prestigious Terry Kay Prize for Fiction. Lee's books are available at Amazon and many other bookstores in the U.S. and Internationally.

For more information about him, please visit his website at: www.LeeGimenez.com. There you can sign up for his free newsletter. You can contact Lee at his email address: LG727@MSN.com. You can also join him on Facebook, LinkedIn, and Goodreads.

***

Novels by Lee Gimenez

Blacksnow Zero
The Sigma Conspiracy
Crossfire
Fireball
FBI Code Red
The Media Murders
Skyflash
Killing West
The Washington Ultimatum
The Nanotech Murders
Death on Zanath
Virtual Thoughtstream
Azul 7
Terralus 4
The Tomorrow Solution

CROSSFIRE, a J.T. Ryan Thriller
is available at Amazon and many other bookstores in the
U.S. and Internationally.
In paperback, Kindle, and all other ebook versions.

The SIGMA CONSPIRACY, a J.T. Ryan Thriller
is available at Amazon and many other bookstores in the
U.S. and Internationally.
In paperback, Kindle, and all other ebook versions.

FIREBALL, a J.T. Ryan Thriller
is available at Amazon and many other bookstores in the
U.S. and Internationally.
In paperback, Kindle, and all other ebook versions.

FBI CODE RED, a J.T. Ryan Thriller
is available at Amazon and many other bookstores in the
U.S. and Internationally.
In paperback, Kindle, and all other ebook versions.

THE MEDIA MURDERS, a J.T. Ryan Thriller
is available at Amazon and many other bookstores in the
U.S. and Internationally.
In paperback, Kindle, and all other ebook versions.

SKYFLASH, a **J.T.** Ryan Thriller
is available at Amazon and many other bookstores in the
U.S. and Internationally.
In paperback, Kindle, and all other ebook versions.

KILLING WEST, a Rachel West Thriller
is available at Amazon and many other bookstores in the
U.S. and Internationally.
In paperback, Kindle, and all other ebook versions.

THE WASHINGTON ULTIMATUM,
a J.T. Ryan Thriller
is available at Amazon and many other bookstores in the U.S. and Internationally. In paperback, Kindle, and all other ebook versions.

Lee Gimenez's other novels, including

- **Blacksnow Zero**
- **The Nanotech Murders**
- **Death on Zanath**
- **Virtual Thoughtstream**
- **Azul 7**
- **Terralus 4**
- **The Tomorrow Solution**

are all available at Amazon and many other bookstores in the U.S. and Internationally.

Here's an excerpt from Lee Gimenez's award-winning novel, CROSSFIRE:

CROSSFIRE

a J.T. Ryan Thriller

A Novel

By

Lee Gimenez

Face-Look is the world's largest social media company. When that company's president is brutally murdered, the FBI investigates. As more people are killed, former Special Forces soldier John (J.T.) Ryan and FBI Assistant Director Erin Welch are assigned to the case. Ryan and Erin delve into the mystery and begin to uncover a vast criminal conspiracy behind the murders. A conspiracy involving not just Face-Look, but also the world's other social media and high-tech corporations. As more people are murdered, Ryan pursues the secret cabal of criminals across the USA, Japan, and Europe. The dangerous and harrowing journey takes him from the mansions of the super-rich to the gritty back streets of the criminal underworld. There he learns the ultimate goal of the secret group, known only as Viper. A goal so explosive it will cause the collapse of the American economy. Can John Ryan and Erin Welch capture the murderous criminals before they themselves are killed?

Chapter 1

Atlanta, Georgia

Feeling energized by the death that was about to happen, the sniper peered through his rifle's scope and adjusted the crosshairs. Although his target was in an office building a half-mile away, the custom-made scope allowed him to see clearly into the man's office on the tenth floor. The target, a tall, heavyset man was at his desk reading a report.

Using his laser finder and a small computer, the sniper made a few final adjustments to account for wind speed and direction. Then he slowed his breathing and slid his finger past the trigger guard until it rested on the trigger itself. He was using a Barrett M107, a high-precision, long-range rifle that was the weapon of choice for those in his profession.

He slowed his breathing even more, took another moment to zero in on the target, and gently pulled the trigger. The suppressed rifle coughed. A split-second later the armor-piercing round cracked the bullet-resistant window a half mile away.

The target's head exploded.

Then his lifeless body slumped forward on his desk and blood began to pool under his head.

Chapter 2

St. Croix
The U.S. Virgin Islands
the Caribbean

It was a sunny, cloudless sky, the temperature in the mid-seventies. The sky was a deep azure blue and the shoreline was crystal clear surf.

Another perfect day in paradise, John (J.T.) Ryan thought, as he exited the cottage and began walking toward the secluded beach. He noticed Rachel was already there, lounging on a chaise, sipping a drink. Ryan had booked the cottage for a week; the bungalow was part of a resort comprised of golf courses, tennis courts, several pools, restaurants, and miles-long beaches of sparkling sand.

Ryan almost reached the beach when his cell phone vibrated in his swim trunk pocket. Pulling it out, he answered the call.

"Ryan here."

"It's Erin," he heard the woman say.

"Erin," he replied with a chuckle. "My favorite ADIC." Erin was the Assistant Director in charge of the FBI's Atlanta office.

Erin sighed, used to his attempts at humor "How many ADICs do you know, J.T.?"

"Besides you? None."

"Then I guess the fact I'm your favorite isn't much of a compliment."

Ryan laughed. "You got me there. Why are you calling?"

"I'm working on a new case and I need your help."

Ryan was a former Special Forces soldier turned private investigator who did security work for law-enforcement agencies.

"My usual fee?" he asked.

There was no response and Ryan could visualize the FBI woman frowning. Finally she said, "Yes. Your usual fee. High as they are."

The PI grinned. "I'm worth it. Otherwise you wouldn't hire me."

"All right, smartass. Enough banter."

"What's the case about, Erin?"

"A high-profile murder. It happened yesterday. Here in Atlanta."

"Who's the DB?"

"The president of Face-Look. The big social media company located here in the city."

Ryan let out a low whistle. "That is high-profile. How was he killed?"

"He was assassinated. From what we've been able to piece together, he was shot by a sniper using a high-powered rifle."

"Any clues?"

"None so far, J.T. That's why I need you on this case. Your unorthodox methods are good at ferreting out information."

"Okay, I'll take the job. But I just got to St. Croix. I'm on vacation. I'll be back in Atlanta in a week."

"I need you here now," Erin said, her voice hard.

Ryan gazed toward the beach and saw Rachel waving at him. She looked delectable in her red bikini.

"No can do," he replied. "Like I said, I'm on vacation. I'll see you in a week."

"That's not good enough."

"Listen, Erin. I like working for you. And the FBI cases you've given me are some of the best work I've done as a PI. But Rachel and I have postponed this vacation too many times."

"I'm not going to change your mind, am I?," she said, a resigned tone in her voice.

"I'm afraid not. But don't worry, I'll be back next week. I'll come to your office the day I get back, okay?"

"All right, J.T."

He hung up the phone and slipped it in the pocket of his swim trunks. Then he strode the short distance to the beach, his bare feet sinking into the warm sand. He sat on a lounge chair next to Rachel's.

She rested her drink on a side table. "Who was that on the phone?"

"Erin from the FBI."

Rachel gave him a worried glance. "Does that mean ...."

"No, beautiful. I told Erin I wasn't going to cancel my vacation." He smiled. "I'll work on the case when I get back."

Her expression brightened and she returned the smile. "That's a relief." She caressed his arm and her smile turned mischievous. "We've got a lot of catching up to do, you and me."

Ryan gave her a long look, taking in her intoxicating beauty. She was a tall, lean, and curvaceous woman in her mid-thirties. With long blonde hair, sparkling blue eyes, and classic good looks, she resembled a model. Besides her looks, she also had a razor-sharp mind and a vivacious wit.

Ryan pointed toward her red bikini, which did little to conceal her curves. "Since you're a CIA operative, you must be working undercover. But looking at your swimsuit, you're barely undercover."

Rachel laughed. "You play your cards right and you may get to see a lot more."

He grinned and they held hands. Then they both looked out toward the rolling surf a few feet away. Ryan felt more at ease and content than he had in a long time.

The warm sun and light breeze lulled him into sleep.

He awoke with a start sometime later and heard the clatter of machinery in the distance. Looking around the secluded beach, he saw nothing except palm trees, rolling surf, and the white sandy beach.

As the sound grew louder, he got up from the lounge chair and shielded his eyes from the bright sun to get a better look.

"What is it?" Rachel asked. "What's that noise?"

Then he spotted it, a black helicopter flying low toward their location. He pointed. "Chopper. Could be military."

Rachel stood next to him as they watched the helicopter land on the relatively flat beach. The rotor wash sprayed sand in all directions.

As the craft powered down, Ryan noticed there were no markings on the chopper, which was a Sikorsky Black Hawk. Its bay door opened and three men climbed out and began trudging towards them, their boots sinking into the sand. All three were wearing U.S. Army fatigues, with Military Police markings on their uniforms. The PI noticed they also had holstered sidearms.

When they were a few feet away, one of the men approached Ryan. "I'm Lieutenant Holder," he said. "Are you John Taylor Ryan?"

"Yes. I'm J.T. Ryan. What's this about?"

"You need to come with us, sir."

"You haven't answered my question, Lieutenant. What's this about?"

"Sir, that will all be explained later. It's a matter of national security. You just need to come with us."

"I'm not going anywhere until I get some answers."

Ryan noticed the MP's hands moved and rested on the butts of their holstered pistols.

"We can do this the easy way," the lieutenant said, "or the hard way. It's totally up to you, sir."

Ryan glared at him, then glanced at Rachel who looked bewildered.

"This is not a request," the lieutenant added. "It's an order."

Angry and confused, Ryan balled his fists.

"You better go," Rachel said in a quiet voice. "You have no choice, J.T."

The PI took a deep breath and let it out slowly. "All right, damn it."

The MPs escorted him to the helicopter and they climbed inside.

The rotor blades spooled faster and the engines whined to a loud roar. The chopper lifted off and seconds later receded into the horizon.

Chapter 3

The Pentagon
U.S. Department of Defense
Washington, D.C.

After a five hour flight from St. Croix to D.C. on a military transport jet, J.T. Ryan had been escorted to the small conference room he was in now.

The three MPs who had put him in the helicopter were still with him, posted outside the conference room. On the flight he had been given food and a change of clothes, but none of his questions had been answered.

Ten minutes later the door to the conference room opened and an Army officer wearing his Class A blue uniform stepped inside. Closing the door behind him, he extended his hand to Ryan. "I'm General Keating."

As they shook hands, Keating said, "Please have a seat, Mr. Ryan."

They sat across from each other at the conference table and Ryan said, "Am I under arrest?"

The general gave him a wry smile. "Of course not." The man was tall and wiry, with close-cropped sandy hair, and looked to be in his mid-fifties. He was a brigadier, a one-star general, and from his military ribbons Ryan knew the man had been posted to a long list of duty stations.

"I'm sorry about the abrupt flight," Keating said. "But in light of recent events, we needed to brief you as soon as possible."

Ryan nodded, relieved he wasn't under arrest, but still confused why he was there. "In that case, General, I'd appreciate an explanation. The MP said it was a matter of national security?"

"That's correct, Ryan. It is." The man leaned forward in his chair. "Everything I'm going to tell you is classified Top Secret. Is that understood?"

"Yes, General."

"All right. Yesterday the president of Face-Look was murdered. Have you heard about this?"

"Actually yes. The FBI has already hired me to work on that, when I get back to Atlanta."

Keating gave him a hard look. "Have they now? Well, our investigation takes priority over that."

Ryan waved a hand in the air as if to encompass the whole room. "What's the Pentagon's interest in this murder?"

"I'll get to that in a moment. Are you familiar with the DIA?"

The PI nodded. "The Defense Intelligence Agency? Sure. The DIA is the military's version of the CIA."

"That's correct. I'm with the DIA. In fact, I'm second in command. And I'm heading up the Face-Look investigation."

"Sir, why is the DIA so interested in this? I would think the FBI would be the best organization to handle a case involving a private company."

"Under normal circumstances you would be correct, Ryan. But we've had Face-Look on our radar for quite some time. We've been monitoring them for years. Do you know much about them?"

"I know they're a large social media company."

Keating nodded. "Not just large, but the biggest. They're larger than Twitter, or Instagram, or Facebook."

"Okay, I'm with you so far. But I still don't see the military's interest."

"Face-Look," the general continued, "has a worldwide audience of 2.2 billion people. And all of these people give up much of their privacy when they join social media networks. They share personal details, photos, posts, friends lists, family names, etc. They take polls online, read news items, find products to buy, and message friends. And all of this vast amount of information is kept in Face-Look's computer databanks for practically forever."

"Face-Look," the general added, "has become the largest intelligence gathering organization in the world."

"I didn't realize how widespread and intrusive they were," Ryan said. "I'm not into social media very much myself. I'm too busy with my PI work."

Keating steepled his hands in front of him. "Normally this intelligence gathering is benign. They store the information about people and it is kept private. But we at the DIA have become concerned that if all of this data falls into the wrong hands, the results could be catastrophic. The potential for blackmail, corruption, and criminal activity is vast."

The general paused as Ryan realized the ominous implications of what the man had just said.

"And now that Face-Look's president has been murdered," Keating continued, "we've decided to become directly involved."

"I understand, sir. But why do you need me, General? I'm sure you have military people who can carry out the investigation."

"That's true. We do. But having you investigate this case has several advantages. First, you're based in Atlanta, where Face-Look's headquarters is located. So you know the area well. Second, we need a civilian face to head this up. The DIA is a secretive organization – we don't want it known that we're interested. And the third reason is obvious – you're former military – you're familiar with our ways."

Ryan nodded. "I can appreciate that, sir. But I've already committed to working on this for the FBI. I can't walk away from that."

Keating waved that away. "You can still keep them in the loop. As long as you understand you work for the DIA. We take priority."

"I don't know about this, General. My whole business as a PI is based on the work I do for the FBI, Homeland Security, and other law-enforcement agencies. I don't want to jeopardize that."

Keating grimaced. "You have no choice, Ryan. This is not a request. I'm giving you a direct order."

"What are you talking about, sir? I left the Army years ago."

The general pointed an index finger at him. "Don't force my hand. Accept this job or you will regret it."

Ryan's blood pressure rose and his hands balled into fists. "With all due respect, sir, what the hell does that mean?"

Keating had brought with him a thick file folder, which he opened now. "This is your U.S. Army service record, Ryan. Very impressive. You served as an Airborne Ranger, then a Green Beret, then finally in Delta Force, Tier 1. The most elite of the Special Forces, even more elite than the Navy SEALS. You received numerous commendations for valor in combat including a Purple Heart and a Silver Star. You were even awarded the Medal of Honor. Impressive stuff."

The general paused, then said, "You left the Army with the rank of Captain. But if you hadn't been such a smartass in the military, I'm sure you would have been promoted to Major or even Colonel."

Keating paused again and he removed a sheaf of papers from the file and slid them across the table toward the PI. "There's a clause in your Army enlistment contract, Ryan, which you signed years ago. The clause is in small print at the every back of contract. I'm sure you never read it – most people don't."

The general gave him a tight, hard grin. "The clause stipulates that in times of a national security need, the Army can re-activate you back into the military. All it takes is a General officer, such as myself, to invoke that national security need."

Ryan had been unaware of the clause in his contract. But as he quickly scanned the document, its meaning was now crystal clear.

General Keating's hard grin remained on his face. "Welcome back to the Army, Captain Ryan."

Chapter 4

Tokyo, Japan

The Asian woman picked up the handset of her desk phone and pressed the encryption button. Then she tapped in a phone number she had committed to memory long ago.

A man answered on the second ring. "Yes?"

"It's me," she said in flawless English. She was Japanese, but spoke five different languages. "The operation has begun. We took the first step in Atlanta."

"Excellent." The man paused a moment. "Is everything else on schedule?"

"Yes."

"Very good. Keep me informed as things progress."

"Of course." She disconnected the call and hung up.

Standing, she went to a corner of her large, luxuriously appointed office. She was an avid chess player and had installed a life-size chess set in that part of the room. The intricately carved ceramic pieces all resembled Samurai warriors from 17th century Japan. She pushed one of the smaller, but still heavy figurines forward two squares. That particular game opening move was called Pawn-to-King-four. She smiled. *It'll be awhile before I can claim Checkmate. The important thing is the game's begun.*

Then she went to a teak cabinet and poured herself a large tumbler of Chivas Regal scotch. Turning around, she faced the floor-to-ceiling windows of her office.

The room, located on the top floor of the skyscraper, gave her a panoramic view of Tokyo's ultra-modern skyline. It was nighttime and the rows and rows of high-rise buildings were lit up in a riot of neon light.

The woman sipped the scotch and mulled over her next steps.

Chapter 5

FBI Field Office
Atlanta, Georgia

Erin Welch heard a knock at her door and glanced up from her laptop.

J.T. Ryan was standing at her office entrance, a worried look on his handsome face. Erin closed the lid on her laptop.

"Come in, J.T. Have a seat."

The man took one of the visitor's chairs fronting her desk.

"Didn't expect you back until next week," she said.

Ryan frowned. "My vacation was cut short."

"What happened?"

"It's a long story."

Erin studied the tall, good-looking man in his late thirties. He was 6'4" and powerfully built, with a weightlifter's physique. He had close-cropped brown hair and brown eyes. As usual he was wearing a blue blazer, slacks, and a white, buttoned-down shirt. He looked tired, as if he hadn't had much sleep.

"What, no banter? No smartass comments?" she said, amazed he hadn't already cracked one of his lame jokes.

"Not today."

"Okay, J.T. You ready to work my case?"

Ryan nodded. "I am. But I need to tell you something before I start. I've got another boss on this besides you."

"What do you mean?"

"I've been reactivated back into the Army."

"How's that possible?"

Ryan grimaced. "Some bullshit clause in my enlistment contract. Like I said, it's a long story. I'm not happy about it, but it is what it is."

"Now I understand your sour mood. What's the military's interest in this case?"

"They've been monitoring Face-Look for some time. They're concerned with the immense data gathering capability of the social media company. When their top executive was murdered, they decided to get more involved."

Erin nodded. "All right."

She opened a desk drawer and took out a file which she handed to Ryan. "In here's the information we have on the murder. The FBI and police reports, the coroner's findings, and CSI information."

Ryan opened the folder and scanned the details. "Not much here."

"You're right, J.T. It was a professional hit. They left virtually no clues behind."

The man closed the folder and stood. "In that case, I'll get to work."

"What's your first stop?"

"The morgue."

Chapter 6

Fulton County Morgue
Atlanta, Georgia

J.T. Ryan drove his Ford Explorer out of the FBI building's underground lot and headed south. A short while later he pulled into the parking lot of the morgue on Pryor Street.

He went through the building's security checkpoint and was shown into the non-descript office of the Medical Examiner. As usual, the whole building smelled of strong antiseptic, the cleaning solvent masking, but not quite erasing the pungent stench of human decomp.

Ryan shook hands with the M.E. and took a chair facing his desk. Ryan had been here many times and knew the man well.

"So, J.T., what brings you here today?" Doctor Mallory asked. The M.E. was a gaunt-looking man with oval wire-rimmed eyeglasses and a pallid complexion.

Ryan leaned forward in the chair. "I'm investigating the murder of Matthew Ross, the CEO of Face-Look."

"Of course."

"You've completed the autopsy, doc?"

"I have." Mallory opened a desk drawer, took out a file, and opened it. "My findings are very straightforward. Ross died of a massive head wound. The bullet that shattered his skull came from a high-powered weapon."

"Could you determine the caliber of the round?"

"Not exactly. But I could give you an educated guess, considering we process an average of 2,500 deaths a year in this building."

Ryan nodded. "Go ahead. You've never steered me wrong before."

"The bullet cracked a shatter-proof window and then penetrated Ross's head. As you can imagine, all we found were the bullet's fragments. But my conclusion is that it was a .50 caliber round."

The PI rubbed his jaw. "That means a very-sophisticated, high-end rifle was used. The type used by professional snipers. No question this was a well-planned assassination."

"I agree, J.T." Doctor Mallory closed the file folder. "Anything else I can tell you?"

"I want to see the body."

"You sure? I know you've got a strong stomach, but this is gruesome."

"I'm sure. I may pick up some clues."

"All right. But I have to make this quick. I've got three more cadavers to process today."

"Don't worry, doc. Those folks aren't going anywhere."

Mallory frowned at Ryan's attempt at levity. He stood and said, "Follow me and I'll take you back there."

The M.E. led Ryan down a long, white-tiled corridor and moments later they entered what the building's employees referred to as the 'meat locker'. It was the storage area where cadavers were kept after autopsies. The room was kept at a frigid 36 degrees and Ryan shivered from the cold.

Mallory strode past a long row of stainless-steel freezer lockers and stopped in front of one of them. He opened the locker door and slid out the metal shelf. Then he removed the sheet covering the corpse and stood aside so that the PI could see.

Ryan had witnessed his share of death, while in combat and later in law-enforcement, but he still swallowed hard. The M.E. had been correct in his assessment – it was a gruesome sight. The dead man's head had literally been blown off. All that remained were bloody chunks of brain matter and skin tissue and cracked skull fragments. His neck resembled raw hamburger meat.

Ryan inspected the cadaver for another minute, then turned back to the M.E. "You can close it up."

Mallory nodded, covered the body with the sheet, and slid the metal tray into the wall.

They left the frigid room and Ryan exited the building, knowing the gruesome sight would haunt his dreams for several days.

Chapter 7

Downtown
Atlanta, Georgia

After reading the FBI report Erin had given him, Ryan pulled out a paper map from his SUV's glove box and studied it carefully. The map, which was a detailed diagram of the downtown area and its nearby surroundings, showed the avenues and all of the side streets. It also identified the numerous high-rises that comprised Atlanta's skyline.

A half-hour later he folded up the map, put it away, and fired up his Explorer. Then he spent the next three hours driving through the areas south of downtown, scouting out possible locations where the sniper had taken the shot. After stopping at multiple buildings to determine a likely sight line, he spotted an abandoned structure about a half-mile from the Face-Look skyscraper.

He parked at the curb, got out, and studied the fifteen-story building, which appeared to be an office complex. It was partially finished – no windows or doors were in place, its construction most likely halted years ago due to lack of financing.

Ryan took out a rucksack from his SUV's hatch and went inside the deserted, dim interior. Using a flashlight, he made his way around the first floor, which was covered with cobwebs and dust. He found a concrete staircase at one side of the space and began climbing the stairs to the tenth floor.

When he got there, he noticed it was a wide-open area, with only support beams in place. He headed toward the north part of it, and stopped just shy of where the glass windows would normally be installed. A light breeze was blowing, swirling dust into the room. He gazed out toward downtown Atlanta.

Taking out a pair of binoculars, he focused on the Face-Look headquarters building a half-mile away. The murdered man's office had been on the tenth floor and thru his binos the PI could clearly see the plywood that now covered the shattered window of his office.

It's a perfect sight line.

Realizing this was an excellent location for the sniper to take his shot, Ryan spent the next hour scouring the large, open space, looking for disturbed areas.

He found it eventually, a spot near the edge of the floor where the windows would normally be. Footprints and other fresh marks were evident on the otherwise dust-covered floor.

He looked for shell casings but found none. *The sniper was a pro. He cleaned up his brass after taking the shot.*

The PI had brought with him a small CSI kit, which he took out of his rucksack. Erin had given him the kit years ago. Although Ryan was not a crime scene expert, he knew enough to carry out several procedures.

Opening the kit, he took out fingerprint tape and DNA tools and started collecting samples from the disturbed area of the dusty floor. That done, he took photos of the footprints. Satisfied he'd collected as much evidence as he could, he packed up the CSI kit. He'd call Erin when he got back to his vehicle to schedule her techs to come out to the scene and do a more thorough job.

Then he made his way down the stairs and headed back to his SUV.

Chapter 8

Salt Lake City, Utah

The man was driving south on Interstate 15, away from the city. The car ahead of him, a gray Lexus sedan, was doing sixty.

The man realized the Lexus was pulling away from him and he floored the accelerator of the big rig he was driving, a Mack semi truck. The truck's large diesel engine growled, it's twin smokestacks spewed a burst of black dust, and the hulking vehicle surged forward.

The man peered into the distance ahead of him, then glanced at his rearview mirrors. There was no traffic on the mostly deserted interstate.

The timing's right. Almost perfect.

He cut the rig's steering wheel left and slid into the passing lane. He kept his foot jammed on the accelerator, the semi picking up speed. The speedometer ticked up. 65 mph. 70 mph, and he was alongside the Lexus.

The man eased off the accelerator and glanced down at the gray sedan, which was dwarfed by the massive truck. He cut the wheel to the right, the big rig edging closer to the car.

For a brief moment he caught the Lexus driver's wide-eyed look of panic, as he realized what was about to happen. The truck driver felt energized by the terrified look. He cut the wheel even further right and the two vehicles collided.

The scraping metal howled, the car's windshield exploded, and its tires shredded. The 5,000 pound Lexus was no match for the 80,000 pound truck and the car was thrown off the interstate, it spun 360 degrees, and crashed head-on into a rocky formation by the road, one of the many rock-strewn buttes that covered large parts of the mountainous state of Utah.

The semi, barely scathed from the collision, kept driving south.

The driver slowed the vehicle and glanced into the rearview just as the gas tank of the Lexus exploded, a ball of fire engulfing the crushed remains of the car.

He sped up again, wanting to quickly put distance between himself and the crash scene.

Half an hour later he pulled off the interstate, slowed the big rig, and stopped. Climbing out of the stolen truck, he started jogging away from it toward his own vehicle, which he'd hidden behind a butte. Ten minutes later he got in his Jeep. He took a swig of water from his canteen and pulled out his SAT cell phone. Turning it on, he pressed the encryption button and tapped in an international phone number.

When the woman answered, he said, "It's done."

"You've taken care of our Utah problem?" she asked in flawless English.

"Yes."

"Excellent."

"When can I expect payment?"

"I'll wire you the money today," she said.

"Good. Will you have other work for me?"

There was no answer for a moment, then the woman said, "I'm sure I will. I'll text you the details."

He heard a click on the line and realized she had hung up.